Burning Bridges

A novel by

Matthew Ross

Burning Chair Limited, Trading As Burning Chair Publishing
61 Bridge Street, Kington HR5 3DJ

www.burningchairpublishing.com

By Matthew Ross
Edited by Simon Finnie and Peter Oxley
Cover by Burning Chair Publishing

First published by Burning Chair Publishing, 2022

ISBN: 978-1-912946-25-9

Praise for Burning Bridges

"A sharp, gritty thriller that grips you from the first page… a riveting, authentic voice that drives the story at a fabulous pace."
– Victoria Dowd, author of "The Smart Woman's Guide to Murder", winner of The People's Book Prize 2020/21 for Fiction

"Jam packed with addictive action… Buckle up, you're in for an explosive read!"
– Sharon Bairden, author of Sins of the Father

"Blisteringly real while elegantly composed, Burning Bridges is an excellent and compelling crime novel - highly recommended."
– Rob Parker, author of the 'Ben Bracken' series and the Audible #1 bestseller «Far From The Tree»

MATTHEW ROSS

Two and a half years ago:

THE CAR STOOD ON ITS SIDE IN THE HEDGEROW, *its wheels still turning. It had come off the road at enough speed to flip it on edge, its own momentum sledging it into the unmade bank. Blue paint smeared along the tarmac for a dozen or so metres. Tiny cubes of broken glass followed in its wake like a far-away meteor shower. The crows, over their initial surprise, regrouped on the telephone wires up above the wreckage, their feathers jagged, black and stiff.*

He jumped out of his BMW, phone in one hand already dialling for an ambulance. He ran to the front of the upturned Audi and dropped to his hands and knees, trying to peer past the white shatter-pattern of jagged crazing that seconds before had been the crystal-clear windscreen, and seeing nothing.

They were only a few miles from the town centre and this single width lane was a back route mostly used by locals. It took the driver between flat featureless fields: empty hectares waiting for the wheat and rapeseed to grow back. There were no buildings or passing traffic anywhere to be seen. He'd never felt so isolated, alone and useless. There were no sirens yet, just the 'caw' of the crows calling their friends back to the wires to watch the drama unfurling below.

With the base of his fist, using his phone as a hammer, he smashed out the windscreen. It peeled away in one long clinging piece and at last he could see clearly.

The female passenger, a make-up demonstrator in a department store and new to him today, was unmistakeably dead. He'd only been introduced to her an hour earlier and struggled to remember her name: Nikki, Nicole, something like that. Still strapped in her seat, suspended high above the ground, her head hung at an unsustainable angle for any living person. The car had ploughed into the edge of the field's bank when it flipped, embedding the pillar of the driver's door into the hard clay earth. The driver's head had bounced and scraped and shredded against the unforgiving ground.

He looked at his lifeless, unmoving brother: face in ruins, body smashed. He howled at the sky. The crows took flight again and a siren in the distance grew louder.

-1-

Now it begins:

THE ISLE OF SHEPPEY: a bleak expanse of marshes and moors hanging off the edge of Kent. The mainlanders call the locals 'swampies', and the place 'Cabbage Island'. Dori Musatova, however, calls it home.

The hour was early but Yemi was late. No apologies, he just clambered into the passenger seat beside Dori. He placed his small bag between his feet and fumbled with the seat belt. The worn wiper blades squealed as they dragged across the screen, sticking then bouncing as they swung across. *They need replacing but it won't be this month, it won't be any time soon, there's too much to pay for already: Viktor needs new school shoes so the wiper blades will need to wait along with everything else, it's a shit car anyway, not worth wasting money on.*

Yemi yawned, stretching his mouth wider than Dori thought possible; his teeth broad, long and yellow. Yemi lived in the flats opposite hers. He also worked at the same supermarket distribution centre, on the other side of the bridge: an enormous place shaped like a box. Lorries would come and go all day, their trailers shaped like boxes, full of boxes, unloaded onto miles and miles of shelves, boxes piled high. Boxes within boxes within boxes within boxes. In Chișinău Dori was an accountant for the local Government. Now she worked from six 'til six, sixty hours a week unpacking boxes. Hard, dirty work but it paid three times what she earned back home. She had a small apartment for her and Viktor paid for by the Government. Viktor liked his school, his English was good, better than hers, he'd almost lost his accent. She thinks he sounds like an Englishman. That pleased her, it meant he'll do well here. Dori's mother, his 'bunica' teases him in their Sunday Skype calls, saying her grandson sounds like Prince Harry, and they all laugh, Dori likes England. England has been good to her.

Yemi on the other hand, she doesn't know. He doesn't talk about his experience leading him to England, but she's seen him chatting and joking with the other African men at work. Although he was in no laughing mood this morning; he just stared through the passenger window, pebbled with rain, at the low grey mist coming in off the river.

The warmth from the two adults in the small tatty car fogged the windscreen. No point turning on the hot air blowers, they don't work. Another thing that needs mending, another thing to go on the list that'll never be ticked off.

'Come on Yemi,' says Dori, handing him a tissue. 'Help me wipe'. Together they formed a clearing in the fog, and Dori pulled away from the kerb. So began the short journey to work. The clock—at least that worked—read 05:17.

*

The Isle of Sheppey, situated as it is in the mouth of the Thames Estuary, was once a place of great military importance. Henry the Eighth built himself a naval dockyard that went on to employ the swampies for the next four hundred years. In later times, the fledgling RAF used the large flat moors as airfields for its Spitfires and Blenheims. But technology and economics evolve; the arrival of the Jet Age saw the airfields close. The dockyards soon followed. That left around thirty thousand swampies on an island twelve kilometres wide: a lot of land, not a lot of people, and not much to do.

There's only one way, by road, on to the island: the fast-moving A249. It splits as it approaches the water and merges back together on the other side, after offering the driver the slow option of the squat square old bridge, or high-speed across the toweringly tall new bridge. Both bridges sit there, like father and son, side-by-side, watching the boats glide by, all the while the traffic thunders across the narrow River Swale. Once across, the road proceeds for about a mile, dead straight, until reaching a junction that only offers the driver left or right. To the left, field after field, tens of thousands of new cars sit empty. The roll on/roll off ships delivering over half a million new cars every year from the Continent, and growing. To the right: prisons. The infamous Sheppey Cluster. Three prisons nestle beside each other: Swaleside, Stanford Hill and Elmley. Running the letters, categories A through D, housing two and a half thousand men a year, and growing. That's what happens, successive Governments find a lot of space with few inhabitants and see it as an easy win—what's a few thousand votes if it gets the unpopular and unwanted off the streets? Out of sight and out of mind for the metropolitan electorate, whether prisoners, acres of unsold Austerity-age cars, or the many immigrants given refuge in the island's towns of Minster and Eastchurch.

*

The morning still hadn't woken up yet. The sky was as grey as a battleship's arse and street lamps threw nicotine-stained speckles of light through the hanging drizzle. The wiper blades' screech across the windscreen glass had become so annoying Dori turned them off, only flicking them on for a single swipe when the screen became too obscured. *It's too early, no one's around, I'll be okay,* she thinks.

Through the mist, Dori saw the new bridge. Its proper name is the Sheppey Crossing, but everyone called it the new bridge. Built about ten years ago, shooting straight up in the air, climbing high and fast and then... dropping just as fast on the other side of the peak, like a rollercoaster. Dori found it crazy: the speeds people drove, not knowing what waited for them over the crest. A few years earlier Dori's fears proved right: a massive pile-up, vehicle after vehicle ploughed into each other, coming at speed blindly over the bridge. Thankfully nobody died, but it was such a big incident, over one hundred and thirty cars crashed, it made the news everywhere. Even Bunica heard about it in Chişinău.

When he noticed she'd passed the approach road to the new bridge, Yemi uttered his first words since getting in the car, 'Not the old bridge? We'll be late.'

'Then you need to wake up on time,' she gently chided. 'Look, you can't see the top today, it's too dangerous.'

Yemi sucked his teeth, passing judgement on Dori's caution. He knew Dori was right. The new bridge soared skyward where the mist and gloom masked its upper reaches. Breaking through the miasma a few blinking red lights gave low flying aircraft an approximate indication where the top was, but it was impossible to see clearly. Foolhardy early commuters hurtled up the new bridge, they climbed high then disappeared, as though eaten by some great unseen beast lurking in the clouds.

'We'll take the old bridge.' She tried keeping a cheerful tone to her voice. She wasn't enjoying Yemi's bad mood this morning but didn't want to fall out, she needed his contribution to the petrol, 'It might take a few minutes longer but at least we'll get there. Anyway, I don't see any ships. It'll be okay.'

The new bridge, the tallest structure for miles around, dominated the flat landscape. An epic ten storeys high; tall enough for the container ships that arrived every day laden with hundreds and hundreds of more new cars. Great idea: the ships went under, the vehicles went over, it all worked fine for everybody, except... who forgot the trains? With no new rail bridge the trains continued to trundle throughout the day across the old road/rail bridge, as they have done every day since it opened in 1960. Despite the new bridge racing sharply up and then straight back down again, like the last day on a heart monitor, every time a ship reached the old bridge everything was forced to stop. And slowly, using ancient technology, the span across the river rose vertically while the traffic and the ships and the trains stop and wait and listen to the reckless drivers hurtle across the new bridge overhead in expectation of another crash. But the early hour favoured Dori: she was right, the warning lights didn't flash, there was no lift imminent, they could glide through and re-join the higher speed A249 once they'd crossed the river.

Ahead looked blurry and underwater. Swirls and waves danced on the windscreen moving through the grey air. With a tap from her little finger the wiper arms rose together but quickly lost synchronicity: they stuck, they skipped, they smeared, they squeaked and then the bit Dori liked best, they flicked. She was lost in thought watching a thin brown stripe trickle down the edge of the screen, merging into the filthy crescents left behind by the wipers rise and fall when Yemi screamed, 'Look out!'

She snapped out of her daydream. Yemi pointed straight ahead, then she saw it too, a shape across the carriageway. A solid shape. A substantial shape.

The decrepit brakes thankfully took anchor against the wet road just in time. The car shuddered to a halt uncomfortably close to the shape. With a crunch of gears Dori backed up. Just a few feet, far enough for them to try and distinguish the shape in the beam of the car's headlights.

'Is... is that a man?' asked Dori, leaning forward, the curls on her forehead brushing the cold, damp windscreen. Yemi didn't speak but nodded.

'Do you think he jumped? From the new bridge?' Dori asked aloud but it was really to herself. 'No, it's too far, that's at least a hundred metres away,' she whispered to herself, looking up at it.

Yemi rubbed his palm over his shaved head and back down across his cheek, then spoke. 'We have to go.'

But Dori had already unclicked her seatbelt and opened the

door.

'Get back in, we have to go', but either Dori hadn't heard Yemi or she'd ignored him. She walked away from the car towards the man.

Dori began to take everything in as she approached the man. He lay on his front. It was his hair she noticed first: too long to be short but too short to be long, like the sort of haircut Viktor and his friends had, like the footballers they worshipped, a young person's haircut. The constant drizzle plastered the hair across his dirty and bleeding face: an older man's face, too old for that haircut, a bit paunchy, slack hung around his jawline. It was a face shaped by punches and preening, fists and fillers. As she surveyed further, the set of his shoulders told Dori he was a strong man, a big man: gym-toned like the young men in this country but his hands and wrists told her he was also powerful, like the manual workers back home. Dori squatted for a closer look, ignoring the chill forming across her back. It was hard to age him in this light, under these circumstances, but he looked a bit like her brother who'd soon be forty, so she estimated the man to be either side of that.

Then she saw it. At first she missed it in the dull lights against his dark clothes, but then she spotted it and immediately recognised what it was.

'He's been shot!' Dori shouted to Yemi, but the wind snatched most of it away. She shouted again.

'Dori, get in the car. Let's go!'

Dori felt biting in her thighs; the squatting had become uncomfortable and a slight wobble caused her palm to fly to the tarmac to steady herself. Then she rose, the discomfort dissipating. As she walked back to the car she became aware of Yemi's shouting, and then his pointing. At what? Her hand?

She turned her hand, the one she had steadied herself with, and saw illuminated in the headlight's beam that it was painted red with blood.

'Yemi, full beam.'

Yemi flicked the stalk and the white lamps burned to their maximum, flooding the area in light. Dori looked at the big man with the bullet hole in his shoulder and realised he lay face down in a puddle of his own blood. Raindrops splashed in it and trickled towards the cast iron storm drain.

Dori got back in the car, and slammed the door behind her, absent-mindedly wiping her damp hands against her coat. 'We need to call the police.'

'No. No police. We must go,' said Yemi. 'Now!'

Dori looked at Yemi. Her twisted face told him she didn't understand, that she was confused.

'Listen, Dori, we must go. I cannot talk to the police.'

Then Dori understood. 'You're illegal, aren't you? False name and documents, is it?'

'And what about you? You told me this car has no tax, no insurance. You want the police? You lose your car you lose your job. You may even go to jail. What about Viktor?'

'An ambulance then?'

'No. We have to go. Now. Anyway, there's nothing we can do. He's dead; trust me.'

The battered little car spluttered back to life and Dori swung it gently past the big man with the bullet hole. He still hadn't moved, giving credence to Yemi's conclusion. The car gathered speed and disappeared across the old bridge towards the mainland.

Around ten minutes later, the battered little car arrived at the cavernous supermarket distribution centre. Its passengers dashed through the rain into the building, desperate to clock on before their shifts started at six. Yemi punched in his timecard with barely one minute to spare and wished Dori a good day then ran on his long thin legs to his work area on the other side of the depot. Dori, about to clock on, paused then returned to the staff room.

Quarter of an hour later, singled out by a fat woman with more tattoos than brain cells, Dori was reprimanded for starting late. She humbly apologised, knowing, being the foreigner, that that was what was expected of her if she wanted to keep her job. The stupid fat slob jabbed her stubby finger in her face as Dori nodded and remained silent. Viktor would have it so much easier if he could pass for an Englishman—no kowtowing to ignorant bullies who think they're better just because by chance they were born under a certain flag.

*

At the same time as Dori was being forced to eat shit, Kent Police slowly cruised the Kingsferry Bridge, responding to an anonymous report of a dead body. The young constable in his waterproof fluorescent jacket swept a high-powered flashlight from side to side in wide arcs as he walked the carriageway, before stopping. He pointed his flashlight to the tarmac in front of him. Under the bright beam the viscous red sheen of blood reflected back at him. Almost the full width of the road was puddled by blood, even the white concrete kerb was rinsed pink where the blood had splashed and gurgled down the storm drain.

The young constable shouted into the radio at his shoulder, trying to compete against the wind rolling in off the river. 'This is definitely the spot...'

Back at Area HQ, the radio controller struggled to hear the message over the howling background noise. 'Repeat please, over.'

'I said,' came the officer's voice over the radio, 'there is no body on the scene. I repeat, the body has gone.'

-2-

QUINN WOKE WITH A JOLT, as though an electric nightmare had rattled through him like an express train. *Blue. Everything is blue.* He faded away.

Quinn woke again. *Is it later? The same day? What time is it?* The walls around him were blue, the ceiling blue. *Is this what death looks like? Benny? Where am I?* He faded away again.

Quinn woke once more, but this time his conscious caught hold of the drive chain and he knew he wouldn't fade, at least not yet anyway. He tried to piece together what he knew. There wasn't much. The only thing he knew for definite was he'd never seen this room before. Lying still, he moved only his eyes, but even that fired an uncomfortable twinge through him. He grimaced at the effort it was taking.

The room was small. Cardboard boxes lined one wall almost to the ceiling: battered and torn old boxes, the sort given away at the back of the supermarket, *'Contents: 48 packs'* in industrial black typeface. The walls of the room were blue, not the vibrant joyful Adriatic blue of summer, but the same cold lifeless blue as mould, as though it had been painted a very long time ago then left to fade forgotten. A square window, too small for the wall, was positioned exactly central and faced Quinn. It took him a moment to realise why it looked odd: no curtains. A lank greying muslin attempted, and failed, to block the outside from coming in. The daylight poured through the small window, ricocheting off the walls and turning the ceiling a pale blue, giving an unsettling undersea sensation. *Water. I was under the water, I fell in the water.*

Quinn shifted his weight to prop himself up on his elbows. A fire burnt through his left shoulder. He looked down and saw a white pad: a medical dressing stuck down by gauze tape. The realisation he was naked brought the cold chill of those blue walls down on top of him; hairs rose all over his body and his skin began to pucker. Quinn pulled the duvet up to his neck. It was thin and smelt dry and dusty. Nobody had used this bed for a long time, a very long time indeed, Quinn was certain of that. His eyes felt heavy and everything faded to black again.

*

'You're awake then,' said a voice. 'I thought I heard you stirring.'

Quinn lifted his head off the weak gutless pillow and found a small man adding another box to the wall of boxes. Quinn tried to speak but no words came out, his mouth dry, his throat seized. Quinn swallowed the miniscule amount of saliva he could muster, then tried again.

'Where am I?' Barely above a whisper, it didn't sound like his own voice. The small man looked about to speak but paused, raised a finger then disappeared from the room. He came back a few seconds later holding a green plastic bottle with a torn and ragged Sprite label.

'Water,' he said, passing it to Quinn, loosening the cap as he did so. Quinn took it hungrily to his lips; it tasted warm and metallic, straight from the tap. He gunned most of it down in one go, the overspill trickling across his face, pooling under his chin. He muttered thanks then coughed, loosening up the rusted workings of his throat.

'Where am I?' he repeated.

'Welcome to Leysdown,' the man said, throwing his arms open wide. 'The Vegas of the South, baby!'

Quinn sipped at the water, more slowly and controlled this

time. His senses phased back into life. His perspective returned; he realised the man wasn't small, but average height. Yet there was something about him that made him seem small, as though he'd learned to project meek and non-threatening. Quinn knew there was only one place you need a skill like that to get by, but said nothing. The man looked underweight: malnourished the way drinkers get—or junkies. Yet his skin and his eyes had a healthy pallor. If he was an addict, he was clean now. Again, Quinn knew a place for getting clean, but remained silent. Quinn tried to age the man, but it was impossible. He looked anywhere from forty to sixty; his face was lined and weather-beaten but his movements were agile and swift. He was someone who'd seen a life and it had come at him hard since day one.

'More water?' he asked. Quinn shook his head. The man pulled an old kitchen chair out from under a chipped melamine dressing table. 'So, time for us to talk I suppose. It's Thursday, in case you were wondering. Remember what happened to you?'

'Thursday? I've been here, what, four days?' Just trying to do the maths hurt Quinn's head.

'Yeah, four... or five... depending what way you look at it,' said the man. 'I found you early Monday. But it was Sunday... wasn't it?'

*

The small boat approached silently, a little after 9pm on Sunday. It was a dark, starless night; perfect conditions for what they had planned. They drew up to the jetty, gliding smoothly after cutting the big powerful outboard motor on the approach sixty metres out. Four of them climbed out while the fifth member stayed perched at the wheel, ready to gun the motor back to life when the time came. Quinn looked back at the wheelman and exchanged a thumbs-up for luck. The dinghy gently rocked up and down on the tide, then a sour taste as he remembered what Jamie said, 'It's not a dinghy you sad old bastard. It is a RIB.

Rigid-hulled Inflatable Boat. Remember that, old man.'

Quinn and four kids: that's all they were, barely in their twenties. *Fucking kids. But a job's a job and a debt's a debt. A couple of hours and it'll all be over and I'll be gone.*

All five of them were dressed in black at Quinn's insistence, but Jamie had to push the boundaries. 'What's your problem, man? It's only a tiny little crocodile. Who cares?'

'I do' said Quinn. 'I care. I said black, plain black, solid black. That means no logos.'

'Relax.' Jamie casually flapped a dissenting hand towards Quinn.

'People remember the unusual. Little things stick in their memory, like logos. Get rid of it.'

'How'm I going to get rid of it now, dickhead?'

'Come here,' demanded Quinn. Jamie advanced, packing attitude and hostility into a mere three strides. Quinn grabbed at the crocodile and blacked it out with a marker pen.

'What? You fucking... Do you know how much this cost you fat fuck? My dad'll hear about this. You'll see.'

Quinn ignored Jamie's angry stare on the short boat trip across. *Silly sulking kids. I'm too old for this.*

*

Small, incidental flashbacks began popping into Quinn's head, then more and more, quicker and quicker, as if the dam had broken, his mind reeling from the deluge. Memories surged in, filling his head so quickly and intensely it made his vision swim. His subconscious mind attempted to sift everything into some sort of order, its processors working overtime. He wanted to stop the giddy ride his head had taken. He looked around his unfamiliar surroundings and hoped focusing on something nearby would anchor him. It occurred to Quinn that nothing in the room matched.

The man pulled a pouch of tobacco from a pocket and

withdrew two thin roll-ups. 'Smoke?' He outstretched an arm toward Quinn.

Quinn declined without speaking and rested his head back on the pillow, again becoming aware of its musty smell. The man returned one cigarette to the pouch and lit the other for himself. He took a drag, then exhaled. Quinn watched the man pick a shred of loose tobacco from his untidy gingery moustache then returned back into his thoughts.

*

They crouched low and ran, single file, along the jetty to the main office building then separated into twos. LJ and Pope peeled off to the left, towards the gatehouse securing the only road access in or out the compound. Quinn and Jamie peeled right. Given the choice Quinn would rather have gone with Pope: he at least seemed half sensible and could probably be good at this if he paid attention. But part of Quinn's job was keeping Jamie—the son and heir—out of trouble, so he was stuck with him.

Quinn hung back, watching LJ and Pope scuttle towards the gatehouse: a fancy name for a plastic kiosk housing the buttons that made the boom gate rise and fall. A bored minimum wage guard hired from the neck down was loafing inside it. Even from this distance Quinn could see the trailing cables of the guard's white earbuds, obviously passing time with music or movies. He was distracted: good, this should be easy. Sure enough, he didn't notice the boys' approach and, before he realised it, they were in his face. *Don't hurt anyone,* that's what Quinn had told them. *It's not them you're robbing; if you're good to them you normally find they're good to you. The companies are insured, they don't give a shit about their people. So as soon as they realise you're more on their side than their employer, they tend to remember less. But give them a clump, well, then they want their own back, that's when they remember everything, even tiny little crocodiles.*

He watched as they easily subdued the guard and cable-tied

his hands together. They'd acted just like he'd asked, smooth and professional. *Good boys,* thought Quinn. *Well done.*

Jamie had pulled a small black device from his pocket; it blinked into life, a GPS tracker. After a few seconds it had calibrated itself.

'This way, come on,' he said to Quinn, then sprinted off before Quinn could advise caution. Quinn struggled but managed to keep up with him and caught his breath back as they crouched behind a small outbuilding: a substation or something.

Quinn surveyed the vista ahead. He'd never seen so many cars: row upon row upon row, stretching as far as he could see. Each one brand new, with only the mileage it took to roll off the factory floor, on to a ship and then off again here. The neat ordered rows made Quinn think of a graveyard. Of Benny.

This late hour on a Sunday night was bathed in light. Tall halogen floodlights stood sentry at regular intervals; the cold white light caught the misty drizzle in the air and made it sparkle like needles as it fell through its beam. Despite the floodlights and the high steel fences the security was pretty minimal; it was what it was, a glorified carpark. Would someone really want the risk and aggravation of breaking in to nick a basic family hatchback? Not when there were plenty of residential areas and retail parks offering easier targets right outside. Quinn's visits over the previous few weeks revealed three men patrolling the compound plus the man in the gatehouse. Quinn had checked the website for the security firm after noting their signs hung around the compound, pleased to find they weren't a specialist, not the type to employ ex-police or military. Instead they were a cheap and cheerful body shop: if you can walk in a straight line and hold a torch, welcome to the firm, son.

'It's about two hundred metres, that direction,' said Jamie, consulting his GPS and pointing roughly west of where they'd hunkered down.

'Okay. We go quietly, we go slowly,' said Quinn, but Jamie was off, charging ahead, weaving between the vehicles. Quinn took off after him, silently muttering profanities about his young partner.

'Someone there?' a voice called out, heavily accented. African perhaps; Quinn neither knew nor cared, all he knew was it belonged to a guard. He dropped to his knees and squeezed low and close to the nearest car, confident its shadow gave enough cover. He hoped Jamie had had enough sense to do the same.

'You. There. What you doing?' The guard's voice sounded agitated; Quinn had been in the game long enough to recognise the sound of panic no matter what language you spoke.

'What are you doing?' the guard said again. 'Come out.'

Jamie, the stupid prick, he must have been spotted. Quinn stretched up and peered across the nose of the cars, just in time to see Jamie lunge from the shadows towards the guard. The guard stepped back and Jamie took a swing. One touch felled him. Jamie dropped on top of him letting fly a frenzy of punches. Quinn spotted a metallic glint every time Jamie released his fist: a knuckleduster. The little bollocks had only gone and brought a knuckleduster with him.

Quinn pulled Jamie off but the fury still coursed through him. He bucked and convulsed in Quinn's grip trying to break free, to return to the unconscious guard at their feet.

'What have you done?' said Quinn. 'We agreed: nobody gets hurt.'

*

The man smoked in silence, he seemed as lost in his own thoughts as Quinn. He ground the cigarette's small nub into a green glass ashtray emblazoned with Becks Bier logos, no doubt lifted from a pub garden somewhere. He swiped his fingertips over his gingery moustache, then broke the silence. 'Well now. There's me going for a drive on a Monday morning and then there you are. Shot. Lying, dying, in the road. No wallet, no ID. I put two and two together. I know you were part of that commotion on Sunday night. Police and Fire going crazy, over at the docks. They're saying now it was just kids, vandals. But I know better. Want to tell me about it?'

Quinn grumbled, and faced the wall.

*

'What have you done? We agreed: nobody gets hurt.'

'No, *you* agreed that. I didn't.' Jamie's face contorted with rage as he spat the words at Quinn. 'He saw me, what was I to do, eh? Answer me that, you fat old *fuck?*'

Before Quinn could answer the air was split by the high-pitched screams of the alarm. Blue lights high up on the main building's walls began flashing. Quinn knelt beside the guard and pointed to the red panic button worn on a lanyard around his neck.

'Well done Jamie. He tripped the alarm. The police are coming, we have to abort. We need to go. Now.'

'No way. It's less than five metres away, it's got to be in that row there.' Jamie sprinted towards a row of identical French family hatchbacks, his GPS device becoming stronger in its readings. Quinn looked back towards the gatehouse but was too far away to see it. He could only hope LJ and Pope had succeeded in the second part of their task to barricade the only entrance and exit with as many vehicles as could be moved.

'This one, over here!' cried Jamie, beside one of the hatchbacks. Quinn came across, reaching behind to his rucksack as he ran, pulling out a wrecking bar. With one hard yank the boot lid sprung open. The car joined in the screaming, letting fly an electronic wail, but this alarm was of no concern, its noise smothered by the site alarm blaring from sounders in every corner of the compound.

Jamie pulled out two folded nylon holdalls from his rucksack whilst Quinn ripped up the carpet and opened the spare wheel compartment to discover... the spare wheel.

18

'Fuck! It definitely says here. It must be this one then,' said Jamie, shaking his GPS device, pointing to the car behind.

Quinn popped the boot and ripped away the carpet. Jackpot. Completely filling the spare wheel void were stacks of high denomination Euro notes shrink-wrapped to the size of building blocks, and just as heavy. Quinn and Jamie began filling the bags with them. They were awkward, cumbersome, wedged in tightly, filling all the space. Cutting through the sound of the alarms came the distinctive two-tone of police sirens. Blue flashing lights reflected against the fascias of the neighbouring buildings as they sped through the darkened streets.

Quinn hoiked the strap over his left shoulder, hanging it across his body. The bag rested on his right hip. *Fuck me that's heavy.* Jamie did the same. Then they both extracted the same thing from their rucksacks: red ships' flares. Simultaneously they capped them to release a red billowing smoke. They tossed them into the opened cars, and within seconds the cars were alight.

Jamie led the way, sprinting back the way they'd come, back towards the jetty. Quinn struggled to keep up, his knees feeling the strain of the extra weight, his man-tits feeling sweaty under his clothes and he was panting like an old dog. *After this I'll take time off to get fit, lose a bit of weight, get back in shape.*

Behind him he could feel the rising heat as the fire in the cars intensified; he glanced over his shoulder and saw it had spread to neighbouring vehicles. Outside the gates the police had arrived, at the moment it was only the single squad car responding to the alarm but the driver had taken stock of the situation, the torched vehicles, the barricaded entrance; no doubt reinforcements were already en-route.

Nearly there, nearly there, come on, screamed the voice inside Quinn's head. His heart was pounding and he had the metallic taste of blood in his mouth. He got to the edge of the office building just as two more police cars and a fire engine pulled up. He could feel the ground changing beneath his feet; he was now on the wooden deck of the jetty. It felt springier, there was less impact tearing through his knees.

Up ahead he heard the mighty roar of the boat's engines fire up: almost there. Behind him the fire brigade had cut through the fence and were clearing the barricade. He tossed the bag into the boat, and, using the last ounces of energy within him, he hurled his body into it too. Over the engines' roar he heard the boys swearing at him as the boat lurched violently at his ungraceful landing, sloshing side to side and splashing them with cold, greasy water. Regardless, the boat pulled away from the jetty and quickly accelerated to a frightening speed. Its prow lifted from the water, and the boat bounced as it thundered through the night.

*

The man hadn't spoken, but Quinn knew he was staring at him, waiting for him. The quiet stretched beyond awkward, it became uncomfortable. Quinn turned to face him. "I don't know what you're talking about,' he said.

The man didn't speak a word, he simply shrugged, but the gesture dripped with sarcasm. He didn't believe Quinn, but he was satisfied that Quinn knew he knew. The man jabbed a finger in his ear and rummaged. 'You're lucky I found you,' he added. 'Anyone else would have left you for dead.'

Something triggered in Quinn's head: loud voices, LJ, Pope, shouting, and Jamie shouting back. Water, cold, cold, greasy water. A siren. A flash of blue light. A woman's face: she looked kind, motherly with soft curls. Were those real memories, or just his brain farting and misfiring back into action?

If the man had noticed Quinn's state of mental confusion he didn't let on; he simply continued his account.

'But I scoops you up in the back of the van—fuck me you're heavy, you might want to think about going on a diet, carrying that much extra, it'll kill you in the end. Anyway, I'm thinking to myself, this could be a nice little winner. You see, I know what you are—' Quinn gave a low growl, expressing disinterest and denial. 'You're the kind of man who travels anonymously, who don't want a hospital, who don't want questions, like how'd you get a bloody great hole in you?' A tone of excitement had crept into the man's voice; he was enjoying this. 'So I thinks, I can get you patched up. Then you'll be valuable to me, a fixer-upper opportunity as they say. Either you'll pay me for saving your life, or I get myself a finder's fee from the person who put that slug in you. I bet they're keen to find out where you are.'

*

The boat's journey time was short, only a few minutes, coming to halt at a pontoon on the mainland side beneath the towering new bridge at the Sheppey road crossing. A popular spot in the summer for jet-skiers to launch themselves, but this time of year, this time of night, there wasn't a soul around. Standing in the darkness ready for the next phase of their journey, stolen yesterday forty-five miles away, was an ambulance. An ideal choice: flick the sirens on, join the A249 and within minutes you'll be on to the motorway network and gone.

The boys whooped and hollered and high-fived whilst Quinn recovered. He waited for his heart rate to slow, his breathing to even out and the thumping pulse in his ears to fade away. The wheelman got them up close to the pontoon, and LJ and Pope clambered out. Jamie and Quinn passed up the bags and then clambered out themselves.

Quinn grabbed the jubilant Jamie around the neck, 'What the bloody hell was all that about? You and your showboating, you almost ruined the whole job.'

'My job!' Jamie broke Quinn's grip and pushed him away. 'This is my job. And I'm fucking sick of you complaining and undermining me all the time. I've had it with you, you pathetic fat old fuck.'

'Yeah, likewise. I'm finished with you. After tonight you

won't see me again.'

'You're right about that, Quinn.'

Jamie drew a pistol from his waistband and pointed it straight at him. 'You've had this coming from the start. Fuck you.'

Quinn felt the bullet rip through him. He stumbled backwards with the impact. Losing his footing, he dropped into the cold shallow water of the Swale.

As he faded out of consciousness he could hear voices: LJ, Pope, shouting, and Jamie shouting back. He sank to the river bed, the mud clinging to him, swallowing him, the water covering his face. The synapses in his brain started to short circuit: information was still being gathered but the processing confused. Above him he heard the plaintive wail of an ambulance siren and the flash of blue light—*is that for me? that's quick*—but then the sound grew fainter and further away.

Then everything turned black.

-3-

QUINN FINISHED THE LAST DREGS OF THE WATER, using the opportunity to get a measure of the man. Saviour or captor? Quinn couldn't tell, but his suspicions about the man were right. 'When did you get out?'

The man didn't seem at all surprised Quinn knew he was an ex-con. 'A little over two years ago' he said. 'Stanford Hill: you know it?'

Quinn was aware of it. One of the three prisons on the island, one of the infamous Sheppey Cluster. But he'd never been in there, he'd never been in any prison. Quinn was clean. As a young man he'd been careful enough and ruthless enough to make sure nothing came back in his direction. Nowadays he was wealthy enough and connected enough to call in favours and afford fancy lawyers to keep everything at an even safer distance. He gave a non-committal murmur and the man continued.

'Eighteen-month stretch. Come out, no one there. First time I've ever come out to find no one there.' He'd lived exactly as Quinn thought: a lifetime in and out of jail, keeping his head down, making himself small, avoiding the attention of the big beasts. But the prison mouse passes through invisible, seeing and hearing everything.

'Nobody.' The man's voice broke with the slightest tremble. He turned away from Quinn, trying to distract himself by adjusting the position of junk on the dressing table. 'But it was mid-May, lovely sunny day. I thought, balls to it, I've nowhere to be, let's go the seaside. I walked around a bit, had no idea where I was going, followed the signs, found the beach, had a lovely day out.'

'You're not local then?' asked Quinn.

'I am, now. Spent a couple of nights sleeping rough, on the long grass above the beach, but then the weather broke and I needed somewhere dry. Came across this place. The owner didn't want it anymore, so I took it.'

Quinn struggled to understand what he meant, and the man read this from his face. 'He's gone, not coming back. Dead.' Then, either to reassure Quinn or to shake off blame—Quinn wasn't sure which—he added, 'I didn't kill him, it wasn't me. No one did. All I was doing was trying door handles. Found the one here unlocked. Let myself in. I only wanted to nick myself something to eat, a bit of cash maybe, you know. Anyway, I find him. Carked out. Stone cold dead. In that bed, funnily enough.'

Quinn suddenly felt itchy. 'I hope you've changed the sheets since then.'

'Yeah,' said the man unconvincingly. 'So, I close the door on him, out of respect like, and I kip down in the other bedroom planning to move on next morning. But then in the daylight I see he'd obviously been gone some time.'

Quinn squirmed in the bed, and felt an overwhelming urge to get out of it. He tried to move but the pain in his shoulder tore through him like barbed wire. His host hadn't seemed to have noticed.

'He looked a bit… you know. And all the food in the fridge had gone off, rotten. So, I figured the poor old sod had been sparko for at least a couple of weeks. And that got me thinking, if it'd been a couple of weeks and no one noticed, then they probably never would. That night he got the old burial at sea treatment and I staked my claim for this place.'

'We're near the sea then?' asked Quinn. He could visualise the layout of the island from when he was researching the job, and hoped any information might help him understand where he was right now.

'I should say so, it's literally right out there.' The man pointed in the opposite direction to Quinn's small window wall. 'Anyhow, I figured I'd hang on a few weeks. If anyone asked I'd say I was his son, but no one's ever asked after him. So, I've stayed. It suits me here. It's quiet, under the radar, there's not even any speed bumps round here never mind any CCTV or plod.'

He took another roll-up from his pouch, this time without offering one to Quinn, and lit it as he moved over to the window. He pulled aside the thin net curtain. The sudden rush of unfiltered sunlight made Quinn squint. Noises seeped into the room. The view offered no clues, just a dimpled red brick wall. Quinn shut his eyes, white blurs lingered from the sunlight and he tried to process the sound: seagulls screeched, waves crashed and road traffic rumbled constantly but distantly.

'The name's McLaren, by the way,' said the man.

'That your real name? Or was it his?'

'Does it matter?' said McLaren. Quinn shrugged, then McLaren asked, 'What's yours?'

'Quinn.'

'Quinn? Got a first name?'

'Does it matter?'

'Fair enough,' said McLaren, laughing through a thick smoker's cough. 'You can probably begin getting back on your feet tomorrow. Probably best if you rest up today though. Want anything to eat?'

Quinn shook his head, but asked for more water. McLaren left then returned a minute or so later with a refilled bottle and a banana, more black than yellow. 'In case you get hungry.'

'Did you patch me up?'

'Me? God no,' said McLaren. 'I know someone. It's okay, he's sound. I supply him now and again with—' He squeezed his finger and thumb together against his lips and sucked. Quinn nodded but didn't know what he meant: weed? Tobacco? Crack? Other?

'From Azerbaijan, but he's all right. Used to be in the Red Army, can you believe that?' He chuckled to himself. 'Medic. But he can't do it over here though, different qualifications or something. Works in the chip shop. Things down by the seafront, round all the pubs and arcades, can get pretty lively, especially in the summer, there's always some pissed-up Herbert causing trouble. He's got himself a nice little earner stitching people back together again, no questions asked, no Old Bill poking noses where they shouldn't, just get back on with your rugby tour or your stag night and then fuck off home. And he done you. I promised him you'd pay him a grand by the way.'

'A grand?'

'And a grand-and-a-half for me,' added McLaren. 'I figure that's cheap. Cheaper than the NHS asking names, addresses and why you've got a bullet in you. And it's also cheaper than I'd get if I contacted your Sunday night shooter, don't you think?'

'You think so?' Quinn didn't like the way the situation had turned. His anger levels were rising and his tone became stern. 'Not as cheap as me just getting up and walking out of here, what are you going to do then, stop me?'

'That won't happen.' McLaren didn't sound worried by Quinn's threats. 'You're not going anywhere. Firstly, you don't have a clue where you are so you won't get far without me. Secondly, you haven't got any clothes on. We had to cut off the ones you were wearing so he could patch you up, then I burnt them to destroy the evidence. You're welcome by the way. Thirdly, you're hardly going to fit in any of my clothes are you, you big lump? And finally, you're still tied to the bed.'

'I'm what?'

'In case you haven't noticed, this isn't exactly a state-of-the-art operating theatre. We're hardly equipped with anaesthetics and the machines that go ping, are we? My man suggested we tie you down to stop you thrashing around when he worked on you. I cut the ties after... except the one around your ankle.'

McLaren raised the corner of the duvet to show Quinn the

thick black cable tie looping around his right ankle then the metal frame of the bed. It was only through seeing it that Quinn was aware of it. *Shit, I must be weak if I can't even feel my legs. One more night of bedrest, one night only, then I have to go.*

'So… we got a deal? Two-and-a-half grand to get you fixed up and on your way home?' McLaren extended a hand. Quinn murmured his agreement and McLaren leant forward. Quinn's huge workman-like hand smothered his, tiny in comparison, and they shook. 'Good lad, now get some rest, I'll see you later.'

-4-

BY THE TIME THE NEXT MORNING'S SUNRISE had clambered through the small window to wake Quinn, the weariness of recovery had worn off. He sat up without even thinking about it, and only afterwards realised it hadn't set off any pain within him. Sitting upright he began to twist his lower body off the bed but his ankle was yanked backwards. *I forgot about the tie. Bollocks.*

Quinn pulled back with his knee, twisted his leg, yanked and tugged, but the cable tie held firm. After some struggling the door opened to reveal a bleary-eyed McLaren in only a baggy pair of grey boxers.

'I need a piss,' said Quinn. McLaren left then returned brandishing a pair of kitchen scissors and, with a snip, cut the tie binding Quinn to the bed. McLaren held both arms outstretched towards Quinn, who took his hands and lowered his feet to the floor. Delicately, with McLaren's help, he raised himself to a standing position.

'Here, it's cold this morning.' McLaren peeled the duvet off the bed and draped it over Quinn's shoulders before leading him by the hand. 'Bathroom's this way.'

After draining off what felt like a week's worth, Quinn washed his hands in the stained, scaled basin. He drew his damp palms across his face, the cold water stinging his skin. Above the basin, a small mirrored cabinet. He looked pale and drained. Rings as grey as sorrow hung under his eyes. His hair fell lank and greasy.

Nearly a week's stubble prickled his chin. A short hunt yielded a packet of disposable razors under the sink. He scraped away the growth and stepped back to examine his handiwork in the small mirror but his eyes were drawn to his chest: high left, shoulder almost, there sat a postcard-sized white dressing.

After what felt like an age, he overcame his prevarication and peeled away the surgical tape taking a small forest of hair with it, a copse at least. The exposed clammy skin immediately itched as it gasped for air and sunlight. Torn edges of skin puckered beneath the stitches holding the wound closed, and shades of purple, grey and yellow radiated out from the point of impact. He touched it and immediately regretted doing so: pain unleashed red noise behind his eyes. He sat on the edge of the toilet until the pain subsided. With a sharp decisive yank he pulled the soiled dressing away entirely, then squeezed his large frame into the compact shower cubicle. From where he stood he caught the reflection of his naked torso. *Fuck, is that what I look like now? I used to spend my days in the gym spotting weights with the chaps, now the only thing I lift these days is pastries, I need to sort myself out.*

Quinn cranked the shower control open. Water began to sputter. McLaren's toiletries, Quinn noticed, largely consisted of small individual bottles and sachets, presumably all lifted from the island's hotels and caravan sites. Using his fingernail, Quinn popped the chalky crusted pimples on the shower head and the flow improved from puny and patchy to underpowered but adequate. Clean hair again felt good, but it was beyond pointless hoping McLaren had any product he could use to style it.

On the back of the bathroom door hung a dressing gown. A snowfall of dust gathered across it. Quinn pulled it on. It was too small, but anything was preferable to being in that duvet again. Short in the sleeve and tight around the shoulders, it gaped open across his chest, but the belt was long enough to tie it closed for modesty. He wiped off the accumulated cobwebs and dust bunnies. Judging by how long it had been hanging there untouched, Quinn assumed it must have belonged to the previous occupant. The thought of him ignited a memory from the darkest depths of his mind: a novelty ashtray in the shape of a skull, something his Dad had pinched from some seaside resort or other, imprinted with the words *"In loving memory of poor old Fred who died in bed".* Quinn pulled the belt, satisfied the robe was securely fastened, and with a wry smile whispered to any lingering ghost of the man: 'Poor old Fred…'

*

Quinn found McLaren in the living room, sitting in a wicker chair beside the panoramic window gazing out to sea. Quinn looked around, wanting to sit himself. He'd not eaten for several days and just the twenty minutes or so out of bed had worn him out. His head spun, giddiness began overwhelming him. Quinn lowered himself on to a green Chesterfield sofa. He gripped the sturdy leather arm and realised the living room was another mismatch of cast-offs. McLaren, Quinn surmised, lived cheaply: handouts, cast offs and whatever he could steal or cadge.

'Look at this view; I can't believe it's mine,' McLaren said without turning his gaze away. Quinn murmured appreciatively but wasn't impressed, it was hardly the Cote D'Azur out there. Instead, a scrubby overgrown patch of grass stood in front of the window before fading into a shingle beach. Low tide. Quinn saw timber groynes poking up irregularly from the sands: ancient, battered and brown like the teeth of an old pisshead his Dad used to hang around with back in the day. The water was grey and unwelcoming, the sky too. On the horizon across the sea stood a herd of alien life-forms. As he looked to the distance, Quinn could make it out as a cluster of spindly legs with crude circular pods atop and realised it must be the old abandoned Sea Forts, and from that Quinn could plot more or less where he was on the island now.

'I got some clothes for you yesterday when you were sleeping.

I've left them on your bed,' said McLaren, rising from his seat. 'Hungry?'

Quinn replied by saying thanks: just the one word but it covered both the clothes and breakfast.

'Expenses: you can add it to what you owe me.' McLaren busied himself where a half complete range of kitchen units lined one of the room's walls on stumpy plastic feet that should have been hidden behind a kickboard. Missing drawer fronts grinned gappily from the range, again reminding him of that old pisshead's smile. McLaren placed an anaemic cup of tea and a dry slice of toast in front of Quinn.

'I had to go all the way to Sittingbourne for them,' said McLaren.

'For what?'

'Clothes, for you. I couldn't go to the Cancer Research here, all the old dears know me, love me: I'm the acceptable face of poverty I guess.' McLaren thought this funny as he chuckled to himself. 'So I can't go in there buying stuff three or four sizes too big—they'd notice believe me—and I don't want any trace of you coming back to me, not yet.'

Quinn appreciated McLaren's caution; he would have done the same.

*

In the bedroom two carrier bags waited for him as promised. Quinn tipped them out on the bed and spread out the contents: one pair of dark blue corduroy trousers, one pair of shiny black office worker trousers, a green rugby shirt with a green shamrock on a white breast patch, and a navy-blue sweatshirt with a small *London 2012 Olympics* logo as the only decoration.

'Here, I got you these too.' McLaren had come in behind him carrying a pair of chunky black shoes on top of a folded black coat. 'Now then, they don't sell underwear in charity shops on account of health and safety. You can borrow a pair of my socks, but for now you'll need to go commando, okay?' He dropped them on the bed and left Quinn to get dressed.

Quinn tried everything and settled for the blue sweatshirt and blue cords. The sweatshirt was slightly too tight, the trousers slightly too loose but at least the shoes were comfortable. He tried the coat too: a black knee-length Crombie style woollen overcoat with a couple of cigarette burns on the sleeve. It fitted well, the pockets were deep and it had a pleasing swing to the tail as he swished back and forth. On the whole McLaren had done all right.

Quinn made to leave the blue bedroom, but curiosity caught him. With the gentlest of nudges to silently close the door he approached the boxes lining the wall. He peered in the nearest to find it packed solid with rolling tobacco. The next box the same, the one after full of branded cigarettes packaged in the holidaymaker's familiar two hundred. All had notices printed in a language he couldn't read. Of course, it made sense now, McLaren being out on the bridge in the wee small hours. He probably picked the pontoon for the same reasons as Quinn: quiet, out of sight, ideal for a small boat to rock up to, unload and then be away again totally unobserved. Perfect for bringing in smuggled tobacco from the Continent. A nice little easy number for a small operator like McLaren to tout all round the pubs, clubs and holiday camps. Good luck to him.

*

A dark oak cabinet dominated one wall of the living room by its total inappropriateness for its surroundings. Big heavy wooden doors concealed its lower portions, and glazed doors with olde-English leaded diamonds displayed its upper. Every square inch of it was covered with random, assorted crap—in, out, on and above. Quinn's eyes were drawn to a cheap wooden frame, possibly because it was the only thing that wasn't dusty. He lifted it off and looked at the happy lady and little boy smiling back at him. 'This your family?' he asked.

McLaren appeared at his side and looked at it as though it was the first time he'd ever seen it. 'Nah, no idea who that is. It's always been there,' he replied, taking it out of Quinn's hands and returning it to the same spot from where it came.

'You have family though?' Quinn found himself asking, which went against his principles: never ask for anything as they'll want it in return. But there was something, he hadn't identified what it was, but something about McLaren he liked.

'Yeah... no... well... you know... it's complicated.' He edged the cheap frame with his fingertips, straightening it up to match its original position in the dust outline and looked at it again. 'My Elaine, she'd had enough, can't complain, it can't have been easy for her with me in and out of nick. Six stretches I've done in all, just shy of thirty years banged up. She'd brought the girls up herself, told me plenty of times if I went down again she'd go. Never believed her. Then, stretch before last, two years in Maidstone, and she's gone.'

'Sorry. That's rough.'

'Yeah, well...' McLaren shrugged. 'The girls. That's the hardest part. The eldest, Louise, she went with her mum, not heard from her since. But my little one, my baby, there's seven years between them, squeezed out between stretches,' he chuckled unconvincingly. 'Claire, she doesn't give up on me, she sticks by me.'

'Nice.'

'Then I fuck it up and I'm back inside, here on the island. Let her down. Her mum says I told you so, her sister says I told you so. They were right. And now she's gone.'

'Have you tried talking to her? Even to let her know you're okay?'

McLaren dropped his head to his chin and blew a sigh through his nose. 'No. They're better off. I'm not too proud to see that. She's doing well though, my Claire. I check in on her now and then on Facebook. In secret of course, using a false name. She's working as a trainee hairdresser, doing a hair and beauty course at college, got a boyfriend, he seems proper. She don't need me pulling her down.'

McLaren turned his back to the cabinet. 'How about you, Quinn? Anyone out there wondering where you are?'

'I'm here. Don't be afraid. I'll protect you. Always.'

'No,' lied Quinn.

-5-

Six weeks earlier:

NOT FAR FROM THE ISLE OF SHEPPEY, heading back towards London, twenty-five miles on the fast roads, give or take, lies Rochester. Nestled in the bend, overlooking the River Medway, Rochester has a nice charm about it, something quaint and oldie-worldy. They've done well to wring every last penny out of its Charles Dickens connection and make it a year-round tourist destination. Even now, well out of season, the colourful summer bunting strung between the historic buildings and ornate lamp posts gives it a picture postcard photogenic quality. Towards the end of the High Street, near the foot of the mountainous Star Hill sits a coffee shop. Its shopfront, with its upper two-thirds glazed and its lower panels of a once deep verdant green now chipped and faded, sits directly against the wide pavement, parallel to the narrow red brick road. In curly gold and black lettering, the coffee shop's name is hand-painted across the glass: *Estella's*.

John Bentley found it easily enough from the directions given. He left the car in the pay and display at the back of a pub and, as he rounded it to get to the High Street, he spotted the coffee shop almost immediately opposite, as promised. The entrance door was set into the shop's chamfered corner, where the High Street met a narrow, cobbled side street. Bentley gripped the polished brass handle and pushed: a little effort needed to counter the stiffness of the ancient door closer overhead. An old-fashioned bell tinkled as the door edge brushed against it. A young woman, not even out of her teens, looked up from the counter as he approached.

Before either Bentley or the girl could speak, a figure emerged from the back-of-house staff area, a tea towel folded lengthwise and draped across his huge shoulder. His eyes met Bentley's and a grin spread to meet them.

'John,' said Quinn with a convincing tone of pleasant surprise. 'What brings you here?'

'I need a quick word; you got a minute?'

'Of course, mate.' Quinn yanked the tea towel from his shoulder, wiped both hands with it and dropped it on the counter top. He gestured towards a pair of mismatched wing-back chairs in the corner. Bentley took the hint and began moving in that direction. 'Zoe,' Quinn shouted to the young girl behind the counter. 'Zoe, cappuccino for John, and one for myself.'

Bentley got comfortable. None of the furniture matched but it all co-ordinated; clearly a style decision. Bentley looked around and noticed this design statement extended to the walls: lots of pictures, no theme, different frames. It gave the place an organic, studenty feel. Quinn settled in the armchair opposite him, filling it entirely. His white designer polo shirt clung tightly around his huge chest, the little horseman logo riding a pectoral as wide, smooth and solid as a panel of a new car. The short sleeves strained over biceps as wide as your thigh. He looked as though he'd given up the 'roids, probably a good thing, make him less volatile—although a sleeping bear is still a bear, and Bentley knew him well enough not to forget that.

'What do you think then, John?' asked Quinn, noticing Bentley's eyes surveying the surroundings.

'Very nice,' he replied genuinely. He approved of its ramshackle junk shop furnishings; it gave it a warmer more welcoming feel than the identikit corporate coffee chains. 'Who's Estella?'

Quinn had possibly never been asked that before because a wrinkle of confusion crossed his brow, if such a thing were possible, as if it were capable to put a crease in an Easter Island statue. He turned his massive shoulders towards the counter, the girl was busy twisting knobs and pulling levers on the elaborate shiny machinery, but undaunted he shouted at the back of her head. 'Zoe, who's Estella?'

Zoe didn't bother turning around, and shouted in response, 'Great Expectations,' then blasted a noisy jet of steam into a small jug.

'Great Expectations,' repeated Quinn, relaying the information to Bentley as though he hadn't heard despite being only eighteen inches further away. 'And now you know.'

Bentley nodded sagely but was still none the wiser. He put it aside, knowing it didn't matter in the long run, and instead used the moment to get a proper good look at Quinn. The signs of middle-age were evident; the once lantern-jaw hung a little looser than before, and Bentley couldn't help but notice a softness spreading around the belly where once it had been as hard and defined as the cobbled alley outside. If he was making any snide implication that Quinn had been *"getting high on his own supply"* in the question, 'So, you're now in the coffee and croissant business, are you?' Quinn either missed it, or ignored it in his reply.

'Yeah. It wasn't in my plans, but I sort of acquired this place—'

'Sort of?'

'Yeah, sort of. Previous owner gave it to me in lieu of payment.'

Bentley didn't comment any further and gave the impression he really didn't want to know the details. He'd find out later, he always did. Zoe brought across two cappuccinos in glass mugs that looked suspiciously like jam jars. She plonked them on the low table in front of the men. They both said thanks but her surly dismissive attitude was noted. 'I'm guessing she came with the fixtures and fittings, did she?'

'Zoe? She's my niece.'

'What… Benny's little girl?' Bentley turned to get a better look at Zoe, but self-conscious of his beady gaze she turned her back and wiped a cloth across the chrome of the machine, 'I can see it now, round here…' his finger circled his face, 'she's got his eyes and his nose.'

Zoe pushed open the door to the back-of-house area with enough force to clatter it against the wall and disappeared within, away from the staring.

'She's all right when you get to know her, she just doesn't like to be reminded of anyone from the business, and her dad, you know…'

'Poor old Benny. Such a shame…' Quinn spotted true sincerity in Bentley's voice and respected it. Bentley took a sip, an appreciative sip as it turned out because, despite her attitude and obvious resentment towards the visitor, Zoe did make a nice coffee.

'So, you're out of the bars and nightclub game, then?'

'Too right,' replied Quinn. 'Nothing but trouble.' Bentley spotted the concerned flick of Quinn's eyes towards where Zoe had been standing only seconds before. Quinn noticed him noticing, and swiftly moved on. 'It's a little goldmine this place.' He wafted a hand to mark out his new territory. 'I should have moved into this field years ago. This is how people spend their money these days. You should have seen how much it cleared during the last Dickens Festival; people can't get enough coffee.'

Bentley nodded. In his head he quickly weighed up the situation and considered the numbers; if Quinn was telling the truth and takings were that good, there must have been something deadly—every pun intended, he meant deadly—serious for the owner to hand it over to him. Bentley had heard Quinn and his brother dabbled in a little money lending on the side, and it was clear Quinn was still keeping his hand in and it was gripping just fine. He made a note to include that little titbit in his report back after the meeting.

'And it's nothing like the bar trade, most of the punters want grab-and-go so you don't need dishwashers on all the time, you don't need bouncers because some idiot's had one too many skinny lattes, and you're certainly not mopping up piles of vomit at two in the morning.' Quinn shifted in his seat, his eyes flicking towards the counter once again. 'And no girl's ever been accused of leading someone on because they'd had a few frappuccinos.' He held his focus for a second too long, but then blinked and returned to Bentley. He leaned back in his chair. He crossed one leg over the other knee, sat up straight and rested his heavy forearms, as thick and muscular as a joint of beef, along the arms of his leather wingback. 'So what brings you here, John? What can I do for you?'

'I was just coming to that. I'm glad you asked.'

-6-

QUINN TURNED THE COLLAR OF THE BLACK OVERCOAT up to batter back the sea breeze around his neck. McLaren had suggested a bit of fresh air after their meagre breakfast, Quinn agreed, and they had transferred themselves to a pitted, sun-bleached patio set outside. Quinn shuffled to get comfortable in the tight embrace of the narrow garden chair.

It was the first time Quinn had seen where he'd been cloistered for the better part of a week: a long, narrow structure, clad in flaky weatherboarding, with a low-pitched roof.

'What is this place? A chalet? A static caravan? What?'

McLaren laughed through a mouthful of smoke. 'This is... I don't know what'd you call it actually... a beach hut, shack, holiday chalet. Don't know, to be honest. But it's mine, all mine, and that's all that matters.'

With his roll-up pinched between two fingers, he used them to point out to towards the distance. 'See that,' he said. Quinn followed the direction indicated and could see a long container ship, faded red, sitting low in the water heading away from land. 'They arrive here all the time, day and night, bringing all sorts from all over the world. Cars, some of them.'

Quinn knew this game. 'Tobacco too,' he said. *There: we both think we know secrets about the other.*

The two men sat in silence and watched the ship sail away to foreign ports.

'Tony Flint has asked for you by name. That's virtually a royal summons,' said Bentley, the frustration at repeating himself laced clear and evident within the nasal tone of his voice.

Quinn looked at him, examined him, got the measure of him, sat there in his coffee shop drinking his cappuccino, giving him orders. Despite looking like an accountant on his day off, the lumpy middle-aged man in the golfing sweater and dad jeans wielded great power and influence, being Tony Flint's sole negotiator and go-between. Quinn connected and held eye contact with him for a second or two, just long enough to make him uneasy. Bentley pushed his glasses back up his sharp thin nose with a pudgy finger, waiting for his response.

'I know Tony. I've no problem with Tony,' said Quinn. 'It's the boy I'm concerned about.'

'Jamie. I've already told you, his name's Jamie.'

'I don't care what his name is. I don't know him.'

'Well this is your chance. He's told Tony he wants to join the family firm; he'll be an important man one day. It'd do you good to get in with him early.'

'Not interested.'

'What's the matter with you? You used to be a big-name player—'

'We got relegated, remember? Excommunicated.'

Bentley sighed inwardly. If he had to massage egos and tickle balls to get a result, then so be it. 'Well this is your chance to get back to the top table.'

'I'm a bit long in the tooth for that. Anyway, I'm out of all that stuff now, retired when Benny... you know. I just want to do what I do.' Quinn had money in the bank, real money with proper audited accounts to legitimise it, as well as other funds and interests kept well out-of-sight that he could draw upon, if ever needed. Glory and infamy were of no concern, he didn't feel the need to prove anything to anyone anymore. He could afford to say no to people, he had enough to get by—and then there was Zoe to think about. He had no urgency to go back to the old life.

'Look, he's clearly going to be the son and heir, one of London's oldest families, and Tony wants you on board as the voice of experience. People have called you a lot of things,' Bentley chuckled. 'But the one thing you are is a safe pair of hands, and Tony wants you to guide him through. He wants his signature job to launch his name. His Securitas, his Brink's-Matt, his Hatton Garden.'

'Hatton Garden got caught!'

*

The ship disappeared slowly over the horizon. Quinn broke the silence. 'Actually, there is someone I need to contact. Have you got a phone?'

'I've my mobile, but you're not using that, I don't want anyone tracing me—'

'Yeah, you've already told me that,' said Quinn, interrupting McLaren mid-sentence. 'Where can I find a phone?'

'There's bound to be one in the club,' said McLaren. 'Just as soon as you're ready to walk, I 'll take you there. It's about ten minutes away.'

That'll be fine, thought Quinn. *I'll speak with Bentley and then be off of Cabbage Island.*

AS QUINN STARED OFF TO SEA, a stranger had arrived on the other side of the island. He'd been given very clear instructions. Get the first flight from Frankfurt to London City Airport, where the promised hire car was waiting, then head straight to the island. As he crested the peak of the new bridge, he saw the acres and acres of cars parked down below and knew he was in the right place.

He drove slowly past the car compound then, finding a roundabout, looped back on himself and drove by in the opposite direction. *There must be twenty thousand cars in there,* he thought. *So how did they know which one to target? An inside man. Must have been. And it's the inside man I must find first.*

There was a reason why he was Europe's best manhunter: he didn't need to advertise, his reputation for always getting his target was enough. He got the call from the Dutchman, his usual intermediary, and as was expected he dropped everything immediately. The small antique watch shop he ran in the financial district of Frankfurt would be closed today, and remain closed until the Hunter had completed his assignment. When he re-opened, should any of his regulars ask where he'd been, he'd inform them an auction of vintage Rolexes had drawn him to Geneva, but no he hadn't bought any, the prices have gone through the roof recently, now then what can I interest you in sir, I have a lovely Patek Phillipe just in, one of a kind—and the matter would never be brought up again—at least not until the

Hunter's next assignment.

The Dutchman, normally cold and aloof, sounded urgent but the brief was clear. The Employer wanted him to recover what had been stolen, which was circa two million Euros, and remove those responsible. He had instructed the Dutchman to confirm acceptance of the assignment back to the Employer. The Hunter would oblige, and the Hunter always kept his promises. He pulled the car over into a drive-thru takeaway and began to strategize how to find the inside man.

*

Sandy was a man without a care in the world. Everyone knew Sandy, Sandy was everyone's mate. Sandy was the character in the colourful socks. The girls in the canteen billed and cooed over him: a free cup of tea now and again, bigger portion of chips on a Friday, he was in there. The rough tough hairy arsed dockers saw him as one of the guys, good for a laugh, keen for a joke, always in on their WhatsApp mucky video swaps. The reception team wanted him in their lottery syndicate—our good luck charm, money goes to money—they'd chuckle. And as for the office staff, he was the life and soul. Nothing happened at the port without Sandy knowing: he was all across it, by his own reckoning he'd be running the place in less than ten years. Yes, Sandy—or Sandeep Ghosh Assistant Logistics Manager according to his name badge—was king of his castle.

It wasn't even as if he had money problems or gruesome skeletons in his closet; he had entered into the situation quite happily, eyes open. Sandy was a geezer, that's how he saw himself: procedures were for losers who couldn't think for themselves. What Sandy lived for was the thrill of going off-piste: giving instructions as he dashed past you on the stairs, taking them two at a time, agreeing deals chattily over a coffee. He was Sandy, he lived on the fly. So when he was offered a sweet little cash bonus it was all his dreams come true. It wasn't the money so much, it was the frisson of knowing it was wrong; he was mixing with the naughty boys and he loved it. Diamond geezer. And how sweet it was—every Friday the roll on/roll off would bring another batch of cars and one of the seamen would find him, five hundred pounds in one hand and a GPS tracker in the other. All he had to do for it was hold on to the tracker, usually accumulating three or four in the back of his desk drawer before a courier would arrive to collect them. What happened to them after that, or what they were for he had no idea. Until...

Eighteen months later, a slow night shift combined with crushing boredom resulted in a flicked switch and a small device blinking in to life. Recognising the device was centring on a point out in the compound, Sandy felt a treasure hunt might relieve the tedium. The signal led him to a medium family hatchback but there was nothing extraordinary about it. Luckily Mr Sandeep Ghosh Assistant Logistics Manager was master of the keys. A rummage of the car yielded zilch then he popped the boot open and discovered the spare wheel compartment. *Fuck me, there must be tens—no hundreds—of thousands. Fuck, this is serious.* Suddenly the gloss had come off: way too deep, less diamond geezer, more cubic zirconia. He sealed the vehicle up, switched off the tracker and never said a word. The business partner, whoever that might be, never noticed; no questions raised, no harm no foul, any panic was quick to subside. The trackers kept coming every week and Sandy kept trousering the bung—happy days were here again. And as he arrived for work that morning he was standing on top of the world. If only he knew the Hunter was looking for him, then he might have wanted to stand somewhere else.

*

At the same time as Sandy's arrival in the office, on a busy street about a mile and a half away, a weasel-faced youth in a grubby white van hollered at a man crossing the road in front of him.

The man—the Hunter—didn't speak but silently flipped him the middle finger. The weasel shouted something else then yanked his van back into the stream of traffic, and roared on down towards the town centre, applying an extra bit of speed to jump the traffic lights at the last second. The Hunter pushed his ear-bud headphones back in, right ear first, then reached across his body with his right hand and simultaneously lowered his head to insert the other in his left ear, all the while holding his smartphone in front of him in his left hand.

Firms nearby were opening for the day's business. The delivery men and sales reps drove by, already re-plotting their routes ahead to counter the rush-hour jams. They hardly noticed him. Just a man, head down checking his phone, walking into town. By the time they'd turned the corner he was all but forgotten, just the slightest memory of yet another phone-zombie: the perfect disguise for anyone following military-grade sat-nav in unfamiliar streets.

He was a small, wiry man with a long chin who was older than he looked, thanks in part to the fashionable way he wore his straight black hair. As he walked his gaze was rooted to the pavement, avoiding eye contact with any passers-by: total anonymity was required.

The Hunter stopped outside an empty shop unit, a former pet store long since closed but beside it stood a red door with a white laminated sign: *Mercury Security*. He had arrived at his destination. He pushed the door; it was locked. He looked both ways, up and down the street: it was clear. He took from his pocket a slim piece of metal, custom tooled for this very purpose, and inserted it into the lock. The door began to swing open at his light touch. He entered and began climbing the stairs to the small office above the disused pet store.

-8-

McLaren had brought Quinn to the clubhouse of a nearby caravan park. Now in the late autumnal off-season with the holidaymakers long gone, it threw its doors open to the public. Signs declared membership cards must be shown on entry, but this wasn't being enforced. A hardcore contingent of hardcore boozers were dotted around the dormant dancefloor taking advantage of the discounted drinks and minding their own counsel.

McLaren, just by the rising of two fingers, had the barman pulling pints for him before he'd even reached the bar. 'Morning, Pat,' he said and gestured for Quinn to find a seat. Given they were in a dancehall that seated over two hundred, with only twelve seats occupied, the choice would have been overwhelming for anyone but Quinn. As always, he chose the seat in the corner opposite the main door: clear sightlines to all other doors and no one behind him. In this case it was a threadbare velvet banquette that had begun life a deep oxblood red but after more than forty summer seasons was now a stained and shiny grey. McLaren pushed a pint in front of Quinn and dropped a packet of peanuts on the table.

'What's the deal you've got with the barman?' Quinn tore at the corner of the silver foil packet, not looking at McLaren as he spoke. 'You didn't pay and he didn't ask. I'm guessing smokes?'

'Pat lets me run up a tab, food *and* drink, I pay him back in fags, two hundred a week.'

'And what's the boss have to say about that?'

'Fuck him! He's in Cyprus. Fucks off as soon as the summer season's over. Leaves everything to Pat to sort out. So, bollocks to him. We're all allowed to have a perk here and there.'

Quinn tipped the contents of the packet in to his mouth. The salt fizzed on his tongue and his blood rushed as his depleted sodium levels replenished. A gulp of the beer sluiced away the giddy sensation it was creating. 'Thanks.'

'Pleasure,' said McLaren, raising his own glass, and then he too took a slurp. He placed his hand flat down on the table and slid it towards Quinn, lifting it away to reveal a basic old-school mobile phone. 'Here you go. Be quick and don't take the piss, it needs to be back in her bag before she notices.'

Quinn followed McLaren's tilt of the head to a weary and baggy-eyed middle-aged woman sitting by herself. She gazed into fresh air, never letting go of the glass in her hand. Quinn showed he understood with a small downward nod.

McLaren pushed a couple of buttons, the screen lit up. Taking it, Quinn headed towards the gents' toilet so as to speak privately away from the deserted ballroom.

*

'Got my money?' said McLaren to the returning Quinn. He waited for Quinn to manoeuvre his midriff between the banquette and the table then added, 'Coming soon, is it?'

Quinn didn't respond, he simply slid the phone across to McLaren. He was done with it. If McLaren noticed the cracked and splintered screen he didn't comment.

McLaren stood and scooped the phone into his palm in one fluid movement, Quinn could appreciate a well-practised thief when he saw one in action. He didn't want to draw attention to McLaren so kept him on the edge of his peripheral vision whilst ostensibly looking at his pint. McLaren weaved between the empty chairs with the grace of a dancer. He returned the phone to the sad faced woman's bag without her ever becoming aware of him standing right behind her. Impressive: the prison mouse had learned himself some useful tricks.

Maintaining his forward momentum in case anyone should be watching, McLaren headed into the gents' toilet, and Quinn replayed the telephone conversation in his head: to say Bentley was surprised to hear from him would be an understatement.

*

'I've been mourning you for a week,' he had said. *'They told me you was dead.'*

Quinn had tried to reassure him that as far as he could tell he was still alive, but Bentley wasn't in the mood for levity; from the sound of his voice he was trying to get him off the phone as quickly as he could.

'Tony Flint himself broke the news, giving his condolences,' Bentley was picking up speed. 'He said you messed up, said because of you they nearly got caught.'

'That's not true.'

'Said you turned on them. Tried to rob them. Pulled a gun on them.'

'John, that's simply not true.'

'Said Jamie was a hero for stepping in, said you were about to blow the head off one of those boys.'

'It's not true. John, it's not true.'

'So you keep saying—'

'Don't you believe me, John?'

A pause, a deep exhale, then finally Bentley replied, 'Yes, of course I believe you,' his words sounded more placating than truthful. 'But listen to me,' Bentley lowered his voice and spoke slowly. 'Jamie Flint was the one who came home, not you, and according to him you're in the wrong so it doesn't matter if it's true or not. He is the son and heir, if Tony Flint says that's what the story is then that's what it is.'

'But John—'

'Look, you've wanted out. I know you have, you told me so yourself, don't deny it.'

'It doesn't matter what I want—' Quinn began to protest.

'Maybe it's for the best.' Bentley either hadn't heard him or wasn't listening. 'You can't come back here. The Flints have a long reach, no one would want to go against them, you can't ask anyone, it wouldn't be fair. Maybe you'd be better off staying dead wherever you are. I'm sorry mate. Take care.'

Bentley killed the call before Quinn had chance to speak again. Quinn knew there'd be no answer if he rang back. He looked out the window, across a field of empty forlorn caravans, and considered his next move. There was someone he needed to call, and from memory he tapped in the number. It immediately went through to voicemail and at the prompt he left the agreed message. 'Hello this is Simon Fisher from Pierhead Insurance calling about your claim for PPI. You can call me back on this number, thanks.'

Quinn sat and looked out the window. He knew it would be a few minutes; she'd need to find a payphone and it's anybody's guess where you find one of them these days. He gazed out over the caravans again, a low-sitting heavy grey cloud slowly rolled behind them. He waited. The phone buzzed in his hand and he snatched it to his ear.

'Zoe, it's me.'

A painful sob hit him from the other end of the line. He didn't need to ask, she'd already heard the news of his apparent demise.

'Zoe, it's not true,' he added although he knew it was redundant, but he couldn't think of what else to say.

'There's been someone coming round every day, saying you were dead—'

'Who?'

'Jamie. He said his name was Jamie…'

Quinn's heart pulsated in his chest, driving rage and anger

through his veins like a mighty engine. Without realising he was doing it he rammed his fist against the wall in impotent fury.

'He says you owe him. He says you messed everything up,'

'It's not true.' He rolled his hand over and looked at his grazed knuckles with curiosity when the pain finally surfaced in the conscious part of his brain. He gripped the phone tightly, 'Are you okay?'

'No. Not really.' She let out another sob that took her a few moments to compose herself from. 'He was at Dad's. He must be following me. I hadn't planned to visit his grave, I just went there and he turned up. This Jamie, I mean.'

'Why? What's he want?'

'He keeps pushing an envelope at me, papers he wants signed.'

'Papers?'

'Power of attorney… for you. They must know I'm your next of kin. At first he tried being all kind, saying he knew how hard it must be, me first losing my Dad and now you…'

'I'm so sorry, Darling—' protested Quinn, but she hadn't heard him and continued.

'Made out he was doing me a favour, telling me signing away power of attorney would make life easier for me, one less thing to worry about, he'd take care of it for me. I told him to fuck right off. He didn't like that.'

Quinn smiled at the thought. Jamie Flint, the flash git, failing at the first fence.

'He kept coming back. The last time, last night, he had someone with him, another man.' Quinn held his breath, waiting, wanting a name so he could pin a target on the rage brewing inside of him, 'Some goon. A massive lump of muscles and tattoos. Nasty looking.' A cold electric shiver ran through Quinn's blood. He knew getting angry was fruitless without someone to unleash it at, but at the same time it was becoming clear there was more to this than he knew about.

'What did they want?'

'Jamie and the goon? He said he wanted your businesses and

your property. Said you owed it to the Flints. The way he said it, his whole manner, it scared me. What's going on? Am I safe?'

Quinn considered his words carefully before responding. 'No. Listen to me, Zoe, listen very carefully, I don't know what's going on but you're not safe. Get out, go, now, right away. Don't tell me where, I don't want to know, just get away as far as you can. Don't have any contact with anyone you know. Don't use your phone, or your email they can trace it, likewise credit cards. There's a few grand in the shop's safe, the code's 9-1-7-4.'

'Dad's birthday.'

'That's right. Take it, it'll keep you going for a while. I need to get to the bottom of this and I need to know you are safely out of it, so go, now.'

'Okay,' she replied but her voice said she didn't understand.

'When it's safe to come back, when it's all over, I'll leave a message on your Dad's voicemail, okay? You'll recognise it when you hear it. Take care Zoe, look after yourself.'

He cut the call before she could say anything else, but if there was any family trait inherited by his niece it was that the Quinn family don't spook easily and not without good reason; he was confident she knew the urgency of the situation and was already on her way into hiding.

Against his better judgment, Quinn redialled Bentley's number, the fury accelerated within him at every dull ring in his ear. He'd dialled knowing full well Bentley wouldn't respond, but fury overwhelmed him: he needed an outlet, he'd scream and holler and threaten, he'd flood Bentley with anger. The ringing noise became a monotone buzz, the call had been rejected. The phone crashed into the wall with enormous ferocity and speed. Faded, dog-eared posters of entertainers and activities from the now defunct holiday season dropped to the floor, released by the flurry of punches to the plaster, fallen opponents hitting the deck.

But Bentley was right about one thing: Quinn wanted out. In fact, Quinn was out, and happy to be so. He had his coffee shop; he had his sidelines. He was looking to acquire a second coffee shop: a pretty little one further up Rochester High Street near the Cathedral, a cute narrow little unit done up all pretty in lavenders and pale blues. He'd buy it and give it to Zoe, to make sure she was set and secure; his promise to Benny. But John Bentley was Flint's negotiator for a reason: he was damn good at it. He knew how to bargain and how to deal, and when Quinn prevaricated he leveraged any objection Quinn had straight off the table. *If you do this, all is forgotten: Redlands, everything, slate wiped clean. Reparations made good.*

Quinn bent and reached out with sore and bleeding knuckles for the phone that had come to rest below the window. His eyes drifted out over the flat expanse, trying to find patterns in the green algae that spread across a nearby caravan like an infection. His mind processed the information available, there were three certainties of which he was sure: He knew he'd been set up. He knew help wouldn't be forthcoming. And he knew he was stranded on Cabbage Island.

-9-

MCLAREN RETURNED TO THE TABLE with a pint in each hand and sat down. Quinn pushed his empty glass aside and took the replacement from McLaren, tilting it slightly towards him in thanks.

'I've got news. But you first: where's my money?' McLaren said raising his beer to his lips, eyes locked on Quinn across the top of the glass.

Quinn didn't respond. McLaren's eyes widened over the rim of the glass as though that'd coax Quinn to speak. Quinn didn't react. McLaren smacked his lips together in appreciation, letting out a contented sigh, then, 'Okay, I'll go first. My news.'

Quinn's body language screamed disinterest as he slumped back into the velvet. He dropped his hands to his lap beneath the table to hide his split, bleeding knuckles from McLaren but he didn't appear to have noticed. Instead, McLaren looked first over his left shoulder then right, then leant forwards on his elbows.

'Just heard from a friend of mine,' he began. Quinn hadn't seen McLaren talk to anyone else other than him and the barman so either, he rationalised, it was the barman, or McLaren was making it up. Quinn kept his silence and waited to hear more before calling bullshit or not. McLaren, sensing his suspicion, explained his source. 'A mate of mine at the car depot—I say mate but more of a business contact, he fancies himself as a bit of a lad—I sell him fags and baccy and he sells it on.'

It sounded plausible to Quinn; he was satisfied with McLaren's credentials. McLaren took it as permission to continue. 'That security guard at the car compound who got battered on Sunday night,'

'What security guard?'

'Yes, whatever, anyway, that security guard who got battered. They released him from hospital on Tuesday morning. Seems he was taken back in again today. Got himself battered all over again.'

Quinn didn't respond. Many people may have replied with a cold-hearted quip but Quinn was too busy thinking.

'They got his address from the security firm,' added McLaren. 'It got turned over first thing this morning. Sounds like someone somewhere thinks he might have known about what happened on Sunday night, like they've come back to tidy up loose ends.'

Quinn didn't give it a second's consideration; he knew the security guard was blameless. 'No,' he said, correcting McLaren. 'What's happening is the owner wants their property back and they're looking for the inside man.'

McLaren didn't look as though he cared one way or the other. 'Whatever. All that matters is at the moment I'm two-and-a-half grand down...' he left the threat hanging unsaid, and took another noisy slurp of his lager. 'So, got my money?'

Quinn hadn't moved from his relaxed posture but his eyes were fixed and angry; the raging fire that had blazed within in him had reignited and was ready to explode. McLaren seemed oblivious, but that was the talent of the prison mouse: don't make eye contact, don't react to anything, and move quietly wherever you go. Quinn knew that McLaren didn't go in for grand dramatic gestures, his style was more subtle than that—he would know in whose ear to drop a few whispers and, in a small place like this, it only needed to pass through a few ears before it landed in the right one. Quinn looked at the small wiry man with disappointment and annoyance, fighting back the urge to lash out and knock that copper ratty 'tache off his face. Under any other circumstance he could quite easily pick him up and snap him in two, but Quinn was all about the details, and he hated that he had none. Quinn realised that, for now, McLaren was in control.

*

Quinn pushed his half-drunk pint to one side, stood up and walked out. A chill breeze riding in on the tide slapped him in the face. He stood the collar of his overcoat up in a futile gesture to keep the cold back and began to walk in the opposite direction to where he'd come from. He'd not passed any sort of town or shops when he'd arrived with McLaren, so set off in the hope they were this way.

McLaren caught up with him after he'd been walking a minute or so. Between puffs and pants McLaren asked Quinn to stop. Quinn shuffled to a halt. McLaren lit himself a roll-up between wheezes, and tried to catch his breath.

'Come here, come here,' McLaren gestured towards a public bench on a grass verge overlooking the beach, and plonked himself down, Quinn followed.

'I don't have your money,' said Quinn.

'I guessed that much. But is that don't have the money *yet*, or don't have the money *ever*?'

'I don't know,' wasn't the best answer Quinn could have given, but it was the most truthful.

'I thought you said you were good for it?'

'I was, when I was alive,' replied Quinn. 'But now I'm presumed dead and I'm guessing certain people want it to become permanent.'

'So is that it then?'

'No. They've stolen from me. I did the job I was hired to do. We agreed the cut, they've taken mine. I want it back. I need it. I will get it back.'

'Great, so it's don't have the money *yet*. Let's go collect.'

'It's not quite that easy. I can't just walk up to Tony Flint and shake him down.'

'Tony Flint?' The colour blanched from McLaren's face. 'You want to rob Tony Flint?'

'I'm not robbing anyone; it's my money.'

'Whatever. I've heard all the stories and rumours about the Flint firm. If they think you're dead, you're probably best off letting them keep thinking that.'

'So I've been told. But I want my money.'

'Why? Can't you write it off, be grateful you're still alive?'

'No. I need it. I have commitments.'

'Wait, you and the Flints, Sunday at the car compound? This is a big deal isn't it? Is that why… the security guard?'

'Yes' replied Quinn. 'This is a big deal, and I need your help. You're part of the network here, you know everything that happens and who connects to who.'

McLaren for the first time looked scared; after a lifetime as the prison mouse hiding in the shadows he'd been thrust into the foreground and the prospect terrified him.

'Before I can get to the Flints, before I can get what's mine, I need to get off this island. And to get off this island I need money, I need a war chest, and I need to keep out of the way of whoever is hunting Sunday's players. Can you help me? I'll pay you double, five grand.'

McLaren scratched his head, his chin, and sighed. 'Okay, All right… but I want ten.'

-10-

TWENTY-FIVE MILES AWAY, on a side turning just off Rochester High Street, a furious conversation was taking place. 'Of course I'm fucking sure, I've just spoken to him.'

The out-of-season tourists walking past the sombre saloon car turned in surprise at the sound and fury emanating from within, and caught a glimpse of the middle-aged driver, red of face, yelling into his cell-phone and jabbing his finger with every word for emphasis. They looked at each other and giggled: another bad day at the office for someone.

The sight of the two backpackers glancing back at him made Bentley realise he was drawing attention. He closed his eyes and held them shut for a couple of seconds, deep breath in, up through the nose, hold it, release through the mouth. Convinced he was calm, he spoke again.

'I'm telling you, Quinn's still alive… No, I don't know where, he didn't say…' Bentley removed his spectacles and pinched the bridge of his nose. He ground the ball of his thumb in his eye socket as though that would somehow release the tension suddenly filling his head. 'No, he didn't sound as though he suspected anything but, as soon as he contacts the girl, he'll know… I'm right outside now… Okay, leave it to me.' Bentley ended the call and dropped the phone on the passenger seat. *Fucking Jamie*, he muttered to himself. Quinn had warned him he was a liability, that he'd mess things up. Bentley gave a small snort, appreciating the irony in it being this task Jamie had failed. In his rear-view mirror he watched a dark four-wheel drive vehicle draw to a slow halt behind him. *Good; they're here.*

You wouldn't survive as long and successfully as Bentley without being a quick thinker and a strategic planner. By the time the back doors had opened and his rear axle lurched under the weight of four hundred pounds of dumb muscle, Bentley knew exactly what needed to be done. He turned to face the two beasts now occupying his back seats. 'Change of plan, listen up…'

Bentley slowly explained their new roles in the patient tones of an attentive parent helping a reluctant child learn long division. These guys were paid based on how many punches to the head they could take, not their thinking, so Bentley kept it simple. 'We don't know where he is, and the only family he's got is his niece, so we need to watch her, follow her, she'll lead us to him. She knows me. You, LJ, came here yesterday with Jamie, and inconspicuous you're not,' he spoke at the big lump with bold black tribal patterns inked from wrist to ear. 'So Marko, it's up to you. Follow her, but keep your distance, let me know what she does, where she goes and who she meets.' The gigantic Russian didn't speak. The only sound he made was the rasp of his ginger beard bristling against his puffa jacket when he nodded his acceptance.

Bentley's car bounced back on its springs as the two men exited. LJ, the tattooed knucklehead, returned to his four-wheel drive. Marko the big red Russian pushed apart the doors to the pub opposite, ordered a soft drink and took up his watching brief of the pretty little coffee shop across the road.

-11-

QUINN SAT FACING MCLAREN. The white melamine table between them had a nasty stickiness that tried holding him down every time he moved his arms. Before them both were coffees in tapered glass mugs. The waitress was a distracted young Eastern European woman more interested in her phone than them; even when delivering their drinks, she had it pinned between ear and shoulder. Right now, she was engaged in a heated conversation in a language neither of the men understood. Quinn wasn't impressed by her presentation skills: there was no layering, the foam was too thin, and no effort had been made to dress the cup with a little artwork or a light sprinkle of cocoa powder. He took a sip and couldn't hold back the wince. *Nasty; you wouldn't last five minutes in my shop serving this muck.*

Despite there being nobody else there, McLaren looked over both shoulders before leaning in conspiratorially, the ingrained survival instincts of the prison mouse. He swirled a long-handled teaspoon around his coffee, licked it clean and then used it as a pointer.

Quinn's eyes followed the direction of the spoon, to the other side of the road. To a small, irregular-shaped spit of land with no attractive redeeming features, just a rough concrete yard. Along its nearest side, galvanised steel railings ran parallel to the road. Its furthest edge shared the boundary with the windowless, weather-beaten wall of a dilapidated warehouse building, two storeys high in greyish/green concrete blocks and sun-bleached crinkly tin sheeting. The yard had, once upon a time, been open storage for a builder or some other similar light industrial use. Today, big banners were fixed to the wall and railings. Bright yellow with plain black letters: *'Drive Thru Car Wash'*, they proclaimed. Grimy, bent traffic cones formed three channels for cars to line up and get cleaned. Business, whilst not busy, was brisk and regular. Quinn counted ten young men working collectively across the first channel closest the road, and the second channel in the middle. The third channel, furthest from the road and nearest the wall, remained empty. Quinn put it down to a mid-week quiet phase and watched the workers. One waited by the entrance welcoming the drivers in off the road. He'd agree what was wanted by pointing at a big yellow menu fixed to the nearest wall. Quinn assumed he had the job because he had the best command of English. Once agreed he'd direct the driver to one of the two channels where his colleagues were waiting with mops, hoses and foam.

'Watch carefully,' said McLaren. 'Look, only one person touches the money, see?' Quinn watched on following a silver estate car pass through the whole cleaning process in the first channel, closest to the road. Just before it rolled through the exit gates to re-join the traffic on the main road McLaren piped up again. 'Watch him.'

A fat swarthy man with thinning hair hauled himself out of a collapsible camping chair. Even from the opposite side of the road, just from the look of him, Quinn knew he'd stink. The man thrust a surly hand through the driver's window only to snatch it back clutching a banknote, never at any time removing the cigarette from the corner of his mouth.

'He's the boss, only him allowed to touch the money. All cash. He must have a couple of hundred quid a day,' McLaren informed him. Quinn knew what he was suggesting: rob the fat man. For a couple of hundred quid, was it worth it? Something didn't add up for Quinn and, when he realised what, it sickened him.

'They're slaves,' he said. 'I'm not robbing slaves.'

McLaren's expression was one of disbelief and revulsion. 'Slaves?'

'I've counted at least ten men there, and all of them working for two hundred pounds a day, you reckon. That won't go far split ten ways, will it?'

McLaren hadn't taken his eyes of the activities over the road but shook his head in response to Quinn's question, no matter it being meant rhetorically.

'Probably forced into doing this by the traffickers that brought them over, told it would pay off their debt for the crossing.'

The fat man got comfortable in his chair and looked along the channels. He barked something they couldn't hear to the workers, who immediately began tidying up the yard. He took the stub of the cigarette from his mouth and used it to light another one, then flicked it towards a puddle of foam suds left behind by the last car.

'The fat man, he's the slave master. Probably holds their papers, pretends he's doing them a favour then works them like dogs. No matter how desperate things get, I'm not robbing him, as it'll be those boys that bear the brunt.'

Quinn gazed out towards the carwash again. The fat man's arrogance triggered something primal in him, making his nostrils flare and lip twitch into a sneer. McLaren looked to Quinn with expectation, waiting for further guidance. Quinn, ready to suggest going home, noticed something of interest, something new. He pushed aside his coffee and called for tea instead, just to justify staying in his window seat.

A car had arrived, the sort of car you heard long before you saw it. Quinn lightly pressed his fingertips to the café's window, wondering if the car's thumping bass made the glass throb.

The worker at the entrance approached the car but, before he'd even got close, he turned away and with a loose flap of the arm gestured towards the third channel, nearest to the wall, furthest from the road. So far Quinn hadn't seen anyone use the third channel. The car aggressively accelerated then slammed to a halt three metres later when it reached the third channel. A previously unseen young man sauntered up to the car. He had a long, rangy walk like a greyhound. He leaned in through the driver's window. The man and the driver spoke, and as they spoke the young man reached in to his jacket pocket then extracted a clenched fist which he passed in through the driver's window. It was swiftly retracted, clutching banknotes that got crammed into the same jacket pocket. The car gunned back into life and accelerated out of the carwash, as dirty and dusty as when it arrived.

Quinn pointed at the young man retreating back to his hiding place, a small non-descript garden shed erected in the corner of the yard. 'He's the boss, that one.'

McLaren looked up and around but had missed it.

'The carwash is a front; they're dealing out of there. That's where the money is. That's what we'll hit.'

McLaren dropped his spoon; it fell to the floor with a noisy clatter. 'What? Now?' Cold, heavy panic struck him like an avalanche.

Quinn laughed seeing him squirm, enjoying holding the upper hand at last. 'No, what we're going to do is sit and wait and watch.'

'What for?'

'That guy, he's the bottom of the food chain. There'll be someone coming for the money at some stage, they won't let him hold it too long and certainly won't let him leave the site with it. Someone will come and collect it from him. We need to know when.'

McLaren wore a rollercoaster face: a shared expression of both fear and excitement. 'Why?'

'Because we get one go at this so firstly we don't want to hit it after the pick-up when he's not holding anything, and more importantly it's just you and me: we don't want to hit it just as a vanload of tooled up gangsters turn up.'

The pieces fell into place before McLaren's eyes and he nodded along, open-mouthed.

'So,' Quinn continued, 'we need to find out when they collect, and if we assume it's a regular thing, we'll hit it twenty minutes or so beforehand tomorrow.'

McLaren nodded on and on, quietly muttering, 'Yeah, yeah,' to himself. Outside in the mid-afternoon sky huge sombre grey clouds loomed into view like a fleet of destroyers. The atmosphere took on a dark tone to match the sky. Sensors in the streetlamps reacted to the dimming of the daylight and began to illuminate.

'Seeing as we're going to be here for a while, why don't you give your pal at the Car Depot a call, find out what else he knows.'

The waitress brought across Quinn's long forgotten cup of tea and slid it across the table, not saying a word. She turned away without even looking at him. McLaren dialled his contact: Sandy Ghosh.

In a synchronised symmetry, at the same time as Quinn was testing the insipid tea, the same time as the waitress was scanning her phone to see if she'd missed anything in the past thirty seconds, and at the same time as McLaren was impatiently listening to an unanswered ring tone, Sandy Ghosh was dying. He lasted five seconds longer, then as the ringing ceased so did he.

'Straight to voicemail. I'll try again later.' McLaren placed his phone on the table top and called out to the engrossed waitress, 'Another coffee here please, darling, and a Kit-Kat.'

-12-

ABDI ZELALEM ANSWERED THE door on the second ring. He was tired and needed sleep. He'd just come off shift; the last thing he wanted was visitors. He'd ignored the doorbell's first ring, but he knew when it chimed again they wouldn't leave him alone until he'd spoken to them. The young Somalian hauled his tall, slender frame off the sofa where he'd been drowsing and rubbed his long narrow fingers across his eyes. The thick swirling pattern of the small glazed panel in the door made everything look underwater, but he could identify a man's head in profile. He looked bored, a salesman going door-to-door, distracted by the passing yummy-mummies pushing prams. Abdi pulled the door open, and as it widened the man turned to face him.

The man smiled; he was small and wiry with straight black hair and a long chin. He thrust a glossy brochure for upvc windows and conservatories straight at Abdi and asked, 'Might I interest you in double glazing?' with the faintest of accents to his voice.

Abdi lived in the house with four other men, and every week he'd pay his bit for a shared bedroom. It wasn't so bad, his room-mate was a motorway labourer from Syria who tended to work different shifts to him, so it was almost like having a room to himself. They'd never once met the landlord who still hadn't done anything about the broken shower despite them asking for months, so it was unlikely replacement windows were a priority.

'Might I interest you in double glazing?' the man repeated,

his accent sounding stronger.

Abdi had no interest or investment in the house, but before he could answer the small, wiry man with the straight black hair and the long chin pushed past him into the property and was closing the door.

*

Sandy Ghosh was at home. He was not, however, at home to visitors. His heart fluttered in panic when the phone in his hand began to ring and vibrate. The caller flashed up on screen, Work: it can wait, I can't be worrying about that today, let voicemail take it.

Carefully, Sandy edged his eyes no more than an inch above the window-board and peered through the gap at the bottom of the blind. *Is anyone out there? Has that van been there all day?*

Sandy knew he was acting paranoid, but that didn't mean he was wrong. Someone was looking for him. He knew that for certain, but did they know it was actually him they were after? He wasn't sure, yet. All he did know was the day after the car depot was robbed both the security guards were visited and hospitalised, or re-hospitalised in the case of the first guard. Someone was looking for the inside man. The guards were new. One of them had only been on the job for a week. They didn't know Sandy. But it wouldn't take long before someone joined the dots and put Sandy in the frame, but nobody knew, nobody could make that link, he hadn't told anyone... except... well, but... they wouldn't... would they?

The day came and went. The children first shuffled past his window to school for morning assembly and then sauntered back home for lunch in the opposite direction. Sandy spent those hours, his last in this world, hiding below the window, popping up occasionally as the paranoia deepened: *Where's that van gone? Has it switched with that red car?*

The afternoon sky darkened, the temperature began to

drop. It gave a taster for the cold night to come. Sandy's fears intensified in the gloom. He knew it broke their agreement; he knew he'd get in trouble but what difference would it make if he was to die imminently anyway? Sandy looked in his phone for his contacts, he pressed "call" and the connection was made. It rang a couple of times before it was answered. Sandy took a deep breath in a failed attempt to relax himself, then he spoke.

'It's me. We need to talk.'

*

'Shit shit shit shit!' Jamie thumped and slapped and slammed the steering wheel. The phone call he'd just had was exactly what he hadn't wanted to hear. *Stupid idiot wannabes, I knew I shouldn't have trusted them.*

To fill the tedium waiting for the lights to change, memories entered Jamie's mind and took him back to the previous summer. Whilst the country had basked under a short-lived heatwave, Jamie had endured a tedious birthday party for a distant family member in a stifling hot white marquee. Its poor air flow meant everything smelt vaguely of plastic and grass under the beating July sun. Finding himself increasingly bored and tetchy, his luck had suddenly changed when he noticed a little cutie in a tight yellow dress eyeing him from the opposite side of the tent. She was hot, she was fun, not looking for anything too serious, and had a thing for naughty boys. Just Jamie's type; maybe the night wasn't such a wash-out after all.

Cassie, for that was her name, could tell she was in the presence of a proper naughty boy; no small-fry tobacco tout, no two-bit hustler flogging counterfeit sunglasses to tourists, no, this guy was the real deal. He was connected. He was dangerous. He ran with the big boys. Cassie wanted to impress him. Cassie wanted to be with him. Cassie wanted some of his stardust to land on her: watch out for Cassie, she knows people who knows people.

The party began drawing to a close: the candles were blown out, the empty champagne bottles lay across the tables like fallen soldiers and Jamie was already beginning to lose interest. Forget about not wanting anything too serious, he'd spotted early on she was a danger-groupie, the sort desperate to play the martyr, the sort desperate to complain loudly about the unpredictability his kind of lifestyle brings whilst loving it at the same time. He'd already accepted a text invitation to meet friends in a nearby nightclub and was counting down the minutes before he could make his farewells when she uttered the magic words to stop the clock.

'Say that again,' he demanded, his attention suddenly snapping back to her. Jamie had filtered out her jibber-jabber as white noise for the past ten minutes or so, allowing his attention to linger on a new cutie in black leggings having fun on the dancefloor, appreciating how she wiggled in time to the music.

Happy to be Jamie's focus again, Cassie eagerly repeated herself. 'I said, the boot of a car, packed solid and I mean solid, absolutely jammed tight, with money. There must have been hundreds of thousands of Euros. And it comes in every week.'

Jamie ushered Cassie to a nearby table, where she proved all his assumptions correct: she had a thing for naughty boys, and the naughtier the better as far as she was concerned. Her latest boyfriend—'More of a dabble, nothing serious,' she was keen to stress, not wanting to distance herself from Jamie by appearing spoken for—had a sweet little scam going on at the car depot where he worked. Turned out Sandy Ghosh had been keener on Cassie than she was on him. Fearing he was losing her affections, he'd tried to prove he wasn't just a fantasist but had proper naughty credentials and had told her all about what he had found in the boot of a car one day, thanks to the trackers he was entrusted with every week.

Jamie could spot her eagerness just as easily as he could spot an opportunity. By dangling the promise of meeting up later in the week, she was persuaded to get him more details. Soppy

Sandy Ghosh, all too flattered by the attention he suddenly received from the oh-so-keen Cassie, recognised how hot it was making her. He was only too happy to tell her everything, not leaving a single detail out, to the point of even the make and model of the tracker devices stored in his desk drawer.

When Jamie met her again, Cassie was as equally desperate to impress her new lover as Sandy was his. It felt dangerous just even talking to him, and she wanted to show him she was up to the task. Jamie nodded and reined in his impatience, knowing she was a "pleaser": if he tried to rush her she'd only tell him an embellished version of what she thought he wanted to hear, rather than the bald facts of what he needed to know. By biding his time, he learnt all about the roll-on/roll-off ships delivering new cars from the continent and the tracker device entrusted to Sandy to look after, and more importantly the regularity of drop-offs and collections.

By the time Jamie left her the next morning, he had himself a project to take to his old man; this was going to be his invitation to the top table.

*

With two electronic beeps the microwave awoke and the small plastic portion of pasta chundered into slow rotation. Cassie watched it turn, the digital numbers on the panel counting down. Her phone rang and roused her from her unintentional meditation. She looked at the name displayed. *Shit, what's he want?* With two minutes thirty-three seconds to kill before her tagliatelle was ready, she reluctantly answered the call.

'It's me. We need to talk,' said Sandy Ghosh.

*

Jamie composed himself; people walking by were staring at him. He reached for a bottle of water in the door pocket and took down a mouthful. It tasted warm and stale and left his mouth feeling drier than it was before. This would never do. This was meant to be his springboard to the next level, his way to prove himself worthy to his dad and, more importantly, to his partners. The Old Man had been genuinely impressed when he brought the scheme to him; he'd told him he could see a future for him in the firm. Jamie was convinced his father would approve of his efforts to seize control of Quinn's businesses: *just need to get Quinn's soppy bitch of a niece to sign the papers and it's sorted,* he thought. *The Old Man might even give them to me, let me run them, kind of like a practice run before I sit in the big chair.*

A sharp twitch of the head shook out any complacency. Jamie knew he couldn't yet go to his father—not with this new problem presenting itself. It was his to own and he knew he'd need to sort it. He didn't know how yet; the only thing he was certain of was that the cutie in the yellow dress had become a liability. Jamie knew that, if anyone was tracking the money and they'd reached her soppy bollocks ex-boyfriend, it wouldn't take long before they got to her. Then it'd be a short step to him, and from Jamie they could very easily make the connection to the Flint firm, and that must never happen. It didn't require a lot of thinking time for Jamie to realise what he needed to do.

He called Cassie back, and arranged to meet her the following morning. Then he made another call. 'LJ, whatever you're doing tomorrow, cancel it. We're going back to Sheppey. Cabbage fucking Island.'

*

Sandy Ghosh felt relieved. He knew he'd been wrong to suspect Cassie. They may have ended it on a sour note, but he should have known she'd never gossip about him or give him away; in fact she sounded quite angry at the very suggestion.

Sandy rose to his feet with such elation it felt as though he'd keep floating up to the ceiling. Whatever weight had been pressing on him was now off his shoulders and he was free. Sandy knew he could sleep soundly in his bed that night, as whatever problem he'd worried about had gone away and could be forgotten.

Nothing to fret about, thought Sandy. He headed upstairs to use the bathroom, but not before a final cautious look out the window. *The red car's still there; maybe I should write down the registration, just in case.*

*

The red car Sandy could see bore him no ill will, belonging as it did to a neighbour a few doors away, a retired gent from the newspaper business. If he'd been in a similar heightened sense of paranoia every day, he'd know that was the same spot the elderly printer parked in since first acquiring the car eighteen months ago. Then again, if he hadn't been so oversensitive to the presence of unfamiliar cars, he may have noticed the pedestrian who'd been past the house at least once every hour since lunchtime.

*

The Hunter had hit a wall with the two security guards, literally and metaphorically. Neither of them knew anything, both were no more than hired bums on seats, but they'd served their purpose each in their own way.

It had been simple work for him to locate Abdi. He'd taken a list of names and addresses from the security firm's offices. Unnoticed by the security firm and unreported in their insurance claim was the glossy junk mail taken from their recycling pile: windows and conservatories at zero percent interest, always a good disguise when doorstepping. Then he visited the first guard in the hospital, the recipient of Jamie's violence. Apart from confirming Abdi had been his shift partner that night, he had had nothing of any use to give to the Hunter. The hospital visit would have been a total waste of time ordinarily, but it had its own rewards. Other practitioners might say it was a disproportionate amount of violence but he'd respond that he loathed early morning flights. It'd been a useful outlet to work out his frustrations and stiffness from the long journey.

The Hunter could tell just by looking at Abdi's terrified, bleeding face he wouldn't yield anything useful to help find his client's money, but he was here now and figured he may as well make the best of a bad lot. He selected the correct app on his phone, then found the best viewpoint to stand it on edge and pressed record. The Hunter had a contact in Berlin, a very wealthy individual. He had a passion for torture and was prepared to pay handsomely for it. That wasn't to say the Hunter didn't take his manhunting work professionally, whatever his clients searched for remained confidential. Any footage sold was first overdubbed with music to obliterate any conversation, that way one client gets the information to find their treasure, the other gets the video to find their pleasure. The Hunter had already selected *'Gymnopédie'* as his soundtrack for this project and hummed it to himself. He wanted the tempo in his head so it would synchronise his movements accordingly. By the time he'd removed his wallet of blades from inside his suit jacket he'd made his mind up: *I'll start with the eyes. He likes eyes.*

*

Lacking any kind of lead, the Hunter realised a new approach was needed. He sought out the closest cafe to the car depot. Sure enough, within half an hour various members of staff drifted in to pick up a sandwich and a coffee or maybe a can of coke. Some drifted straight back out again, but others stayed, grateful for a short respite from the office. None of them noticed the small, wiry man with the straight black hair on the next table. They never noticed how he hadn't turned a single page of the newspaper laid out in front of him. Instead of reading, he listened to their conversations. And one topic kept coming up: *'Not like Sandy to take the day off, just like that, is it', 'Is Sandy sick, he didn't seem himself yesterday', 'No one's heard from him so I don't know if he'll be back tomorrow.'* The absent Sandy sounded like someone the Hunter should be interested in.

It didn't take long to get a home address for Sandy Ghosh, and lacking any other leads, the Hunter began to make regular passes by the house looking for signs of life within: there wasn't.

Eventually, as the afternoon daylight began to fail, a lamp illuminated a window upstairs. Looking at the weak buttery yellow glow the Hunter correctly assumed it was from a bedside lamp rather than the main overhead fitting, but had a timer activated it? The Hunter waited and watched. A shadow passed across the window in one direction and then a minute or two later it returned back the other way. Sandy Ghosh was in the house, he was upstairs. Within ninety seconds so was the Hunter.

-13-

JAMIE WALKED FROM THE CARPARK without looking back and turned right into the main drag of the high street. Ahead of him were the patchworked tarmac and the cracked pavements and the dull empty shopfronts, some seasonal, some long-term closures. And lots of people on the move, too many for an out-of-season seaside resort, especially at that time of the morning. Policy decisions by successive governments had dumped people there in their droves, but without enough to keep them busy they wandered the streets aimlessly hoping something would happen. Jamie could see up ahead the maroon frontage of the meeting place, and he slowed his walking pace, not wanting to arrive too soon.

The shop girls in green uniforms about to start their shifts eyed him with interest and curiosity as they approached him in the street but Jamie pretended not to notice, acting lost in thought as though questioning his whereabouts. As they passed they caught his eye and gave flirty smiles, he blanked them, offering no response; but inside, any self-doubt was chased away and an extra bounce joined his swagger. *'Yep, still got it,'* it seemed to say.

He was tall and lean, with broad square shoulders and long, toned arms. He wore a neat grey collared t-shirt with a small but significant logo that proved its value, new black jeans that the washing machine would never get the chance to fade, with trainers that were all black, including the brand logos: Jamie's idea of anonymous smart casual, a camouflage to blend in to any public space. He wore his straw blond hair in a scruffy crop, and although a pleasant looking man he carried his looks with more confidence than they actually deserved, privilege writ large on his face, in his walk and his attitude.

Jamie was the son and heir to the empire, and he wanted everyone to know it; despite only wanting it himself for a couple of months. He'd devoted himself to proving it to those who mattered, every single day, that the future belonged to him: a feat only to be embarked on by those with an ingrained sense of entitlement. Having a rich, powerful daddy happy to exert his influence to indulge every whim also helped. There'd been the junior pro contract with a Championship football team that failed when his talent and his attitude weren't good enough to get him a first-team game. Reality TV became the next port of call, where easy money and easy fame beckoned—and all he had to do was hang around in front of the cameras looking pretty to be paired up with gorgeous airheads—what could go wrong? But sure enough, wrong it went. Tony soon pulled Jamie out of that scene in double quick time. And so, with opportunities for easy cash and celebrity dwindling, Jamie decided there was no alternative other than join the family firm. Tony was only too keen to pipe the young captain on board, hearing but ignoring the resentful snipes from others who'd worked for their opportunities by putting in the long yards and facing down the risks, hoping for similar reward. Jamie knew others were jealous of his nepotistic rise through the ranks. He didn't care, but he knew he couldn't afford to let the scheme he'd suggested to Daddy fail: they'd love that, the bastards. No, he couldn't let it fail, not now, not for the sake of a little cutie in a tight yellow dress.

Speak of the devil, up ahead Jamie saw Cassie rounding the brightly coloured clocktower and into the high street. Bang on time. Jamie glanced back the way he came. He spotted LJ in his red cap hanging back as instructed, loitering in the narrow fire escape route between two neighbouring discount stores. LJ, the proverbial blunt instrument, broad and lumpy and slow-witted. He'd been door security for the clubs, among the pill poppers and the ravers, but too much ecstasy and too much speed had scrambled his head. These days, being big and menacing was the most complicated thing he could handle.

With everything in order, Jamie made the meeting place in a few strides. He grabbed the flat maroon door handle and entered.

*

Cassie hadn't noticed anything amiss when she left home that morning. If she'd shared the same heightened level of paranoia as Sandy, she might have been aware of the white hatchback parked halfway up the road. She might have seen it pull out moments after her. She might even have noticed it consistently two cars behind all the way into the town centre. Maybe she'd have recognised its small, wiry, black-haired driver walking about twenty metres behind her on the opposite pavement. But she didn't. She did, however, notice Jamie approaching from the other direction. Something pleasing fluttered within her at the sight of him again so many months after he'd finished with her. She waved but he didn't notice; it didn't matter, she'd arrived. She grabbed the flat maroon door handle and entered. She found a seat facing the door and struck a pose. She had it prepared: she looked gorgeous even down to wearing the same yellow dress she had seduced him in the first time they met. Jamie would walk in to find her moments later, and beg her to come back: she was sure of it.

*

Finding the girl had been easy: the idiot with the colourful socks had given her name up within seconds. And a few seconds after that he'd given away her telephone number, home address and where she worked. It hadn't taken any time at all to track the girl down. Tailing her had been even easier; she hadn't suspected him for a second. Was this a sign of innocence or complacency? The Hunter knew the benefit of patience; there was nothing to be gained from jumping at conclusions; not yet.

The girl walked with a wiggle and a bounce, as if she had her sights on someone to impress, but then she stopped suddenly at a red, white and blue Victorian clocktower marking the centre-point between three roads: the one he'd followed the girl along, another to the right and the third to the left, a perfect capital T. Planters and stone furniture laid out around the clocktower designated it as a meeting and gathering place for shoppers. The Hunter paused, pretending to take interest in the latest odds offered in a bookmaker's window. On the edge of his peripheral vision he saw her wave, but who to? There were lots of people on the move that morning. The Hunter felt suitably hidden enough in plain sight to come closer, close enough to look along the road joining from the right. Nobody responded to the wave.

Crestfallen, she turned and disappeared through a nearby doorway. The Hunter moved closer still until he was almost upon the clocktower, keen to see where she'd gone. It was a coffee shop, the same colourings as one of the big chains but he didn't recognise the name: Café Azteca. From where he stood he could see plenty of empty tables within and contemplated taking a seat inside to keep a closer eye on her, when to his right he spotted the young man up ahead also watching her intently. He was blonde and lean; he glanced back across his shoulder catching the eye of a tank of a man lurking in an alleyway. The Hunter's patience struggled to be heard over the conclusions crashing into creation: this was a definite meet, and if they were bringing back-up then there was some serious intent.

-14-

IT WAS THE SOCKS QUINN NOTICED FIRST: colourful socks, the type of socks only worn by someone with a suit because they wanted people to notice their socks and to comment about their socks— *'Oh, you're such a character'*—idiots, the lot of them. But it wasn't the bright red and green watermelon slices against the black cotton that caught Quinn's eye, it was the fact they were bone dry.

Quinn had been resistant to McLaren's idea initially. They'd camped out in the grotty café, enduring the hostile glares of the unwelcoming waitress all afternoon. They watched the carwash, waiting. It wasn't until seven in the evening when Quinn finally had the measure of the place: where the stash was hidden, where the money was secured, and when it was collected. Through observing the glances and unspoken gestures, Quinn worked out the chain of command: who was in charge and who was back-up if things got ugly. Quinn had it all worked out; he was a man of great detail and planning and as the afternoon moved to evening and the waitress grew more impatient with them he was confident of a robust strategy for hitting the carwash.

Maybe it was the recovery from his injury, maybe he was tired, maybe he was just too old, whatever, but the day had exhausted him. The walk back to McLaren's shack just about did for him. He flopped on to the green Chesterfield sofa and immediately struggled to keep awake, his eyelids creaking as much as the stiff leather beneath him.

A short fat glass with a chalky white tidemark was pressed into his hand. 'Dutch gin,' said McLaren, a gift from one of his smuggling boats. The caustic aroma wrinkled Quinn's nose even at an arm's length away; McLaren, it seemed, was generous with his measures. He looked around, reminding himself of the room's hit-and-miss approach to decorations, and lingered on the cumbersome oak cabinet beside him. He saw again the photograph of the happy lady and the little boy, the only thing there that wasn't dusty: her loose soft curls, her boy shared her dark shining eyes. Quinn took a sip, and a reflex in his neck spasmed at the hit of strong alcohol. The mum and her boy looked so happy together. Quinn's eyes closed and stayed that way.

His stiff back woke him early next morning. He stretched and flexed; the dried and solidified blood around his wound cracked with the movement and poked him with a jolt of pain that was not totally unpleasurable. The next sensation to register was the faint sweet smell of cigarette smoke. He found the source outside: McLaren perched on the lounge's panoramic windowsill looking out to sea. The sun, a perfect semi-circle, rose over the horizon. He held a mug in one hand, a roll-up in the other, master of all he surveyed, and to his own amazement Quinn envied McLaren's contentment.

McLaren presented his idea to Quinn with his first coffee of the morning. The idea was no more welcome than the coffee: cheap, instant rubbish. The coffee may as well have been sawdust for the flavour in it. And as for the idea, Quinn was happy to pass but he couldn't say why. Maybe too much walking the day before and a bit of rest was needed, maybe his recovery taking too much out of him, maybe he was happy just to wake up and watch the sun emerge each morning from the sea from now on. Whatever the reason might have been, he didn't fancy McLaren's idea in the slightest.

'All I'm saying is if we go now, we can catch him before he leaves for work.' McLaren seemed quite agitated. Quinn wondered if this had kept McLaren awake or whether he was a naturally early riser. McLaren explained he'd tried a couple more times during the night to contact Sandy Ghosh but when all calls rang through to voicemail McLaren became convinced he was avoiding him. 'He knows something about what's going on down at the car depot, that's why he's gone into hiding. So if he's avoiding calls let's go doorstep him. He'll find it harder to ignore us if we're banging on his door, especially with you, you big lump.'

Quinn had to admit it sounded plausible and reluctantly agreed. Within ten minutes they were back on the march, and within twenty-five they were outside the home of Sandy Ghosh: a modest former council semi in red wire-cut bricks.

'You hear something?' asked Quinn. 'Listen.'

McLaren craned his head toward the house, as though bringing one ear two inches closer would make any difference. 'No.'

Quinn had lost the sound too; it had become blurred and indistinct amongst the noise of the street. Whatever it was had gone. Quinn gestured to McLaren to approach the front door.

'Hello? Anyone home?' McLaren rapped against the stippled glass of the plastic front door. It swung open under the gentle impact of his knuckles. McLaren turned a confused expression to Quinn, who returned a frustrated one urging him to enter. McLaren slowly stepped inside, calling 'Hello?' as he did so. Quinn followed.

The sound Quinn had heard outside returned immediately, and in the context of a home he instantly knew what it was: running water. He began climbing the stairs, following the sound. With each ascending step the carpet beneath his feet became softer, moister, looser until he reached the waterlogged landing. A continuous flow was escaping from under the door closest to him. Quinn suddenly escalated to a state of heightened awareness. Convinced something serious was in play, Quinn used his elbow against the lever handle to push the door open. It revealed a small but modern bathroom.

The bath tub was full to the brim. Water constantly spilled over the lip and fell to the floor. The taps were open full bore, perpetually adding more water at a faster rate than the small overflow cut-out could discharge. Quinn grabbed a towel from a rail and through it twisted the taps to a closed position then he stepped back to let McLaren get his first full view of Sandy Ghosh.

Ghosh was bent over the wall of the bath, his hands bound behind him with a plastic zip-tie. His body formed three distinct folds: the first, his head and chest submerged face down under the water; the second, from his waist to his knees perpendicular to the wall of the bath clamping him over the edge; and the third, his knees on the floor but his shins pointed upwards at forty-five degrees, crossed at the ankles and again zip-tied. Quinn could see that, by lever action, all they had to do was gently raise his feet to force Sandy's head under the water.

The water level began to recede to below the rim of the tub, and the choppy turbulent surface calmed. For the first time Quinn clearly saw Ghosh's face at the bottom of the bath: his eyes wide open and staring, the whites red with burst capillaries. He looked along the length of his body, but the lack of any other damage made Quinn suspect this exercise was for intelligence gathering; it wasn't retribution or punishment.

Quinn would never know how correct he was. Ghosh had proven a very malleable and eager informant readily giving up the girl, Cassie. Grateful to have his first solid substantial lead, the Hunter quickly despatched Ghosh so he could pursue it. The torture fan in Berlin wouldn't be getting much out of this encounter.

Quinn turned his gaze away and found his eyes drawn to the socks: bright colourful socks, hoisted aloft on the raised ankles. They were bone dry.

McLaren made as though he was about to vomit, but assured Quinn he wouldn't. On Quinn's instruction he headed back downstairs. Quinn followed behind, still clutching the towel, rubbing down every surface they passed, eliminating every trace they'd been there. At the bottom of the stairs, McLaren paused and extended a finger towards something just inside the entrance door: a nine-inch wooden board fixed to the wall, with half a dozen small brass hooks in a line, keys dangling from each. Quinn understood McLaren's gesture and nodded his agreement. McLaren, using his little finger, expertly extracted a black and silver key fob without touching anything else. They left the house. Quinn looped the towel around the door handle and pulled the door firmly shut behind them, whilst McLaren unlocked the car on the driveway. Slowly, sensibly, without any reason for anyone to give them a second look, they drove away in Sandy Ghosh's motor.

*

After a few minutes driving in silence, McLaren spoke first. 'I guess that answers why he wasn't taking any calls. So, you think he was the inside man?'

Quinn had been using the quiet journey to consider what they'd uncovered. 'I honestly don't know. We're given the target of the job to discuss the strategy for delivering it, but as for how it comes about, that's strictly need-to-know.'

Quinn watched the flat marshland give way to narrow streets of tall terraced houses opening straight onto the pavement. All of a sudden a sense of claustrophobia caught up with him. 'Where are we going?'

'Your plan. You wanted transport to hit the carwash with, so this saves us the trouble of nicking a motor. Now, we don't know when anyone's going to come looking for poor old Sandy, but when they do they'll spot his car's gone straight away so I've got an idea. We're almost there.'

McLaren navigated the narrow streets to a small pay and display carpark tucked behind the parade of shops and cafes in the town centre. He found a space with ease and slotted the car comfortably into it. He read the confused look on Quinn's face. 'Look around you, this is probably the most low-tech carpark you'll ever find.'

Quinn's shoulders shrugged a *"so what?"* response.

'Before anyone reports Sandy's car missing, we can very quickly and quietly swap the number plates in here, and just to be safe we can mix it up a bit. You see that red one facing the wall? We'll have the front plate off that, they won't spot it's gone until they've driven off and got back out again at the other end. And that white one reverse-parked over there, take the back one off that, again they won't notice coming back. And that way we've different numbers front and back just to confuse the plate reading software on the main roads.'

Quinn nodded his understanding. McLaren had gone up in his estimation: he'd proposed a very smart idea. McLaren pulled a small Swiss Army knife from a pocket, half-an-inch thick with a choice of bits. He extended a small screwdriver blade, then scurried off to retrieve the plates. Quinn headed toward the entrance to keep watch.

-15-

QUINN SAW HIM WAY BEFORE HE SAW QUINN. He never saw Quinn until he was almost nose-to-nose with him, and even then it was doubtful, him never being the sharpest of tools.

McLaren had worked with quick, urgent efficiency. The plates were switched in minutes, the car now anonymous. The thought of food brought Quinn to the shopping parade. 'I've got a friend, works in one of the pubs, she'll sort us out with a bit of breakfast,' promised McLaren, leading them along a narrow pedestrianised lane, a short cut to the main thoroughfare.

They joined it where the offices of the local newspaper faced the head of the lane. Quinn swept his eyes back and forth to take in his surroundings: partly out of curiosity, partly survival instinct. The road had been narrowed to one car width, and the pavements widened. People bustled all around, lots of people. Old Victorian buildings lined one side, squat post-War buildings the other; at least as far as he could see because the road had a long slow curve to the right obscuring what lay further beyond. Quinn stepped across to the opposite footpath and stood with his back to the newspaper building. It gave him the vantage point he wanted; he could now see to the end of the street. An old style clocktower stood at the site where the street met two others; marking the town centre. It stood about two storeys tall, a miniature Big Ben in red, white and blue carnival colours.

Quinn assessed the area, just a slight flicking movement of

his head side-to-side, but enough to give total visibility along the length of the street, and that's when he saw him. He'd missed him earlier tucked inside a recessed fire escape doorway: a shadowy dark cavern clad vertically in drab grey and sea green tiles. When he stepped out, just for a second, the flash of colour, a red hat, Quinn spotted him: LJ.

Questions spun through Quinn's mind as quickly and randomly as icons on a fruit machine. He knew he couldn't wait until something came up nice and neat, three bells in a row, and so began walking towards LJ in a slow, cautious prowl. Aware of McLaren behind him, he flapped a hand low at his waist, patting the air. McLaren instantly understood the meaning of this signal: *stay quiet, stay small, questions later*. Dutifully, he stepped in behind Quinn. The prison mouse skulked with such practised stealth he was invisible to everyone, unlike the big lump creeping with the subtlety of a juggernaut just ahead of him. Yet somehow LJ never noticed him approach until it was too late.

LJ was looking ahead to the distance, his focus not breaking. Quinn realised as he inched closer to him, and the vista widened out, that his hidey-hole's position gave a full unfettered view beyond the curve in the road all the way down to the clocktower. Virtually on LJ's shoulder, Quinn finally caught what he was fixated on: Jamie. Up ahead, as clear as day, standing under a green and white shop awning: Jamie. Definitely, Jamie. Something was definitely afoot; Quinn was convinced of that.

'Morning LJ,' said Quinn quietly into the big man's ear. LJ twisted his head around, curious to see who had recognised him, but his eyes stayed faithful to Jamie and were reluctant to make the turn. By the time they'd broken off Jamie and attempted to focus on the man behind him it was already too late. Quinn drove a hard, powerful fist into his guts. All the air spilled out of him in rapid surprise, and he struggled to breathe it back in. Quinn grabbed him around the neck and dragged him deep into the dark recess of the fire escape.

'What's going on LJ? Why are you here? You and Jamie.'

The whites of LJ's dopey, punch-drunk eyes enlarged and gave away his surprise: Quinn knew about Jamie! LJ's primitive instinct to solve his problems switched on: he swung at Quinn. Quinn had been expecting it. LJ's approach was slow and clumsy, and Quinn easily dodged it. Quinn followed up with his own jab, catching LJ squarely on the cheek. LJ stumbled. The solid fire-door he felt behind him was the only reason he didn't topple backwards to the ground. He'd been penned in. His only way out was past Quinn, and the peculiar little man with the raggedy ginger moustache lurking behind him.

'Give me your knife,' said Quinn, talking over his shoulder. He stared at LJ but presented his expectant open palm back towards McLaren. McLaren obliged, pressing it into Quinn's hand. His fingers folded into a huge fist around it.

Quinn looked at the signal-red Swiss Army knife in his hand and unfolded various arms, searching for a blade, but the best he could find was a disappointing thin little piece of pointed steel about an inch and a half long. Quinn brushed the pad of his thumb over its edge. It was sharp, that was something at least.

Quinn's left fist reached out to clench a clump of LJ's shirt. He pressed his left forearm down hard across LJ's breastbone, pinning him to the door. He raised the tiny knife blade up close to LJ's eye, then held it tightly against the underside of his nose. It wouldn't be fatal if he sliced him there, but it'd sting like fuck and cause a lot of blood. LJ understood. LJ didn't fight back. LJ remained motionless.

LJ tried to speak but couldn't find the words. 'You're…'

'Dead? I got better,' replied Quinn. 'Now, where's the money? Where's my money?'

'Bentley's got it. Looking after it. Until this Sunday.'

'Still sticking to the same plan?' Quinn asked, more as a musing for himself, but LJ muttered confirmation all the same. That was a good result, at least for Quinn. They'd agreed beforehand to separate after the robbery. They'd agreed: no contact with each other for an entire week, let the heat die down and the trail go cold. If the plan was still the same, Quinn knew where and when the reunion and distribution was planned. Something wasn't right with this scenario though and it was so obvious it hit Quinn in a lightning bolt.

'If the plan's unchanged, what are you doing here with Jamie, today?'

'Jamie said he'd been told someone was looking for us.' LJ paused, a thought had occurred to him. 'Was it you?'

Quinn shook his head. He was about to voice his denial when McLaren cut in, speaking over the top of him. 'Sandy! Must be the same that did for him.'

'What's Jamie doing?'

'Meeting some bird, she called him yesterday, to warn him.'

'And she has information? She knows who it is?'

'No.'

'So, why's he meeting her then?' asked McLaren. Neither LJ nor Quinn responded. A silence hung too long between them. 'What? What's going on?' demanded McLaren.

'He's going to kill her,' replied Quinn quietly. 'This hunter doesn't have much, he's relying on stepping stones, person to person along the chain. Jamie kills her, he breaks the chain. The hunter can't make the link to him. Am I right?'

LJ, keen to please, nodded with a bit too much vigour and the thin blade nicked a fine cut between his nostrils. His eyes watered and blinked in reaction to the sharp pain. A red bead trickled down the number-eleven muscle above his lip.

Quinn had got everything there was to get out of LJ; he'd served his purpose. A swift rabbit punch to the temple knocked him out cold. McLaren scuttled in past Quinn and, using old newspapers and scraps of cardboard littering the fire escape, covered LJ's unconscious body. They pulled his red baseball cap over his eyes and left him. To anyone passing by, he was yet another homeless bum sleeping it off in a doorway.

-16-

MCLAREN KNEW EXACTLY WHAT QUINN WAS LOOKING FOR, but the sight of him flapping his big square head about like a dog on a windy day rather amused him so he let him look a little bit longer. Eventually, he put Quinn out of his misery. 'Café Azteca.'

Quinn shot McLaren a hard *"what the fuck?"* glance.

McLaren expanded further. 'The young lad you're after. Tall guy, grey shirt, black jeans.' Quinn gave a slow, gentle nod; he was one part confused to two parts astonished by McLaren's talent for noticing everything everywhere.

McLaren took the lead and headed towards the clocktower; Quinn silently dropped in behind him. Within less than a minute they reached it, dead centre of the three streets. A very short distance ahead of them, Quinn located Café Azteca. His quick evaluation: *maroon shopfront and signage with a lot of exposed brickwork inside suggests it was once one of the big national chains. Possibly it was such a successful location the operators didn't feel the need to renew the franchise and peeled off all the labels to invent their own brand?* McLaren approached the entrance door. Quinn followed keenly behind. Then realisation hit him hard and the cold tingle of fear pimpled the skin on his arms.

Quinn now understood: if his first thoughts were checking out the menu and their presentation for new ideas, then he was as good as dead. He scolded himself; he'd got soft, he was thinking like a civilian, was he now a coffee and pastry man first

and everything else second? 'Wait, stop,' he called out. 'I just…
I just want a minute to clear my head first.'

'Fair enough.' McLaren pulled a crumpled, question-mark
shaped roll-up from the back pocket of his jeans, plumped it
back into something more familiar, put it between his lips and
sparked up. 'I'll have myself a little bit of fresh air then.'

The pair of them sat on the low stone plinth at the base of
the helter-skelter painted clocktower and neither of them spoke,
both lost in their own thoughts. The constant flow of people
kept passing by and no one noticed them, just the big man and
the little man perched like ornaments.

*

McLaren ground the cigarette stub out with a twist of his toe,
'Got your head where it needs to be? Ready yet?'

Quinn was ready. Thoughts, the right kind of thoughts, had
galvanised his mind, and got him back in the game: thoughts
of Benny, of Zoe, of falling backwards into the cold dark water,
of the pain and of the humiliation, and of what was his being
taken away. He slapped both palms against his knees, an overly
dramatic gesture to signify his readiness to stand up, but it
somehow felt appropriate. Peering between the Machu Pichu
logos on the polished plate glass shopfront, he recognised the
back of Jamie's head seated in roughly the centre of the café.
Time to get back to work.

'Wait.' McLaren remained seated but raised a soft arm in
front of Quinn's waist. 'Don't turn around straight away, be
subtle, but there's a man watching. Behind us, up a bit, outside
the bookies.'

Quinn stretched both arms out and gave a convincing yawn,
then mussed his hair with the open fingers of both hands and
stamped his feet, slowly revolving on the spot. He gave a passable
impression of someone chasing out the stiffness from being on
a cold stone bench too long. He rolled his head, right ear to

shoulder, chin to chest, left ear to shoulder whilst revolving back to face the café once more. 'Navy suit, black hair, long chin? Looks like the Germany football manager?'

'Klinsmann?'

'Klinsmann? No, he came after Klinsmann.'

'Oh... yeah... I know who you mean. Anyway, yes, him.' McLaren didn't look back when replying to Quinn, instead keeping his eyes down to the paving slabs. 'He's been standing there watching the café since we arrived. Is he with your mate inside?'

'I don't recognise him. Never seen him before.'

'He must be police then,' concluded McLaren. Quinn agreed: it sounded most likely. He'd need a few minutes more now before going in; if the Law was watching he wanted an exit strategy first.

*

The Hunter waited outside the bookmakers and watched Café Azteca up ahead in the close distance, less than one hundred metres from where he loitered. Occasionally his focus wandered and drifted to the bets on offer for the Champions League matches. They were offering pretty long odds for Schalke that evening, better than they were offering back home in Frankfurt, which surprised him given the good run they'd been on recently; was it just local British prejudice at work again, another jibe at the foreigners? He was tempted to put a bet on, he fancied their chances, especially at those prices. But he didn't want to be there another day to collect any winnings, he wanted this wrapped up as soon as he could, so he tried to forget about it.

He glanced back toward the café. The girl still hadn't come out yet. He checked his watch: ten minutes since the young man had followed her in. He decided to give the young man another five: that'd be enough time for the pair of them to get comfortable and relax a little. Then he would go in and observe.

As he surveyed the scene, he noticed two men settling under the clock: one small and fidgety the other huge and slow, both dressed in tatty cast-offs and charity shop clothing. They sat idly doing nothing, didn't ever appear to be speaking to one another. *Drunks or vagrants or both,* thought the Hunter and with that, they, along with any thought of placing a bet, were dismissed from any further consideration.

*

Jamie spotted her as soon as he stepped inside the coffee shop; she'd made sure of that. Cassie had picked a seat facing the doorway and draped herself across it. She looked good, mighty fine; in other circumstances Jamie wouldn't have minded another go with her despite all her clingy, high-maintenance nonsense that annoyed him so much last time. But now he just wanted rid as quickly as he could.

He made her go through everything she'd told him on the phone the day before, twice. And when it came to Sandy Ghosh, 'You definitely didn't tell him my name?' insisted Jamie.

She protested she hadn't.

'You didn't tell him anything about me? Nothing that could identify me?'

Again, she protested she hadn't. Jamie believed her; she'd done enough to convince him, now all he had to do was deal with her and he was in the clear. His plan: get her in the car, then let LJ join them. That should scare her. Then drive to some desolate place in the middle of nowhere—there were plenty of flat expansive fields to choose from: they didn't call it Cabbage Island for no reason—and bish-bash-bosh, she was gone, problem solved. All he had to do was persuade her into his car. The way she was coming on to him suggested she wouldn't need much persuading. Jamie felt confident: *I've got this in hand, I'll be home by lunchtime.*

'Hello, Jamie mate. You and me need to have a talk,' said an unexpected, but familiar voice from behind him.

-17-

THE HUNTER WATCHED THE BIG VAGRANT enter Café Azteca and knew he had to get inside quickly before the vagrant repulsed the girl going table-to-table begging for money. He didn't want her on the move again before he was ready. He knew the tall young man played a part in this but, until he knew what, he didn't want them splitting up: he could only follow one of them if the vagrant forced them back out on the street. He strode with a pace quick enough to look hurried, but not enough to look out of the ordinary: just another man suited and booted and late for a meeting. He approached the entrance door with his attention fixed on the interior. From the outside looking in, between the silhouettes of ancient temples decorating the glass, he recognised the young man he'd seen earlier. He was sitting with the girl in the yellow dress.

'Spare us some change for a cup of tea.' The smaller, fidgety vagrant had appeared out of nowhere and blocked his path, his palm open expectantly. 'Spare us some change, anything'll be appreciated.' His voice sounded forlorn and pathetic, but he moved with a lightness of foot that'd put a boxer to shame. He skipped and weaved; no matter which way the Hunter turned he found his path blocked, the damn vagrant got there first, jabbing his palm back and forth as part of the dance. 'Just a few coins, please.'

The Hunter moved to manhandle him out of the way, but it was as if the vagrant knew what he was going to do before the

Hunter himself. He increased the speed of his weaving until it was almost a fit of nervous energy, at the same time as increasing the volume of his demands. 'A few coins, that's all, help an old soldier buy a hot drink on a cold day.' Passers-by were beginning to take notice, their paces slowing; in couples, one would give their partner a point or a nod to the commotion taking place.

The Hunter stood perfectly still and reached into his pockets. The last thing he wanted was a scene; no, the very last thing he wanted was to be caught in such a scene that rubberneckers felt the need to make video recordings to share with their social media buddies. His entire reputation and his ability to earn the big bucks was based on absolute discretion, on passing through without so much as a footprint, and he had no intention now of becoming a viral internet sensation. He looked at the pocket flotsam he'd dredged up: there was a little over thirteen pounds in coins and notes. He slapped all of it into the vagrant's grubby thrusting palm with one hand, whilst the other gripped his upper arm and swept him out of his path. The Hunter, by now annoyed and struggling to contain it, entered the café. His head snapped towards the central section where the young man and woman were sitting—it was empty; no one there.

*

McLaren felt quite proud of his performance, he'd delivered what was required of him and he'd earned himself a few beers out of it too. He only hoped Quinn managed to achieve what he needed to.

Their plan had been, if the man watching began to move, McLaren was to distract him and block his path for as long as possible while Quinn got Jamie out through the fire exit at the back of the shop. It had been simpler than Quinn anticipated. Jamie's head had snapped round, his face a white pallor, as the words 'Hello, Jamie mate. You and me need to have a talk,' dropped gently into his ear: the voice of a ghost, the voice of a man last seen sinking to the riverbed shot a point blank range.

Jamie was stunned. He still hadn't spoken by the time Quinn had gripped him tight by the shirt collar and hauled him up out of his seat. He still hadn't spoken by the time Quinn, arm outstretched and elbow locked, marched him through the open counter flap to the kitchen prep area. He didn't speak until they were through the fire exit and he was on his knees in a litter-strewn alleyway behind the coffee shop. His first words surprised him as much as they did Quinn: 'Cassie…' he said. 'Get out of here. Now.'

Quinn followed Jamie's eyes and twisted his neck to peer over his shoulder. The young woman in the yellow dress stood shell-shocked in between the open leaves of the fire escape, her eyes damp and glassy. Tears had mustered and were about to fall.

'He's right,' Quinn looked directly at her as he spoke, but never loosening his grip on Jamie. 'Get out of here, forget any of this ever happened.' She wavered on the spot, unsure what to do. 'Go!' Quinn shouted at her, his voice a deep threatening growl. She ran past them both, along the alley then, turning a corner, disappeared from sight.

Quinn's attention returned to Jamie. 'I've probably saved her life and she'll never even realise, will she? She'll always remember me as the bad guy today, won't she?'

Jamie, unsure how to react to his questions, remained silent and surly in Quinn's tight grasp but didn't resist, instead remaining pliant and docile. It was with a morbid curiosity that Quinn watched Jamie process the situation. Previously he'd let Jamie press a few buttons, provoke a few reactions, and now Quinn found himself hoping he'd have kept up that same attitude: it'd make it easier for him to reconcile his killing to his conscience, make it seem far more righteous and deserved.

As if granting his wish, Jamie found a flash of defiance. 'My dad will have you fucking butchered, you sad fuck!'. Quinn responded with a sharp clout to the side of the head.

'The money… my money… still at Bentley's for the pay-out

on Sunday?' Quinn phrased it as a question but delivered it as a statement of fact. Jamie didn't answer but his eyes gave him away: Quinn was satisfied the plan hadn't been changed.

'The girl,' began Quinn. 'You obviously weren't going to do it here in front of all these people.' Quinn rolled his index finger in the vague direction of the clocktower and all the people on the street. 'So, you can tell me: how were you going to do it? What was the plan?'

'Drive her out somewhere remote, shoot her in the back of the head before she even realises what's going on, dump her somewhere where she won't be found and then drive like fuck to get off this godforsaken place and never come back.'

'You've got a shooter? Of course you have, how could I forget. Where is it?' Quinn demanded to know, his free hand patting all across Jamie's hunched over body.

'It's in the car,' replied Jamie.

'Well that sounds like a good place to start then,' Quinn's rigid arm, locked at the elbow, controlled Jamie like a puppet. He hoisted Jamie back up into a standing position, and a shove got his feet stepping forwards involuntarily. 'Lead on, MacDuff.'

THE SMALL BUTTON AT HIS COLLAR dug into his throat.
Jamie swallowed to try to relieve the discomfort but his mouth
was too dry. He'd grown up listening to the stories of Quinn
and his sainted brother, and then he met him: this overweight
middle-aged old fart moaning about instant coffee. Why did
his old man have such a hard-on for this guy? Why had he let
this flabby old nothing and his dumbfuck brother control the
Medway Towns for so long? Where was the man they spoke of
in hushed tones, the hard man forged from iron and stone? Was
it all just bullshit storytelling, was he just a passenger on his
brother's reputation, or had he gone to seed? Jamie rolled his
head hoping it'd release the button from where it dug painfully
just below his Adam's apple. He'd so far resisted the impulse to
reach up and unfasten his collar: no sudden movements, just in
case the ruthless man of stone was still in there somewhere.

'That way,' Jamie nodded towards a narrow passage between
two buildings. He got a shove in the back in reply. Responding
to the cue he walked on but never let the insolence drop. 'My old
man will fucking rip you apart for this.'

The passageway opened out on a small, untidy yard lined with
designated parking bays for occupants of the buildings abutting
it. Judging by the empty windows and the many and various *'To
Let'* notices the parking had become an opportunist's free-for-all.

'There.' Jamie gestured towards a spotless, new red Golf GTi.
A solid slap landed against his hip and strong probing fingers

searched for the key fob. 'Okay, here, look, nice and slow.' With a long, balletic scoop of his left arm Jamie pulled the square black fob from his pocket and held it out extended, the silver ring speared at the end of his finger. 'There.'

Jamie remained still and calm, always facing forwards, his collar tight around his neck. The sensation of the weight pulling on his one finger disappeared. The key had been lifted from him: very lightly done, you wouldn't have credited a big man like that with such nimble fingers. Jamie didn't turn back, he waited and focused on his breathing, trying to control it, to show he wasn't afraid, then 'You'll get yours Quinn, like your fucking brother, you'll get yours.'

The grip around his collar loosened, silence hung for a long moment, then Quinn spoke slowly and quietly. 'What did you say?'

'I know all about your arsehole brother. What happened to him is coming for you, you bastard.'

The grip to Jamie's collar intensified, throttling him, the button pressing hard against his windpipe. 'Say that again. What do you know?'

'Everything.' Jamie's voice was now no more than a croak. 'Him, you, Redlands.'

Jamie squirmed, trying to get his breath and at the same time waited, he'd said too much, he knew that and waited for Quinn's response.

The sound of breaking glass.

The grip around his collar tightened.

He got rammed from behind with such force it felt as though a bull had charged him.

He dropped to the ground.

The felled body of Quinn forced every last gasp of air out of him and pinned him to the floor.

*

The Hunter left the coffee shop, cursing with the best Germanic swearwords. He'd been played; the fidgety little vagrant with the ratty moustache, he was in on it. The Hunter strode over towards the clocktower, its location dead centre between the three streets made it the perfect spot to reappraise the situation.

There was no sign of the little fidget, he'd had the good sense to make himself scarce, but a minute or so later the girl in the yellow dress appeared from an alley in great distress. She looked up and down the road, getting her bearings, then ran straight past the Hunter back along the route he'd first followed her earlier. The Hunter didn't bother giving chase: *let her go, I know where to find her again. Anyway, it's the young man and the big vagrant I'm interested in; they seem key to this.*

The Hunter debated his next move: retrace the girl's steps, see if the alley leads to the men, or wait a little longer? His patience, or perhaps his procrastination, paid off: up ahead in the distance the two men suddenly surfaced in the surging flow of pedestrians, heading with purpose in the opposite direction to him. He set off after them, his quick stride not quite a run but enough to get a reaction from the slow-moving strollers he pushed past. He wanted to keep them in sight, close but not too close: a distance of about twenty feet should do. The young man had been leading, but as he neared them he could see the big man's grip around his collar. The big man was very clearly in charge of the situation and this added a new complexity to the Hunter's investigation: how does an old dosser fit in with this?

The two men ducked down a tight passageway between two buildings, the Hunter hesitated: any closer and they might spot him but this could be his only chance. He patted his lapel, taking reassurance from the bulge beneath his palm, a nine-inch commando knife—ideal to take down one man, but two? If he could come upon them when distracted, overpower one and then the other, then he was in business. What a pity he hadn't brought a gun with him; it would have been so much easier with a gun, people are far more obliging when you wave a gun in their face. Too late for what-ifs, they won't achieve anything. The Hunter's fingertips hovered around his suit lapel, never too far from the hilt of his knife and he headed toward the passageway opening.

*

He followed them down the passageway. They were so focused on themselves they didn't notice him matching them step-for-step. Then they stopped, an extended arm dangled a key. They were obviously getting ready to drive away, he couldn't let that happen. Fortune must have been smiling on him that day, as inspiration winked at him in the sunlight: nearby on a low brick planter, a favourite hangout for drunks, with a carpeting of dog ends and burnt matches, was the proverbial one green bottle standing on a wall. The reflected sun sparkled at him. He gripped it by the neck and crept up behind them. He raised it above his head, sticky sour beads of flat warm beer dribbled over his wrist, and with all the force he could muster he brought it down. He turned his face away on point of impact, avoiding the splintering shards of glass exploding in all directions off the man's skull. When he looked back again they were gone. Then he saw them. They had fallen, one on top of the other on the ground in front of him. He looked at the men sprawled at his feet and a hot flush of pride raced through him. He'd done good, the champion, the king of the jungle. A smile forced itself across his face, completely beyond his control but he liked the feeling: for once in his life he was the winner. The knife blade sunk between his shoulder blades. He fell forwards. He was dead before he collapsed on top of the men.

*

The Hunter cautiously approached the entrance to the passageway. He was trying to see what lay at the other end before committing himself, when he was shoulder-barged out the way. A tank of a man in a red baseball cap scurried down the passageway ahead of him. The man was so wide he could barely fit, needing to twist his shoulders slightly and lead with his right in order to walk down the passageway without scraping the sides. The Tank seemed to be on a mission, he had himself a reason to be there. The Hunter was curious. The Hunter followed, giving the Tank a ten second head start.

The Hunter emerged from the passageway to find his two targets by a red Volkswagen. They weren't aware of the Tank directly behind them, bottle in hand. He didn't know what the Tank wanted, but he couldn't let him get in the way of his quarry. By the time the Tank had reached the top of his backswing, the Hunter was up close to him. By the moment of impact, when the sound of breaking glass rang out across the empty yard, his blade was drawn and poised. By the time the big man had toppled forwards, the knife had been driven to its hilt in his back; with expert efficiency piercing his heart. His knees lost tension, and gravity did the rest. The dead weight of the Tank dropped on top of the men with all the grace of a collapsing chimney. The Hunter reached forwards and extracted his knife. He wiped the blade clean against the Tank's denim jeans, then re-sheathed it under his jacket.

*

Quinn opened his eyes with a startled gasp. *Have I been sleeping? What's happened? Where am I? What am I lying on? What's on top of me?* So many questions collided inside his mind in a fraction of a second and then just as quickly they disappeared: he already knew the answers. Except for one: what was pinning him down? The weight was immense and all-consuming, it smothered him across two thirds of his body, from his shoulders to his knees as though they'd picked up and rolled the concrete footpath across him whilst he slept. Placing both palms flat on the ground he tried levering himself up. The weight, though heavy, had no resistance. Once it began to slide it got carried by its own momentum and slumped to the side of Quinn. He turned, curious to see what had been trapping him, and looked into the face of LJ. He was quite obviously dead, but also looked strangely smug, as if pleased with himself for simply being there.

Quinn spent a moment or two looking at LJ, and tried to fit the jigsaw together: clearly he'd awoken in the fire escape and thought he was coming to Jamie's rescue, but then what? It was then Quinn saw beyond the lifeless body of LJ and found the man with the black hair and the long chin standing close by. The man's suit jacket hung open, from which he withdrew a big knife holstered beneath his arm. His and McLaren's first thought had been wrong, he wasn't police.

'Who are you? What do you want?'

*

The big man got up and adopted a defensive stance. The Hunter observed him with the same sort of interest as a botanist finding an errant bug on a prized bloom: an interesting diversion, a novelty to look at, but mustn't distract from the main event, so examine then pick off and destroy. Now, up close, he could tell he was no vagrant—there must be a reason for the shabby clothing, but he wasn't interested. This man exuded a power and ferocity that he didn't earlier. That, the Hunter concluded, made him dangerous: he knew how to control his raw brute force, when to turn it on and how to turn it off again. He wasn't simply hot-headed dumb muscle; he directed his strength with precision. This was a man to treat with respect, as a peer, as a professional equal. The Hunter took a neutral stance, his hands dropped to his waist, the tip of the knife pointing toward the ground. He noticed the big man's shoulders soften a little in response; this was a good sign.

'My client was robbed. I've been employed to track down who

stole from him, and to get his belongings back,' he explained in flawless English with the faintest of accents. 'I believe this young man knows all about it and where I might find it.'

They both looked at Jamie, still lying on the floor. Jamie wore an air of bewilderment, unsure of what to do or what was happening. He, too, had seen the change in Quinn: from middle-aged wanker to the hardman of urban myth. Quinn extended a hand and helped haul him to his feet. Under the scrutiny of the two men, both of whom he knew wanted to kill him for different reasons, Jamie lost his sheen of cockiness. He resembled an awkward young boy and blinked back the sting of moisture around his eyes.

The man with the black hair faced Quinn. 'I think now that you also know all about it and where I can find it. I think he works for you. Your apprentice, perhaps.' A derisory snort of laughter burst involuntarily from both Quinn and Jamie, while the Hunter looked on confused. 'Perhaps no?'

'LJ? You killed LJ?' Jamie had finally spotted him, lying to the side of them. The Hunter gave a downward turn to his mouth and a small shrug, as if to say *"It was unfortunate, but needs must."*

'And the security guards? And the lad in the bath? That was you?' asked Quinn. The Hunter responded in the same manner.

Quinn considered his situation, then, 'All right, okay. What you want, it's in the car, the boy was bringing me to it.' Quinn slowly reached into his coat pocket and withdrew the key fob. Orange lights flashed, locks whirred and bolts slid back with a reassuringly solid clunk at the press of the button. 'Okay,' he said, turning to make eye contact with Jamie. 'You told me *it* was in the car, where is it?'

Quinn hoped Jamie still had the awareness to pick up on his emphasis. He did. 'Glove compartment, front passenger side.'

Quinn edged around the car, placed one hand on the passenger door handle and glanced over to the Hunter, who gave a short nod signifying permission granted. Quinn pulled the door open. Leaning in, he flipped the latch of the glove compartment. The hatch dropped open. He reached inside and found it exactly as promised by Jamie. Quinn grasped the pistol, slid his finger over the trigger and, in a movement quicker and more fluid than you'd expect from someone of his size, he turned and faced the Hunter, weapon drawn. The Hunter showed experience of being in these situations before; he slowly raised his hands either side of him to head height and released his grip on the deadly commando knife. It dropped to the tarmac with a clatter but it didn't distract Quinn, his focus was fixed. He took aim squarely at the man's chest and squeezed the trigger. He was prepared for the recoil of the blast. He was not prepared for the pathetic hollow click of a misfire.

The participants stood like waxworks in a moment of confused stupor. The Hunter was first to react and sprinted away. In the split-second or so it took Quinn and Jamie to realise, he'd disappeared into the passageway. By the time Quinn reached the passageway there was no sign of him, with any number of shops, cafes, bars and offices he could have ducked into to hide. Quinn turned back but Jamie was gone.

-19-

MARKO THE BIG RUSSIAN YAWNED AGAIN and arched his back to chase out the stiffness that had been building. Five long hours in Rochester, sat in the same window seat watching the green coffee shop with the gold writing. Five long hours it'd remained closed and empty. Once or twice someone had approached, shaken the door handle, then moved on to the next café once they'd realised it was shut. Other than that, nothing had happened. A waste of a day really but he was getting paid so why complain. And he'd made a new friend. The barmaid turned out to be from St Petersburg, from a neighbourhood close to his grandmother. They chatted until her impatient boss called her back to serve. She'd lent him her magazine she kept behind the bar: a glossy import from home, celebrity gossip in the Russian language. He leafed through it, more out of politeness than interest, not recognising half the people in it: *I've lost touch with what's hot at home, been in this country too long.*

He sat by the window, watching and waiting. She obviously liked him; she hadn't charged him for the last bottle of fizzy water, or the one before that, now he thought about it. *Maybe the day's not been completely wasted.* Marko began to daydream happy-ever-afters and saw her blush as he caught her looking at him, then on the edge of his vision something happened outside. Instantly he was back on duty.

*

The door clicked shut behind her. A gentle tug told her it was firm but she knew if they wanted to come in it didn't matter how many bolts or locks she secured, they'd come in regardless. Zoe hoiked the strap of the gym bag over her shoulder. It was heavier than it looked, containing a few days change of clothes, the contents of Quinn's safe and—just in case—the largest, sharpest knife she could find in the kitchen.

It had been a few hours since Quinn's warning to flee. She'd scurried across from the house they shared close to the shop with the caution of a timid cat, every noise startling her. Once packed she needed to choose the right moment: were they out there, watching, waiting? Twice the door had rattled, eager hands pulling against the resistance of the locks, both times the cold fear gripped her heart so tightly it wanted to explode in her chest. Relief fizzed through her veins when the tourists realised their mistake and headed away hungry; a laugh came out by reflex reaction, but the dread didn't quite go away, not entirely.

Eventually, with dusk approaching but no one else, she figured it was time. From the rear door, exiting through the back-of-house kitchen area, she stepped out on to the narrow, cobbled side street. She raised the hood of her sweater and pulled the visor of her baseball cap down in front of her face. She fixed her gaze to the ground, a few feet in front of her, determined not to make eye contact with anyone. Zoe took a deep breath, a superstitious act to bring her good luck, and started walking.

*

Marko saw the girl stepping out of the cobbled side street and rounding the corner that the coffee shop sat on, joining the High Street. She looked like someone with something to hide, the way she'd used her hoodie and her hat to disguise her face entirely. Could this be the girl? A pause and a backward glance to the coffee shop convinced him that it was. He pressed *Send* on

a pre-prepared text message to confirm target sighted and got to
his feet, pulling on his jacket. From the other side of the room he
was aware of the barmaid's interest, wearing a look that accused
him of being just another timewaster all along. He patted down
his pockets and found a pen.

'I have to go,' he said, then picking up on her mood added,
'Sorry.' He handed the magazine back to her, and pointed to
where he'd written his name and phone number on the back
cover. 'Please?' She smiled and nodded, he smiled back, the
impatient manager shouted at her again, and Marko left to start
his pursuit.

Where was the girl? *She was right there, where's she got to?*

*

Marko's good mood faded for a foul one, since he'd lost sight of
Quinn's niece. He trundled his car at almost walking pace along
the brick-paved street, determined to find her but with no idea
where to begin. He'd sent the text message to confirm she was
on the move; people were coming, he couldn't tell them he'd
lost her already. Especially not because he'd been distracted by
a barmaid; they wouldn't be amused. He needed to pick up her
trail, and fast.

When she came out of the carpark behind the pub, moving at
a fair speed, he perked up. She was pushing her Fiat 500 too fast
for the semi-pedestrianised tourist trap. He liked that, it meant
at last something was happening. Marko didn't fully understand
his brief, but then he wasn't meant to. All he knew was someone
special was at large and this girl in the little white car would lead
him right to them.

Except she was Quinn's niece, she was on heightened alert.
She'd easily spotted the huge man with the red beard following
her. His attempt to blend into his surroundings was about as
subtle as a full moon on a dark night.

To prove her suspicions she turned right and right again,

circling the block, making the same turns. He was still close behind. She took him away from the High Street, to Rochester's residential avenues where Victoriana mass-built thousands of homes for its industrial workers and loyal servants of the Empire. Up where they named their new streets with patriotic pride after the great poets, the great statesmen and explorers, the great battles, and the great territories won. In the heart of the Victorian terraces, in amongst the small and narrow flat-fronted houses, he followed the small Fiat: Cecil Road to Thomas Street to Rose Street back to Cecil Road, the big fish chased its prey.

Quarter of a mile ahead, she took a right turn very tight and hard and fast without indicating, angering the oncoming driver forced to emergency brake to avoid hitting her. The lightweight little car leaned into the tight turn, its outer wheels momentarily lifting off the tarmac as she went around the corner and out of sight. Marko slowed to allow the oncoming driver to compose himself and resume his journey, then crossed the carriageway to take the right turning to catch up with the girl. Another narrow residential street, he noted, and laughed when he spotted the sign: dead end. No way out. Marko had this, he was in control, a smug warmth filled him, it felt good to be a winner.

He reached for his phone to inform his associates, when— *Goddamit, the little white car's coming back the other way! How did she do that?* An impossibly tight and nimble U-turn by the tiny little car. She headed straight past him whilst he was still completing his own clumsy manoeuvre. He gaped at her and she pretended he wasn't even there as she zipped past him.

He heard the screech of her tyres before he'd managed to twist himself around in his seat, and by the time he had a clear view through his back window she was long gone. He slumped in his seat, his white knuckles strangled the steering wheel and he uttered some colourful Cossack swearing.

-20-

QUINN BROUGHT THE RED GOLF GTI to a slow halt; braking, a lumpiness juddered up through his toe from the offside front wheel suggesting a worn-out suspension arm. Quinn thought that typical of Jamie: looks nice on the outside, rotten on the inside.

Quinn trundled Jamie's red Golf off the road at less than walking pace across loose shingle and patchy grass, slowing to an eventual halt at the blind side of McLaren's chalet. The agreement before they had separated at the clocktower was to meet up again back there, and Quinn wanted the car hidden from general view just in case anyone was looking for it. McLaren must have had the same thought, Quinn realised, coming to a stop beside Sandy Ghosh's car.

'Where'd you get that from?' McLaren's voice came from behind. Quinn turned to face him.

'It's Jamie's, the young lad's.'

'Oh yeah. He lent it to you for the weekend, did he?'

'Something like that,' Quinn replied, and both of them expelled a laugh that was more a loud exhale and boasted of coming out best.

'Did you get what you wanted?'

'Well, I got this.' Quinn reached into the deep pocket of his overcoat and pulled out the gun.

McLaren's eyes widened and his lips pursed appreciatively. 'Nice' he muttered.

'And I also got this.' Quinn withdrew the commando knife from his other coat pocket; the semi-circular serrations intended for tearing flesh apart sparkled romantically in the sunlight.

McLaren gave a lemony wince. 'Nasty,' he muttered.

Quinn flicked the tailgate latch, it hissed open on hydraulic arms. He pointed towards the shadowy boot-space 'And finally, I bring you...'

'What the...' McLaren recoiled in shock. 'What's that?'

'That's LJ,' replied Quinn. 'You met him earlier.'

'I remember,' snapped McLaren. 'What I mean is, what the... why... what...'

Quinn lowered the tailgate. '...Is he dead and why's he here? Is that what you're asking?' Without waiting for a response, Quinn answered his own question. 'Yes he is, and I couldn't very well leave him lying in the middle of the road for someone to trip over, could I?'

McLaren struggled to get his head around what had suddenly landed on his quiet little chalet by the seaside with the welcome surprise of a drone strike. 'No, I guess not,' he mustered as a reply then finally summoned up the question he'd been building up to. 'Did you...?'

Quinn felt strangely affronted by the question, so much so he found himself protesting, 'No I bloody well didn't. But I saw who did do it. Remember the fella watching the coffee shop, the one you thought was Old Bill? Seems he's not a copper. He did for your mate in the bath as well.'

'So that makes him... what?'

'A manhunter,' replied Quinn. 'He's chasing down what we stole, he's here to recover it. Whatever means necessary.'

'Who's he work for? Who's it belong to?'

'I've no idea. Like I told you, it was all done on a need-to-know basis. The only thing I know is they're not bloody happy about it, and he's not going to stop until he's got it back.'

'But where is it, do you even know?'

'Yes. I found that out at least. The plan's not changed: it's being looked after by a fella called Bentley, he's the Flint family's go-between man. It's the normal routine: he looks after any haul from any job for a week, it's the nearest thing they've got to neutral territory.'

'That's fine,' McLaren's tone was ponderous, as though his thoughts were forming in his mouth, 'but that was on the basis you were dead. If they know you're alive and angry, they going to keep it there?'

Quinn sucked the inside of his cheek, giving the question some serious thought. After a long moment he replied, 'I honestly don't know,' then began a slow long-paced saunter towards the shingle beach. He stopped at the edge and looked out to where the sea met the sky. McLaren joined him. 'So where's the lad now?'

'No idea. He did a legger as soon my back was turned. I'm guessing he's trying to get off this bloody rock as fast as he can. I'd be amazed if he's not already on a train hurtling towards London.'

'Think he's warned them?'

'Probably.' Then a thought trickled into Quinn's awareness. 'Bentley! I spoke to Bentley yesterday, when you got me the phone. He knows.'

'So that means… what?'

'If they've not moved the haul somewhere else by now, they will very, very soon. Time's definitely of the essence now. I've got to get there today, tonight at the latest.'

McLaren took a pouch of loose tobacco from his pocket and extracted a pre-prepared roll-up. 'Aren't you forgetting something?' He lit the cigarette, the sweet, rich aroma of freshly lit tobacco smelt delicious to Quinn: twenty years since he quit but that first burn was always so enticing. 'You still owe me, remember, ten grand.'

Quinn kept looking out to sea. The sweet aroma had worn off and the air hung with the harsh heavy smoke that always made him cough. As he took a sidestep downwind, he caught

McLaren glancing back over his shoulder. 'I suppose there's the cars. Polish Mick might give me something for them, but it wouldn't cover the ten large I'm owed.'

'No it wouldn't,' agreed Quinn. 'But I'm keeping the boy's Golf, I've got a plan for it.'

'And what about matey in the boot? I suppose he gets the old burial at sea treatment tonight?'

'No, I've got a plan for him.'

'Another plan, eh?'

'Same plan,' replied Quinn.

*

Around the same time Quinn explained his plan to McLaren, Jamie Flint watched the scenery flicker past. Quinn had guessed correctly: Jamie had found the railway station and boarded the first train out of there. It wasn't until he'd crossed the bridge and seen the water beneath his window, until he knew he was properly off the island, that he felt he could breathe out. It took another twenty minutes before the survival adrenalin rush wore off and he could think with a clear head. He knew he needed to tell his father Quinn was still alive. He knew he needed to tell his father there was someone else. And he knew he needed to tell his father they both wanted him dead and were coming after him. He'd plead if he had to, but never before had he needed the protection of dear old dad than today.

He got off at Sittingbourne to change for the London-bound service. The panic built again during an agonising ten minutes exposed on the platform waiting for the connecting train. Seated and moving again, he mentally rehearsed and fine-tuned his plea to his father, but one thing was for sure: LJ wouldn't get mentioned. There was no way he was going to admit to going off-piste, responding to a potential threat to the family without first informing its head, especially as it had cost LJ his life. Then another regret introduced itself to him with the welcome touch of an icy cold blade between his ribs: *Redlands. I shouldn't have said anything about Redlands.*

*

'How many times do I need to tell you John, I'm not interested.'

Bentley—passive, unflinching—sat quietly, allowing a long moment of silence to extend. In his many years he'd mediated tenser conversations than this. He'd delivered on decisions that were quite literally matters of life or death, so persuading a man to do the job he was bred for was nothing by comparison. He blew gently across the top of his coffee and maintained his silence, watching the soft waves ripple across the foam.

'I'm serious, John. I'm not doing it. Sorry.'

Got you, thought Bentley, never apologise—it makes it personal— and if it's personal then I've got my in on you. 'It's a simple little get-in-get-out-get-away nothing sort of job: low security, middle of nowhere, middle of the night. There's nothing to it.'

'In that case you don't need me, do you,' countered Quinn.

'Tony wants you,' replied Bentley.

'No way. I'm no babysitter. Now you've said your piece, it's time to go,' Quinn lifted both coffee cups from the table, not caring Bentley's was still two-thirds undrunk, and moved towards the counter.

'Tony says you owe him,' Bentley spoke in clear level tones, any chumminess stripped out, down to business. 'I didn't want to go this route, but you owe him. You know you do. It's time, he's calling in your debts.'

Quinn dropped the cups with a clatter to the counter and spun around, his face showing the anger within. 'Owe? Are you insane? We got cast out, cut off, that was our penance. I owe Tony Flint nothing.'

Bentley remained unfazed; he'd negotiated and beaten far more aggressive opponents. 'Redlands,' his one word reply.

Veins in Quinn's neck twitched, his head fixed rigid, and his eyes locked on to Bentley. 'Say that again.'

'Redlands,' repeated Bentley. 'You owe Tony for Redlands. And here's how you repay him. Now, can I finish my coffee? And one of those lemon muffins while you're up?'

-21-

Three Years Earlier:

DOWN IN THE FORMER PRINTWORKS, *any sign of industry had long since been grubbed out to create the sweaty black box. The crowd swayed and pounded to the amplified sound, the electric beats and the echoing bass. But in the attic office above, the music was just a faint vibration rumbling through the structure; no more than a gentle pulse rising through the carpeted surface of the floor to ripple the whiskeys on the table.*

Bentley, always the accountant, always in the golfing casuals, was uncomfortable. His discomfort came as much from the message he'd been sent to deliver as his surroundings. Quinn and Benny sat facing him. This fish was well out of his water, and they suspected they knew why but they bided their time, waiting for him to speak first.

Quinn noticed the soft tremor beneath him change slightly; the DJ was raising the tempo. Quinn pictured the revellers downstairs moving as one, writhing as a wave following the music. A yawn rose deep within him but he managed to force it back without anyone noticing. He was tired, too tired for this place. Having the nightclub was always Benny's dream, and he'd been happy to go along with it. They'd had a fun few years but it was beginning to take its toll. Too many late nights. It's a young man's game. *Quinn knew his time in clubland was reaching the end; in a year or two he intended to be out, preferably with Benny doing something new, but whatever Benny's plans were Quinn knew he was definitely finished with clubs.*

'We need to talk about the other night,' said Bentley, finally breaking the silence. 'About the Redlands disaster. It needs to be resolved. It's unacceptable. So, what have you got to say for yourself?'

Benny leaned forward in his chair. 'Three things. That's all. Just three things.' He stood, his posture stiffened ready for conflict, then counted them off by extending his fingers one at a time: 'Fuck that! Fuck you! And fuck off!'

Bentley looked embarrassed under the weight of Benny's outburst. Quinn watched on and a faint amusement began sparkling in his eyes. Benny left the room without looking back, slamming the door behind him.

'If you've come expecting an apology, you're wasting your time,' Quinn said to Bentley. 'He won't give you one. Nor will I.'

*

'You look like you're miles away. What are you thinking about?' asked McLaren, shattering his daydream.

'Nothing,' replied Quinn, 'Just ancient history, that's all.'

They'd arranged to meet in the café with the sticky tables. Waiting for McLaren to arrive, Quinn took a seat in the window overlooking the carwash and his thoughts wandered. Redlands, was this really what it was all about? The Redlands incident, unfortunate as it was, was foreseeable by everyone—apart from Tony Flint, it seemed. Could he really have festered a grudge for all this time?

The carwash was approaching closing time. If they kept to the same routine, the pick-up was due in about half an hour's time. Quinn knew he had to focus; time was short, he needed to get his head back in the game. Yet his thoughts kept returning to Redlands: *Fuck you, Jamie, saying Benny paid for Redlands, saying I was due too. And fuck Bentley. I owe Tony Flint he said: hadn't the Flints already taken enough from me already because of Redlands?*

117

Bentley had already riled one of the Quinn brothers; he didn't want to go head-to-head with the other. To buy himself some time, hoping the pause in conversation might release a little tension, he raised the whiskey to his lips and savoured a sip. A smoky warmness filled his mouth and escaped through his nose as he exhaled then, judging the moment right, continued. 'Look, this situation can be managed, but you know how things are. He can't be seen to be walking away from this without even an apology. Reparations must be paid.'

'You heard him: it's never going to happen.'

Before going into any mediation, Bentley always made sure his bargaining position was clear and unequivocal. He hadn't felt comfortable in the drive over tonight because, from whatever perspective he took, his positions were weak. He knew it, and more importantly so did the brothers Quinn.

'So we're back at square one.' Bentley couldn't hide the frustration in his voice, but wasn't sure if it was at Quinn's intransigence to bend, or for Redlands being the disaster everyone had been waiting to happen. 'If Benny's not willing to apologise, then he's outside. He's no longer part of the group, he doesn't get any Flint protection, he doesn't get any of the benefits or opportunities of being a Flint associate. Understand?'

Quinn had been expecting that, but to be honest he'd also expected a lot worse; he was relieved on Benny's behalf and nodded agreement to Bentley.

'There's no point me asking you to choose firm over family is there? You're with him all the way, aren't you?'

Quinn knew exactly what Bentley was suggesting. He didn't like it but Bentley was right, he could only vote one way: every time, family first. Quinn nodded again, knowing that by doing so he was excommunicating himself. A lifetime's work, a hard-fought reputation, given away. Was it a price worth paying? Without a second's doubt: yes.

*

McLaren slid into the seat opposite and brought him into the here-and-now with the words: 'Ready to do this?'

Quinn rose to his feet. He left a neat short stack of coins to cover the cost of the tea that sat cold and untouched, still exactly where it had been deposited by the surly waitress with the phone addiction. Quinn thanked her and said goodbye as he walked out but she never looked up from her screen.

-22-

IN A FURY OF NOISE AND SPEED the red Golf GTi hurtled into the open gateway of the car-wash, kicking its back-end out far enough to block the entrance to any other vehicles. The workforce to a man stopped, stared and began drifting over to check the commotion. In the distraction and largely unnoticed, McLaren brought Sandy Ghosh's car around and blocked the exit gateway.

Since his late teens Quinn had been one of the best armed robbers in the business. He combined the right amount of noise and fury to instil fear and co-operation, the right degree of violence threatened but very rarely carried out, and an uncanny instinct as to who would comply and who would have a go. As a result, his fearsome reputation grew as the man who got the good returns and never got caught. So even on his own, with an unreliable handgun as his only tool, he burst on to the carwash forecourt like a tornado, totally in charge.

As expected, the slave labour force took two paces back and dropped to their knees: too in fear of their masters to run away, but not enough to take a bullet for them. They held back and watched passively, like cattle in the field.

The taskmasters reacted exactly how Quinn had anticipated: the first came for him then hesitated at the sight of the gun. Just for a second, but it was long enough. A fast, hard elbow between the eyes quickly did for him and he dropped to the ground. The other two were similarly dispatched by hard fists and elbows, rounded off with a kick across the face for good measure. In a little under forty seconds from getting out the car he was at the small garden shed in the corner of the yard: the hub of operations.

The flimsy boarded door of the shed flew open and a man charged at him, brandishing a baseball bat. He was tall, lean and sinewy. He swung but it was high and reckless, without aim or strategy. Quinn easily sidestepped it and let its momentum pull the man off-balance. Quinn slammed the butt of the pistol into the back of the man's head; he hit the concrete face first and made no sign of getting up. Quinn headed toward the shed, confident the hard work was over, but there'd been another one out there that he'd missed. He landed on Quinn's back and his limbs snaked around his shoulders and chest, clamping him on tight. Quinn threw himself down backwards, hoping to crush the man underneath him on impact. But he'd pre-empted Quinn's move and twisted himself mid-flight. Quinn landed awkwardly on his shoulder, a ferocious pain flaring through his recovering wound, causing him to release the gun in reaction. It skittered across the rough concrete surface, coming to a halt about six feet away.

The workers stood, dumbly watching the two men wrestle around on the ground, neither seeming to outdo the other. The man clung tightly to Quinn's back like a tick on a dog. Nothing Quinn could do broke his grasp. Quinn's fingers reached out for the rough-sawn wavy edged panels of the shed and dug in to the open grain of the timber. Using every last reserve of energy, his fingers climbed up the face of the shed, hauling him to his knees and then up on to his feet. Quinn's breathing became shallow, unable to fully extend his diaphragm as the legs squeezed tighter, clamping his lower ribcage. The assailant's arm locked hard under Quinn's jaw in an attempted choke-hold, his other arm lashed about slapping him all around the face. Behind Quinn was the low brick boundary wall, about three feet high with metal palisade railings set above it like spears. Quinn ran towards it full pelt, jumping at the last second and dropping a shoulder mid-air to try and force a turn. He collided with the man on impact. He took a few paces forward from the wall, then did it again, and then a third. This time Quinn felt the grip loosen around him, and in a sharp sudden movement ducked, bending himself straight from the waist. The man, thrown off like a vanquished rodeo-rider, crashed to the floor. A backheel to the side of the head nullified the threat, and he was out of the game.

Quinn picked up the gun and entered the shed. The young man he'd seen dealing through car windows the day before cowered in an old armchair in the corner. Beside the armchair was a battered old three-drawer filing cabinet. There was no other furniture or decoration inside the shed.

'What do you want?' stammered the young man. English was not his first language, his accent strongly East European.

'You're dealing on our territory,' said Quinn, speaking very slowly to make sure the man understood. 'This land belongs to the Flint family. Understand?'

The young man stared at him, either in terror or disbelief, Quinn wasn't sure, so he repeated, 'This land belongs to the Flint family. Understand?' and from under his coat he withdrew the long, ugly commando knife. The young man became spellbound by its shiny sharp tip, his eyes never leaving it, prompting Quinn to say, 'Repeat back to me what I just said.'

'Flint family. The Flint family own this land.'

'Good lad,' Quinn extended his arm out straight, lining the tip of the blade to the bridge of the man's nose, a gesture to tell him with just the minimal amount of effort he could skewer him clean through. 'Now, where's the gear?'

The man gave a small nod in the direction of the filing cabinet, never taking his eyes away from the blade. Quinn side-stepped across, pulled open the top drawer and peered inside. 'Good lad. Now, on your knees. I'm going to tie you up. Come on.'

The young man meekly slid from the armchair to his knees on the floor. He knelt in front of Quinn, his head bowed and his hands held out before him. Quinn thought he looked like a supplicant waiting Holy Communion. He rabbit-punched the young man into immediate unconsciousness. 'Silly gullible bastard', he muttered.

*

McLaren watched Quinn run from the shed with the same slow, rolling gait of an old overweight Labrador he once owned. A rucksack hung from one shoulder, and a thin, unbranded carrier bag was clasped in his fist. McLaren put the car into first gear and released the handbrake, ready to get them out of there pronto. This wasn't his life, he was never a smash-and-grab merchant, he was a sneak-thief – lift it out an open handbag, slip it off a table-top, never ever had he done anything as big and brash and brazen as this. His guts churned over. Ice-cold slurry liquified his insides. It'd been that way all afternoon, but despite everything he was quite enjoying the rush. He just needed Quinn to get in the car. They needed to get out of there.

Quinn had stopped halfway across the yard, where the workers had congregated: vulnerable people, safety in numbers. McLaren watched on as Quinn handed the flimsy carrier bag to the man closest to him: he looked middle eastern in origin, with short dark hair in tight curls. He peered inside the bag and pulled out a handful of thin stiff squares in different colours. Most were blue but some greens, some maroons: passports. Then Quinn reached into the rucksack and pulled out a fistful of notes. He thrust them towards the man, and McLaren could read his gestures. 'For all of you, share.' The man beamed a grateful gappy smile and opened the first passport, looked at the photograph then handed it to its owner. Then opened the second, but was stopped by Quinn flapping both his arms as though shooing pigeons. 'Go. Go. Get out of here. Go.' The men didn't need telling again and, as a herd, they ran. They thundered past McLaren's car. They didn't know where they were headed but they were going there with speed and excitement. McLaren watched them in the rear-view mirror until they disappeared from view when the bend in the road became obscured by houses.

McLaren looked back for Quinn and found him by the Golf with the tailgate open. With a grunt and a heave, he hauled the deadweight of LJ out and dragged him across the yard, dropping him in front of the shed. Polishing the commando knife on his sweatshirt he stepped back inside the shed, just for a few seconds, then came out without it. In a gambol that was part-walk-part-run he lolloped across to McLaren and jumped in the car. 'Go, go, go!'

McLaren gunned the accelerator. They sped away. Across the road, in the cafe, the only potential witness never saw a thing, too busily engrossed in her phone screen throughout.

*

'You took your bloody time,' shouted McLaren once they'd put enough distance behind them for the thrill-rush to be replaced by anger, 'What happened to "in-and-out, job done"?'

'I got distracted,' replied Quinn, clutching the rucksack closely to his chest. 'I found the passports for the slave crew. I had to give them back. Had to.'

'Very noble of you I'm sure,' said McLaren, turning the car into a narrow back road. 'And what else d'you give them?'

'I don't know. I didn't count. Not much though, only a grand or so.'

'A grand?' from McLaren's tone it was clear he considered the amount substantially more than *"not much"*.

'Between all of them,' countered Quinn, annoyed at the attitude McLaren was giving him. 'Won't be much when shared out. Probably enough for a train ticket away from here and a couple of meals. Hopefully enough to start again somewhere else.'

McLaren murmured a low grumble but didn't speak. He knew Quinn had done the right thing but at the same time he had left him hanging on the perch whilst going on his white-knight crusade, so he wasn't going to give him too much credit.

'And LJ? That went okay did it?'

Quinn laughed to himself, leading McLaren to understand it had. His many years of conditioning as the prison mouse told him not to push it any further, but let it come to you. Sure enough, after the briefest of pauses, Quinn spoke. 'All went to plan. As far as the carwash mateys are concerned, they've been turned over by the Flint family. So when the local plod pay a visit, which I'd hope will be very soon, they'll find LJ, known associate of the Flints, lying in the middle of the yard, and the knife that killed him—covered with the fingerprints of the nasty little dealer—will be found in that shed. Straight away, gang warfare, serious crime squad.'

'They'll concentrate on the big boys, and not even look down at us?'

'That's the intention.'

'Lovely. Job well done,' cheered McLaren, drawing the car to halt behind his chalet. He killed the engine and pulled the keys from the steering column, 'Tea?'

*

Inside the chalet, Quinn tipped the contents of the rucksack across the kitchen table, and together they counted out the total haul.

'Eight thousand, one hundred and thirteen pounds,' recounted Quinn pointing to the neat pile of notes and coins. 'And all this horrible shit.' He waved a hand over a large pyramid shaped pile of small paper wraps. 'I've no idea how much that's all worth, do you?'

'There's what, fifty or sixty of them, so probably another three or four grand,' replied McLaren, with a degree of certainty to his voice. 'I know someone who might be interested in having it.'

Quinn was relieved; the haul was less than he'd hoped and not helped by his sudden act of salvation. McLaren had unwittingly solved a problem for him.

'Good,' he began. 'So, you said a grand to the medic,' he carved off one thousand pounds and set it aside as small pile. 'And then,' Quinn peeled off some more notes, and made an identically sized pile to sit beside the medic's pile. 'That leaves six thousand one hundred and thirteen pounds, say three and half in product, and the car outside, that's all for you. As promised. That's me, paid in full. Agreed?'

'Hold on a minute,' protested McLaren, 'Eight thousand, less one for the medic, that's seven. So, what's that?' McLaren dropped a probing finger on the small pile in front of Quinn.

'Ah, that. I'm glad you asked,' replied Quinn with a smile. He reached across, plucked the cheap wooden frame from the dusty oak cabinet. He placed the photograph of the happy woman with the soft brown curls and the happy boy with the smiling dark eyes on top of the pile in question. 'It's for them.'

McLaren's face was a mix of surprise and confusion. 'But... why?'

'It took me a while to make the connection, but I knew I'd seen her before. She found me, didn't she? When I was left for dead, she's the one that saved me, isn't she? She contacted you, or were you with her? How did it happen?'

'How did you know?'

'It's the only thing that's not covered in dust. It's obviously important to you, means something special.'

'Dori, that's her name, Dori. She called me, it was early in the morning, about six, but as you know I'm an early riser anyway. She was in a panic, said she'd found a dead body on the bridge and was worried she'd get in trouble for not reporting it. I assured her she wouldn't, and promised I'd go and have a look. I found you, you weren't dead, and you know the rest.'

'So I want her to have this, her reward for saving my life. You okay with that?' asked Quinn, getting a non-committal shrug of the shoulders in response that he took to mean there was no opinion one way or the other. 'How does she know you then? I mean why call you instead of anyone else? Are you two a couple?'

'I don't know, kind of,' was the most honest answer McLaren could give him. 'It's early days, and its complicated. She's got her boy and doesn't want to confuse him by bringing anyone home, I can understand that. And me... well, me and Elaine, we was married almost thirty years, she was my first proper girlfriend. It sounds soft, but I'm a bit nervous about getting too much involved with anyone.'

'Yeah, I get it,' replied Quinn. McLaren's experiences and caution resonated with his own but he was in no mood for sharing and instead asked, 'But do you like her?'

'I do, yeah,' McLaren's voice had a wistful edge, recalling Sunday strolls along the sea-wall, picnic lunches on the beach, skimming stones at low tide. 'I do.'

'Good luck to you then,' said Quinn. 'Good luck to you both, I hope it works out.'

McLaren gave a slightly embarrassed but appreciative smile, then returned the frame back to its place on the cabinet, ensuring with a few fine tweaks it sat in exactly the same spot it had always occupied: Dori's smile facing directly on to McLaren's chair by the window.

-23-

THE HUNTER HAD TAKEN REFUGE in a charity shop, it being the closest door to the passageway. He was surprised the big man hadn't noticed it when he chased after him; instead he had stopped at the head of the passageway and swivelled his head side to side along the shopping thoroughfare before giving up and mooching back to the carpark.

The Hunter lurked beside the window behind a revolving carousel tower of yellowing, broken-spine paperback novels: *"50p each, 3 for £1"*. The Hunter feigned interest, slowly turning it around, releasing the funky, dusty smell of old books, watching the activities in the carpark outside.

From his vantage point he'd watched the youth run for it as soon as the big man's back was turned; he'd sprinted through the vehicle entrance in the opposite corner of the carpark and was long gone by the time the big man returned. The man's massive head flopped left and right searching for the boy, like a dopey big dog on the scent of a rabbit, but the boy was nowhere to be seen. From the comfortable safe distance of the window the Hunter couldn't hear the big man, but he could tell he was angry. The big man stooped low and picked up the commando knife, rotating it back and forth in his grip, appreciating its weight and size, then wrapped its blade in the red baseball cap and carefully slipped it into his overcoat pocket. *Shame. I was fond of that knife, one of my favourites. Maybe I'll get the chance to claim it back.*

The Hunter lifted the nearest novel off the carousel; a tatty old specimen, it fell open in his palm. He raised it as if to read but his eyes never left the big man in the carpark outside. He could tell from the big man's furtive movements and glances that he was planning something. Sure enough, the big man then flipped the tailgate of the Volkswagen and walked across to the body on the ground. The Hunter knew immediately he was planning on concealing the body. He also knew that body was at least one hundred and forty kilos of deadweight. Recognising that was an awful lot to shift by one man, the Hunter knew it gave him some time. Exiting the charity shop, he quickly made it to his own car, parked some streets away, and drove it round to the vehicular entrance that the boy had escaped from. He parked up just a little further along the road and waited. A few minutes later the red Golf GTi, driven by the big man, nosed out and joined the flow of traffic.

The Hunter kept a discreet distance for several miles. He followed the big man until he pulled into what was signposted a dead-end, spurring off from a very quiet single width road. This whole area had been given over to holiday chalets, in varying stages of decrepitude: *so this is where he's holed up*, surmised the Hunter. Most of the chalets looked closed and sealed up for the season, and the amount of traffic had thinned considerably; the Hunter thought it prudent to hang back, it was a dead-end after all, there was no way out. The Hunter parked his rental car between two very obviously sealed-up chalets: no chance of anyone coming out and questioning his reasons for being there. He waited.

After twenty minutes or so, curiosity overwhelmed his patience. He got out of the car. He walked a slow, circuitous route around the chalets, eventually spotting the red Golf hidden from general view behind a particularly shabby structure—*one strong wind would blow it into the sea*, thought the Hunter uncharitably. Up ahead he saw the big man with the small vagrant he'd tussled with outside the coffee shop; they were deep in conversation and looking out to sea. He couldn't hear what they were saying from where he'd positioned himself, but every so often the small one would wave his hands around to illustrate his point and the big man would laugh. Just two friends shooting the shit, decided the Hunter. He didn't need to search the chalet or the car: they didn't have the money. If they did, they wouldn't still be there in that hovel. The Hunter went back to the warmth of his car, cranked the seat back slightly, switched on the radio and decided to relax: *they'll be on the move soon enough*, he thought.

The Hunter's waiting game paid off. Ninety minutes later, just as the daylight was beginning to dim into evening, the big man trundled past him in the red Golf, followed by the small vagrant in a silver Kia. He looked at his watch and counted down thirty seconds, then put the car into gear and set off after them.

The convoy took him to a run-down light industrial area he wasn't familiar with, and not particularly enamoured by. The red Golf stopped in the access mouth of an empty warehouse unit, but the silver Kia continued further along past the carwash on the corner. He followed as it turned the corner and headed on for another two hundred metres or so before swinging a sharp U-turn in the middle of the street without indicating first. *Has the vagrant spotted me?* The vacant expression of the driver showed he was oblivious to the Hunter as he passed him in the opposite direction and then pulled in close to the corner. Knowing it would be impossible to perform a U-turn of his own without alerting him, the Hunter pulled in behind a line of parked cars outside a thriving fried chicken store. He set his gaze in the rear-view mirror and cursed that he was unable to see the Golf from that position. It was only a minute or so before the vagrant gave him the opportunity he needed: the Kia's door opened and the vagrant stepped out and walked away, back in the direction towards the Golf. Seizing upon his good fortune, the Hunter turned his car around and took up a new position, stopping the car outside a builder's merchant on the corner of a side turning. Through the merchant's mesh-fencing he could see along the full curve of the road with the Kia nearest him, the

Golf at the other end and the car-wash in between. The Hunter was curious: *what have they got planned?* Then he spotted them both leaving a grimy café opposite and all became apparent.

*

Six minutes later, the Hunter laughed a delirious whooping chortle. The silver car shot off at speed in one direction. A dozen malnourished men in tatty clothes too thin for the weather stampeded in the opposite, they moved with the enthusiasm and general sense of direction of an avalanche; they didn't know where they were going but they were pleased to be on the way. The Hunter couldn't help his delight: magnificent, like watching a movie, worth coming just for that. He couldn't help finding himself a little aroused at how swiftly and brutally the big man had dealt with five attackers. *I was right about him; he's not the lumbering fool he looks.*

The Hunter rolled up for a closer look. If anyone appeared, he'd just say he wanted a carwash and act dumb. The Golf blocked the access gate, its doors wide open, ramraid-style. As he walked the length of the carwash middle lane, one or two of the fallen groaned, but the sight of another stranger made them stay down. Then he saw it, lying in front of the small garden shed was the man he'd killed earlier that day, the huge tank of a man. The Hunter began to get an idea of the tableau laid out before him. Sure enough, inside the shed he saw his commando knife gripped in the fist of a man on the floor. Part of him wanted to retrieve his knife, it seemed a shame to leave it there, but he understood the plan and left it where it was. As he assessed the battlefield he noticed a baseball bat on the ground. He picked it up and returned inside the shed.

'Wake up. Hear me? Wake up.' the fat blunt end of the bat nudged against the man's cheek. After the third or fourth attempt he roused from his slumbers, his blinking signifying confusion.

'What happened here? Can you tell me? What happened?'

131

'Flint,' murmured the man in a low groan. 'Flint family want this site.' He dropped his chin to the floor with another groan.

'I see,' replied the Hunter and connected a home-run swing against his head, and then a couple of more as a bit of a flourish for the video.

Before he left to return to the chalet, certain that was where they would have gone, he wiped the bat clean of his prints. He pressed it into the tank's grip, knowing it now made a better narrative for the territorial dispute the big man was aiming for.

-24-

MCLAREN WAS THE FIRST TO NOTICE IT. The Prison Mouse's whiskers twitched at the unexpected crowd: too many people loitering outside the railway station, too many for that time of day, too many confused and angry faces. He looked on with a curiosity that verged on the wary, as if they were hurtling into an ambush with all the speed of a glacier. The line of traffic held them stuck tight and had no intention of releasing them just yet, the station entrance enticingly close. McLaren watched on: something was wrong.

'Did you say the next train out's at 18:03?' Quinn already knew the answer but asked anyway, as though it would add urgency to their situation, as though the universe would hear and suddenly part the traffic just for him.

McLaren merely nodded a response; years of watching crowds had sharpened his sense of suspicion. His attention didn't leave the mass of people.

'I'm going to miss it sitting here. I'll hop out now.' Quinn thrust a hand across towards McLaren. 'I guess this is goodbye, then.'

McLaren took Quinn's hand without looking down, and murmured 'See you,' but all the while watched the people. Something didn't feel right.

Using long strides somewhere between a walk and a jog, Quinn covered the short distance to the station building. McLaren released a long breath he hadn't been aware he was holding and flicked the indicator down with his little finger.

Inch by inch he nosed out of the stationary line towards the main flow of traffic. *Bastard, bastard, come on, somebody let me in you bunch of bastards.*

Success! An elderly lady in a small yellow Nissan flashed him both a pleasant smile and her headlights, inviting him to pull out in front of her. McLaren responded with a thumbs-up in her direction. He pulled the wheel tightly to the right and the car started a slow trundle across the lanes.

Thump!

A short, sharp boom to his blindside. *Shit! What have I hit?*

His head snapped around in panic at the same time as the sunlight disappeared. A thick solid wall filled the passenger window and eclipsed everything else. Before he could comprehend what was happening the door opened and the balance of the car see-sawed to the left.

'Come on, drive, let's get out of here,' commanded Quinn, fumbling for the seatbelt. McLaren dumbly nodded and stepped too heavy on the pedal. The car lurched away with a squeal. The elderly lady in the small yellow Nissan shook her head, dismayed at his bad driving: he'd seemed so polite.

*

'No trains,' said Quinn by way of explanation pre-empting McLaren's question. 'Every single train cancelled. In and out.'

'That'll be the police. They've found the carwash, now they're locking down the island.'

Quinn slammed a heavy hand down upon the dashboard, and again, and again, and then again. *I should've guessed this would happen. A gang battle: that's big news on a small shithole rock like this. Of course they'd want to regain control, and the easiest way to do that is to close down the island. No one gets off.*

As they drove the congestion grew more noticeable: the traffic still flowed but it was heavier, thicker, slower, a gradual change from soup to syrup, the knock-on effect of the bridges' closure, the traffic circled with nowhere to go.

'What do you want to do? You're welcome to spend another night at mine, get your head down. It'll all be cleared and open again in the morning. I'll take you down for the first train out,' offered McLaren.

Quinn shook his head. 'No good. I need to get to Bentley's tonight. Jamie's on his way there right now, I'll bet you, and as soon as he gets there and tells them he's seen me they'll pack up and go. All that'll be left there for me tomorrow will be John's Russian minder and a twelve-bore. I've got to get out of here today... now.'

'But how? No one's getting off, the place is in lockdown.'

Quinn stared out the window, the flat featureless fields stretching out before him. In the distance the new bridge stood high on the horizon, the tallest structure for miles around, designed to let the container ships pass under. A thought chimed in a distant corner of Quinn's mind, setting off a relay, in the blink of an eye the connections had been made and he knew the answer. 'I need a boat.'

'A boat? And where are you going to magic a boat from?'

Quinn turned and smiled at McLaren. 'Well, you're the smuggler.'

*

Half an hour later, McLaren gave Quinn a nudge. 'Wake up, he's here.'

They'd parked up in the middle of nowhere beside a stretch of shingle and not much else. Quinn had no idea where he was. McLaren had called in a favour from one of his contacts, but it hadn't come cheap. 'Five grand? I don't want to buy the bloody boat,' Quinn had protested, but McLaren had snapped back, 'No, you want to buy a getaway driver from the scene of a bloody massacre in the middle of a full-scale island lockdown. If you want someone proper who'll do it no questions asked, then

it's five grand. It's not open for negotiation, it's take it or leave it!'
Quinn took it—but he wasn't happy about it.

The fat man in the leather jacket didn't ask his name, and
Quinn didn't offer it. He stood back and let McLaren shake
hands with the man.

'Got the money?' asked the man.

McLaren shook his head. 'Tomorrow.'

The man replied with a volley of profanity and began to
walk back in the direction he'd come from. McLaren scuttled
ahead, blocking his path, protesting, promising tomorrow was
guaranteed. McLaren pointed with an outstretched arm, and the
man looked to where directed. McLaren pressed something into
the man's palm. The man pursed his lips and scratched the back
of his neck for a second or two. A decision made, a handshake to
seal. McLaren returned to Quinn to break the news.

'He'll take us. Come on, he wants to go now.'

'Us?'

'I promised him you were good for the money, because
you promised me you were. I've given him the car as deposit,'
explained McLaren. 'So until I see the money, I'm sticking right
by you.'

'Fair enough,' Quinn sighed, and they followed the man
towards the water's edge.

*

The boat was an ageing pleasure cruiser, the sort favoured by
retired middle-managers who'd always dreamt of a yacht but
whose pension pots made them settle for this: twenty-five feet
long, with a fibre glass hull as white and fragile as an eggshell. A
few pitted brass fittings and some salt-bleached hardwood trim
gave a bit of decoration.

A small external seating pit at the back housed the wheel
and instruments on a panel. A low door stepped down into an
enclosed lower cabin. Quinn poked his nose below deck and

saw bench-seating either side: the blue fabric covers were heavily stained and the foam cushioning looked thin. The same meagre furnishings made up the two-person bunk in the prow. Two small gas rings, an oven under and a tiny stainless-steel sink adjacent offered domestic opportunities for longer journeys. A label stuck to a narrow wooden door identified the toilet facilities. The whole area smelt strongly of fuel and solvents and made Quinn's stomach roll. Preferring the chill evening air to overwhelming nausea he sat himself down in the small pit at the back and tried to get comfortable against the hard sides.

Thankfully none of the meagre creature comforts below deck would be necessary tonight: McLaren had explained Rochester was less than twenty nautical miles away, and yes the boat looked a bit of a wreck but that was the intention. Below the water it boasted a mighty new diesel engine more at home in a powerboat: journey time to Rochester, under thirty minutes. Quinn shuffled again then realised he'd never get comfortable so gave up trying. He flipped up the collar of his coat to hold back the chill. His feet vibrated when the engine roared into life, and the tremor shuttled from ankle to knee and back again all the way to Rochester.

*

Rochester Castle's silhouette stood against the dusk: old and jagged and isolated, like a rotten tooth. Like from the mouth of that old pisshead his dad used to hang about with back in the day. Quinn had been thinking a lot about his dad recently. God alone knows why. I bet he never thought about us again: *'Here's two hundred pound. Take it. For you and your idiot brother. Now fuck off. I've done my bit. You're a man now. Get out.'* Happy seventeenth birthday, Benny: you used to say that was the happiest day of your life, perhaps you were right.

Rochester High Street comprises of hair salons and antique shops, and if it's not either then it's a probably a bar. It was between shifts as the big man lumbered along its cobble setts, his little friend scampering behind. The day-trippers had gone home and the night-owls weren't out yet; Quinn walked its length barely seeing another person. Without hordes of tourists or flocks of partygoers to block the pavements, he made it in no time at all.

'This is me,' Quinn shot a lacklustre point towards his coffee shop.

McLaren surveyed the full majesty of Quinn's emporium. 'Who's Estella?'

Quinn heard but didn't reply; it didn't warrant a response. Instead, he scanned the area, searching for anything out of the ordinary. The coffee shop was in darkness, a few days' mail visible inside the door piled snowdrift style. *Good, she's not here; she got away in time.*

McLaren peered through the glass door, into the darkness. It resembled the morning after a party: uncleared cups and plates lay across tables, crumbs across the carpet.

Quinn took off, darting up the side alley. McLaren followed, a pace or two behind, and arrived to find Quinn pushing buttons on a combination lock. Seconds later the rear door to the coffee shop opened. Immediately came the low-tone *peep-peep-peep* of an awoken alarm system. Quinn tapped on a white panel just inside the door and the alarm went back to sleep. *Another good sign; no one's been in since Zoe got away.*

Quinn entered, McLaren followed. Without speaking, just head gestures and darting eye movements, Quinn instructed him to firmly but quietly close the door. McLaren had seen men like this before, men with their senses heightened to the max, men ready to launch an attack in a heartbeat. McLaren knew well enough to remain quiet, remain small, and let them process whatever it was that had got them so twitchy. He stood back and waited; Quinn would be back from whatever planet he'd gone to soon enough.

The kitchen area was untidy, messy: unwashed cups and

unemptied jugs of milk that would start smelling pretty funky if they weren't rinsed out soon. McLaren recognised the signs of an urgent escape. Him and the girl, they must be close, for her to drop everything without question, to get out the moment she was told to. Thinking it must be nice to have someone trust you that much, McLaren's thoughts wandered. *Maybe I should drop Claire a note, let her know I'm okay. Maybe a Christmas card this year, test the water. Maybe when Quinn pays me out I could give her some money, help with her hairdressing course, maybe.*

McLaren, returning from his daydream, found Quinn gone. He'd moved to a windowless office, little more than a cupboard, small and cluttered, barely space for a battered desk and a swivel chair. A small cube-shaped safe sat under the desk. McLaren looked on hungrily when Quinn swung open its thick door: was this where he would get his big-time bonus? The boatman had only wanted two, but McLaren had persuaded Quinn it was more; only to cover his time and management costs, of course. Five large, thank you very much, don't mind if I do, and the boatman can keep the car; what am I going to do with a stolen motor, anyway?

From where he stood, McLaren could see directly into it: nothing but shadows. Empty. Quinn, however, seemed happy about this, ecstatic almost. *Well done girl, you did it.*

From a small orange metal cabinet mounted to the wall, Quinn plucked a bunch of keys. 'Come on, let's go,' he commanded, ushering McLaren back out the way they'd come.

Quinn pulled the rear door firmly shut and shook the handle. Confident it was secure, he beckoned McLaren to follow him to a side road opposite with elegant, tall, three-storey townhouses in yellow brickwork. He began unlocking the assorted locks to the first front door in the terrace.

'Wait, whose house is this?' protested McLaren.

'Mine,' said Quinn. 'And Zoe's got the basement flat below.' Both men looked down at the shallow well beside them, that too in darkness, nobody home.

'Relax,' said Quinn, finally getting the door open. 'No one knows about this place; I've not had it long.' Quinn didn't feel the need to add that all business was done on the coffee shop premises: keep business and personal separate, never let them meet.

*

McLaren was impressed with Quinn's home: very smart, sleek and modern, even the pale cream carpet looked expensive. Old habits die hard, and McLaren felt subservient enough to discard his shoes without asking.

'Make yourself comfortable.' Quinn's tone sounded more in duty than in welcome. He gestured towards a large kitchen area at the back of the house. 'Help yourself. I don't know if anything's still good in the fridge, but feel free. Otherwise the takeaways are by the phone, order whatever you want. I'm going for a shower.' Quinn took one tread of the staircase then stopped, and growled over his shoulder. 'Don't go nicking anything when I'm upstairs!'

McLaren meekly nodded—was he joking?—he didn't know but thought it best not to antagonise him any further. The very ungenial host climbed the stairs and turned the dog leg halfway up, disappearing from view. The rattle of pipes came from somewhere deep within the walls, immediately followed by the whoosh of a powerful shower.

McLaren padded softly across the plush carpet to the kitchen and pulled the fridge door handle—a chrome pole as long as he was tall—it opened with a reassuring resistance. Inside, staples such as milk, eggs and meat all past their best-befores, not that that ever meant much to McLaren, taking them as advisories rather than warnings. He gave a packet of sliced ham a cautious sniff, decided against it and reached instead for a packet of chocolate biscuits and a bottle of beer. He took his treats across to a plump leather sofa facing an enormous TV and got himself comfortable, as commanded by his host and benefactor.

*

Whilst McLaren was drinking Quinn's lager and enjoying his Sky Sports, Quinn was upstairs. No matter how much he scrubbed, no matter how much expensive soap he lathered on, he couldn't rid himself of the stench of Cabbage Island. It filled every pore and contaminated every follicle.

In an act of resignation, Quinn placed his palms flat against the wall, pressed his forehead against the cool tiles and let the water rain down on top of him. The drumming against his back and the way it cascaded across his body was hypnotic and soothing. Eyes shut, thoughts took over. He let them run, free to go wherever they wanted. *Keep business and personal separate, never let them meet*, that was the rule, it echoed inside his head until it took flight and spiralled off on its trajectory. It never used to be that way, but then the personal clashed with the business, the boundaries got lost, the innocent got hurt. Nicki, Nicole, whatever her name was, Benny was keen on her, watching the firefighters cut her out of the wreckage, no need to be gentle, no need for restraint, she was dead already. And Zoe, crouching, crying, frightened. When the disaster everyone expected struck, the carnage that went with it was immeasurable.

*

McLaren's head toppled backwards, waking him into startled surprise. *Fuck, I hadn't even realised I was that tired: been a long day.* He wriggled on the sofa, getting more comfortable, this time pressing his head against a cushion and closed his eyes ready to welcome sleep.

'Wake up,' came quickly followed by a tapping of his knees, 'Wake up.'

With bleary eyes and a dry mouth McLaren emerged from his doze. A glance at a nearby mantel clock told him he'd been asleep for about twenty-five minutes. After a few blinks to drive away the tiredness, he discovered a very different Quinn stood before him. This Quinn looked ten years younger thanks to a shave, a shower and fragrant products styling his hair with a modern look. Dressed in his own clothes—a white long-sleeved t-shirt and black track pants with discreet brand logos picked out in gold thread verifying their expense—he looked healthy, wealthy and respectable.

McLaren didn't speak, just nodded, hoping the small talk was over, feeling the lure of sleep pull strongly, when, 'Better pay you out, I suppose,' suddenly snapped him wide awake and any trace of fatigue was forgotten.

Quinn beckoned McLaren. 'This way.' McLaren followed him to a utility room at the back of the kitchen: small but plenty big enough for a washing machine, dryer and butler sink to co-exist side-by-side. Quinn dropped to his knees and gave a sharp tug to the plinth board across the bottom of the sink unit: it popped off with very little force. Quinn reached inside the void under the kitchen cabinet and slid out a slim black metal drawer on smooth runners.

Peering over Quinn's shoulder, McLaren felt like Howard Carter: *'What do you see? Wonderful things!'*.

Quinn extracted a handgun from the drawer and lay it beside his knees, then he retrieved and placed beside it two fully-loaded magazines. Next, he plucked out a roll of banknotes, tightly coiled into a cylinder about an inch thick; no need to unwrap and count it, he knew how much it held, it was exactly the same as all the others lined up in two neat rows the full length of the drawer. Without looking, he tossed it over his shoulder in McLaren's general direction, knowing McLaren would be waiting expectantly, stretching out like an eager seal in a circus to catch his treat. 'Five Kay. That's how much the boatman wanted, wasn't it? There you go, paid in full.'

McLaren snatched the bundle in mid-air. There was something immensely satisfying holding it in his hand, it felt heavy and reassuring. Quinn rose to his feet, slotted a magazine into the butt handle of the gun and slipped it behind his back into his waistband. A muscle pulsed in his jaw. 'That's us settled. Happy?' he asked. McLaren nodded his response as Quinn continued. 'Good. I've got to go. What are you doing?'

McLaren hadn't given the matter any thought beforehand and had no answer now. Quinn looked at the open-mouthed simpleton for a couple of seconds before putting him out of his misery. 'You can stay here tonight. Spare bed's second door on the left upstairs. I'll sort you out a ride home in the morning, okay?' He didn't wait for a response and pushed past McLaren to get out. 'I should be back in a couple of hours but can you do me a favour … please?' He waited for McLaren to nod before he continued, 'If I'm not back here by morning can you call the number on the board by the fridge, the one that says Benny's mobile. It'll connect you to Zoe, let her know please. Thanks.'

Quinn threw on a black hoodie jacket that matched his track pants, grabbed a key fob from hook near the door and headed outside. McLaren realised he'd left without waiting for an answer, but nonetheless muttered in a quiet voice. 'Sure, no problem.'

-25-

TONY FLINT DIDN'T KNOW HOW TO DEAL WITH THIS: he knew he was mad letting Jamie in on the firm, but what else could the boy do? He'd given Jamie everything he wanted, and more, all his life—what father wouldn't, especially considering how tough he'd had it growing up. His own old man was self-made and never let him forget it. His old man had built his firm, hardly a sprawling empire but still a pretty impressive foothold for a one-man band in the lawless wild west era just after the War. When every spiv, chancer and crook tried to fill the gaps left by austerity his old man held his nerve, forged his own way and earnt the trust and protection from all the major firms in London. His old man grew up tough and made sure Tony did too; he had nothing that wasn't earnt, stolen or fought for. After fifteen years of life-lessons toughening his son up he gave him the ultimate test by dying suddenly. At sixteen, Tony had to step up or the firm his father created would be snatched from him.

There was no denying it, life had been a challenge every single day for Tony Flint. So if he had the money to make life a little more comfortable, a little more colourful for his one and only son then how could anyone begrudge him that? But you don't become the man Tony Flint became by making people a little more comfortable and their lives a little more colourful, you get there by being a cold, ruthless, nasty bastard. You only bring close those you can trust and you don't accept failure: you fail, you're out. But now he faced a dilemma entirely of his own making and he didn't know which path to take: forgive Jamie and be seen as weak and nepotistic, or punish Jamie and risk losing him? So, he behaved like he always did when strategic thinking let him down: he shouted a lot.

There's a chief inspector whose kids' school fees are paid courtesy of Mr Flint. In return he passes on insider gossip, quite literally the Police Informer. He'd just finished downloading Tony Flint with recent events on the Isle of Sheppey, and quite frankly was glad to get off the call because he could sense Flint's patience was burning down like a fuse and he certainly had no intention of being anywhere nearby when he exploded.

Jamie, slouched in an armchair, silently looked out at the garden whilst his father took the chief inspector's call. Tony put the phone down and looked across at his son, who returned him a sullen scowl that took every ounce of self-restraint not to slap off his face. Tony decided to approach matters from the side rather than go head-on and so began with, 'Tell me about your car. Where is it now?'

'Don't know. Sheppey. Somewhere.'

Somewhere? Was he really being that flippant? That bloody car he insisted on having, wanting it in his own name, legit? The same car he signed a ridiculous leasing agreement for, and spent a fortune insuring? Just left... somewhere?

'What do you mean *somewhere*?'

'Somewhere. A carpark, near the high street, that's where.'

'Oh, bloody is it?' replied Tony. 'Your car is actually in the middle of a murder scene that the police are chalking up to gang warfare. Exhibit number one, in fact.'

'It's what? That's nothing to do with me!'

'Well, first things first, what you're going to have to do is work out an alibi for yesterday and today, make it absolutely waterproof, and then you're going to make a phone call and report the car stolen.' Tony didn't break eye contact with Jamie when delivering his instructions, he had to be sure the boy understood the severity of the situation, but when all he got was a derisory shrug Tony chucked in his hand grenade. 'Get LJ to back up your alibi, get him to say he was with you all day.'

Jamie fidgeted in his armchair, not much but enough for Tony to notice. *Good, that got through to you, perhaps you'll pay attention and do as you're told from now on.*

'Got something to tell me, Jamie?' Tony re-connected eye-contact, there was something in his gaze now that made Jamie take notice, he sat up straight and looked attentive. 'Didn't think I knew about LJ, did you?'

Jamie nodded then shook his head, unsure of the correct answer his old man hoped for. 'It wasn't my fault,' he said.

Tony levered forward on his elbows, his fingers steepled against his chin. 'Who killed LJ?'

'I don't know, I've never seen him before, some bloke—'

'Some bloke?' exploded Tony. 'Some bloke you've never seen before suddenly decided to have a pop at LJ?'

'Yeah, well, no—it wasn't like that, this guy was like a… a… manhunter.'

'A manhunter?'

The composure in Tony's voice gave Jamie confidence, he began to feel as though he was edging out of trouble. He started to add to his story unbidden. 'Yeah, this manhunter, he must've been sent to track down the money we stole. I got a call from this bird I had a little dabble with, the one who gave me the idea for the gig in the first place. She said she'd been called by her ex who worked at the car depot—'

'Wait,' commanded Tony, raising his hand to emphasise his point. 'How many people? This is sounding very shaky so far.'

'But this manhunter, he'd been working his way through people, like links in the chain, that's why this bird's ex got in touch, he was panicking he was next.'

'And was he?'

'I've no idea. Probably.'

'So, if this manhunter is any good… how long before he gets

to us?'

'Well, you see, that's why me and LJ went there. I'd given her a lot of blah-blah-blah to calm her down, telling her I'd protect her, stop her panicking, going to the police and all that, but all I wanted to do was take her out somewhere quiet and, well, take her out.'

Tony gave an appreciative nod; perhaps the boy had potential after all. He'd shown he was capable of making good tactical decisions when called upon. 'So did you do it?'

'No. I was all prepared and ready to,' Jamie noticed his father stiffen at the implication of failure. 'I'd got her alone, got her guard down. Then Quinn blunders in, scares her away—'

'Quinn?' asked Tony, but the way he said suggested it didn't come as a surprise to him. Ever since Bentley had spoken to him the day before, Tony had been fuming, waiting for Jamie to broach the subject of Quinn with him. Now came that moment. 'You told me you'd dealt with Quinn. That was the one job I needed you to do.' Jamie gave a meek nod to the sudden aggression in his father's questioning. 'You promised me he was gone.'

'He was. I shot him. He dropped in the river. He never came back up again.'

'Well quite clearly he bloody well did!'

The muscles in Jamie's jaw twitched, he didn't have a response for his father—at least not one that wouldn't result in getting his head torn off—instead he slumped in his armchair and raised his hands in a shrug: a gesture more incendiary than any answer he could have given.

Tony jabbed a finger in Jamie's direction. 'You need to watch your back. If you've got Quinn after you, then you're in big trouble.'

Jamie, never appreciating what his father saw in Quinn, couldn't help himself. 'He's a useless fat old fuck!'

The lightning-fast slap across his face wiped the sneer clean off. Tony had gone too far and he knew it, but he also knew he wouldn't apologise: if the boy wants to be in my world, he needs to respect me.

'Think.' Tony jabbed his forefinger to Jamie's temple. 'Think. What did he say, what did he want?'

Jamie's face glowed an angry red: partly slap, mostly shame. 'I don't know. About the money mainly. He wanted his share, wanted to know where it was—'

'You told him?'

'He knew it was at Bentley's, that's always been the plan, nothing changed because he was supposed to be dead,' protested Jamie.

'Have you told John Bentley?' Tony asked and was oddly relieved to find out he'd come straight home after escaping Quinn and not spoken to anyone. 'Okay, fine, that's okay. So we know where he's headed at least. Round up the men, make sure they're armed, tell them to meet us outside that pub near John's in one hour. Think you can manage that?' Jamie made the right-sounding promises, he'd do it right away but Tony hadn't finished. 'What else did you two talk about?'

'He wanted to know what it was all about—'

'And?'

'I told him.'

An icy cold chill washed over Tony Flint. The stupid boy. The force of the slap this time knocked him off his feet, and the one after that kept him down.

-26-

QUINN KNOCKED ON THE DOOR AND WAITED: one second, two second. He knocked again and waited: one second, two second. He called their name and waited one more time, one more second… When no response came, he smashed the door in. He channelled all his brute force down through his raised foot, through the flimsy flush door. It burst open, the small cheap barrel bolt holding it closed offered no resistance, the thin ply skin split and tore apart with a fast snap.

The door shot open, the handle driven against the wall with such ferocity it sent a spiderwebbed shatter pattern racing across the square white tiles. Quinn stood aside to let Benny pass and waited in the lobby: boxed catering supplies piled high, the cloying smell of cooking oil thick in the air. He waited. He listened.

When Quinn heard the repeated thud of something dull and heavy hitting something hard and immoveable, coupled with the sound of screaming, he knew it was time for him to act. He entered, becoming the fourth person to occupy the small windowless lavatory. Despite each wall being covered floor to ceiling in glazed white tiles, it had a dank, cave-like feel due to the single weak bulb overhead and the feeble ventilation. In one corner, cowering on the floor beside the toilet bowl, seeking protection in the narrow space between the scratched plastic cistern and the wall, a young woman screamed, her clothes ripped and torn, a girl not even out of her teens: Zoe. In the other corner her father, Benny, gripped a man called Redlands by the hair. He'd already rammed Redlands's face against the hard porcelain edge of the wash hand basin twice, and he had no intention of stopping. He worked with the unceasing rhythm of a piston stoking some great engine: push-push-push. The basin shuddered under each blow but still held firm to the wall. Under the dismal bare bulb, the blood that sprayed up across the tiled walls took on the colour of dark thick communion wine.

Quinn looked on as his brother destroyed the man's face and his niece screamed. An observer, but only for a moment or two, then he snapped out of his inertia and knew it was time to intervene. Out front, in the restaurant, they must have noticed them coming back here, and they certainly must have heard the commotion even over the party melee. As if on cue, the 'staff-only' door, connecting the restaurant to back-of-house, opened. A quizzical head peered round. Seeing enough and assuming more, it summoned support. The sound of chairs scraping back in urgent surprise alerted Quinn: company was on its way.

Quinn reached in, his big strong hands landing firmly on his brother's shoulders. 'Benny, that's enough. Stop now. Let him go.'

Benny smacked Redlands one more time against the lip of the basin then dropped him. Redlands fell face first to the floor and didn't move. Quinn held out both hands, beckoning for Zoe to take them, his wordless gesture assuring her she was safe, it was over. She gripped hold, her hands tiny in his, and he pulled her to her feet. She embraced him tightly then released him. She switched her embrace to her father, Benny, this time not wanting to let go.

Quinn stepped across and used his size to block the doorway from the gathering crowd. The men, tough uncompromising guys the lot of them, stood around unsure what to do next. A shuffle rippled the crowd as a man pushed his way to the front,

Tony Flint.

'What the hell is going on here?'

-27-

IN THE LEAFY COMMUTER SUBURB OF CHISLEHURST, John Bentley gazed out across his lawn. The gardeners had cleared the fallen leaves and it looked beautiful. The shrubs and the mature trees turning their autumnal yellows and reds, the grass a deep emerald green - rich and lush, nicely recovered from the parching of the dry summer. At home John Bentley was completely different to the man he was at work. At home he was a family man in his well-to-do South London idyll, throwing himself extensively into local life. Tomorrow he would chair the resident's meeting for the final run-through of this year's charity fireworks night: John, the pillar of the community, doing his bit.

Bentley had a nice respectable life: two grown-up children, a wide circle of friends and on nodding terms with most in the area. But not one of these people knew what Bentley really did for a living, except his wife Helen. Helen had been with him since the very beginning, from her mum's council flat in Deptford.

John and Helen Bentley, from the nice house with the immaculate garden. If asked, John would say 'I was the head of procurement for a large regional building contractor.' It was an answer that was vague enough yet at the same time specific enough, and usually boring enough to end any further questions, but on the rare occasions someone persisted he would add, 'New owners, a national firm, came in and offered me a golden parachute. A severance package. I couldn't say no to early retirement.' Most believed it, not that anyone cared: he wouldn't have been the first crook to settle on the wealthy outer fringes of South London. But the Bentleys enjoyed the anonymity and veneer of respectability they'd crafted—if Bentley had known Tony Flint was currently rounding up a militia to set up camp on his gravel driveway, he'd have thrown a shit-fit. Perhaps it was just as well he didn't.

The chime from his laptop brought him back from the window to his desk: online banking confirmed a transaction had successfully gone through; *need to plan ahead for our retirement.* He printed off the confirmation, clipped it into a folder in his desk drawer then closed down his computer. At the threshold of his small home-office he glanced back towards the locked understairs cupboard set into the opposite wall. The grand sum of the car depot takings were safely stowed within. He closed the office door and cursed when he found his pocket empty; he'd have to go find where he'd left the key. By the time he'd released the doorknob he'd made his mind up; the door was closed, he'd leave it tonight. He couldn't be bothered turning the house upside down looking for his keys to lock it, it could wait until tomorrow and anyway, he was hungry.

Helen, having booked herself on a cruise with her sister, had provided him with a selection of meals in the freezer: tonight's fare being a shepherd's pie. He read the handwritten note she'd attached to it and tapped her recommended timings into the microwave control panel. He pressed *go*. It began to slowly turn and his mind wandered. *Corsica today, I think that's what Helen said, or maybe it's Sardinia.* The minutes counted down slowly and he quickly grew bored with his wife's itinerary. Instead he thought about Quinn; perhaps he shouldn't have told Tony he'd been in touch, maybe found an alternative solution, but ifs and ands achieve nothing. The fact was he had, and plans had been put in motion.

The microwave pinged its completion; the glass dish was hot to the touch. It burned his fingertips. He had to move quickly getting it out. The gravy bubbled around the edges and it smelt delicious. It was a big portion, big enough for two—just as well seeing as he had a guest that evening.

*

'We need to talk about the other night.'

Ever since he'd discovered Quinn was still alive, Bentley had replayed his historic confrontation with the Quinn brothers. In hindsight perhaps he could have dealt with them differently. Once again, it entered his mind and lodged there, looping over again from the start.

'We need to talk about the other night. It needs to be resolved. It's unacceptable. So, what have you got to say for yourself?'

The way Benny, that huge beast of a man, leaned over him, and spat the words: 'I've got three things to say—Fuck that! Fuck you! And fuck off!'

It took every ounce of restraint not to flinch or show any intimidation and maintain a calm composure, to stare down the beast, but it seemed to work.

'If you've come expecting an apology you're wasting your time,' Quinn said to break the silence after Benny left the room with a dramatic slam of the door. 'He won't give you one, and I agree with him.'

And so, to the matter in hand: 'He can't batter Lee Redlands to a bloody pulp and not expect any comeback.'

'Why not? He deserved it.'

'Because Lee Redlands, as you know perfectly well, is an important man. Him and Tony Flint have been best friends since the first day of primary school. They're more like brothers.'

'So what?'—was Quinn playing dumb? *There's an etiquette to be followed, a hierarchy to be respected, or did he simply not get it?*—*'Doesn't entitle him to rape kids, does it?'*

'He didn't rape anyone—'

'Only because Benny stopped him in time!'

'And don't you go starting rumours about him and kids—'

'She's fifteen, John. She is a kid.'

Recognising the warning signs of rising tempers, diplomacy was required, try to take the emotion out of the conversation. 'It can be managed: it was a misunderstanding, he was drunk, something like that. But you know how things are. He can't be seen to be walking away from this without even an apology. Reparations must be paid.'

'A misunderstanding?' Quinn was clearly entrenched, he wasn't going to drop the emotion. 'She's a fifteen-year-old girl. There was no misunderstanding. And don't go saying she was giving him any kind of come on. She was waitressing to earn a bit of extra money; what's to be misunderstood?'

*

It was imprinted clearly on Bentley's memory just how angry Quinn had become, how much passion and fire burned within him. Bentley took some runner beans from the freezer and heated them through in the microwave. He'd risen to the role of negotiator and mediator for the Flint family because of his talent for strategic thinking and his ability to read a room. He'd often thought if chance had born him to different circumstances, slipped him a silver spoon, he'd have made a superior politician and diplomat—but then the money wouldn't have been so good. He smiled at his own wit, but it was faint respite as Quinn's unbending obstinacy elbowed and barged its way back into his mind-space like an angry bull...

'Benny needs to apologise to Lee Redlands.'

'You heard him; it's never going to happen.'

Before going into any mediation Bentley always made sure his bargaining position was clear and unequivocal. But he still carried the very distinct memory of not feeling comfortable that night because, from whatever perspective he took, his positions were weak. He knew it, and more importantly so did the brothers Quinn.

'He's regained conscious, you know? Thirty-six hours he was unconscious for. Four teeth gone, nose and jaw bust, fractured skull.'

Quinn shrugged his shoulders, a surly gesture to signal he lacked interest or compassion for the patient.

'That means a few months' lost earnings.' It was a distraction comment thrown in to try to deflect attention away from the girl, but Quinn replied entirely as predicted.

'He's got his rents coming in, he'll be fine.'

Quinn was right. Redlands was so comfortable at the top of the totem pole he didn't need to dirty his hands working; he got his management fee from those further down which he invested in his rental properties generating him a solid, legitimate income. Apart from Tony Flint himself, Redlands hadn't endeared himself to anybody. It was a struggle to find a sympathetic strand to cling on to, all that was left to rely on was the protocol.

'He's an important man, it's a matter of respect.'

'I don't respect someone who rapes kids... Do you?'

'So, we're back at square one.'

It was frustrating, but was the frustration at Quinn's intransigence to bend, or at Redlands for bringing the situation on himself? It was becoming harder and harder to tell.

'If Benny's not willing to apologise, then he's outside. He's no longer part of the group, he doesn't get any Flint protection, he doesn't get any of the benefits or opportunities of being a Flint associate. Understand?'

From Quinn's sullen nod it was evident he'd been expecting that kind of judgment, and he appeared to accept on behalf of his brother, but it didn't end there, it couldn't.

'There's no point me asking you to choose firm over family is there? You're with him all the way, aren't you?'

Quinn nodded again, and from that moment forth he and Bentley were on different paths.

*

Even with the benefit of hindsight, Bentley still didn't know whether Quinn had done the right thing. Yes, he believed in the principle of what he was doing, but was it really worth everything he gave up for that principle?

Bentley didn't think so, but then he and Helen never had to make that choice. Mr and Mrs Bentley had been blessed with two children, both boys, but neither had followed in his footsteps. Partly because of the great lengths he'd gone to in brushing away his footsteps from behind him, covering up any path back to exactly where he'd made his money, hopeful that that world and theirs should never meet. Yes, he'd made himself a nice living out of it, but he'd seen plenty fall foul of it with many meeting danger, disaster or death. He recognised the hypocrisy of his position and knew many who regarded it the family trade, fathers and sons—Tony and Jamie being the latest example—but he didn't want it for his boys.

Bentley had tried to gently nudge his boys down the routes that seemed the best fit for their talents and encouraged them to pursue professions they could find enjoyment from, and he was quite pleased it seemed to be working out. Dan, the eldest, was doing something with websites and computers, and Tom was at university in Bristol, doing Geology and thinking he might try to find a job in oil and gas when he graduated. Bentley was proud of them, and happy the way they'd turned out.

The microwave beeped its completion. He formed a neat stack of runner beans beside the shepherd's pie. No matter how he tried to force the subject from his mind he couldn't escape the suspicion that perhaps, in hindsight, he was starting to think Quinn was right: this was a shit business.

-28-

THE THREE-CAR CONVOY MOVED SLOWLY along the tree-lined streets, narrowed almost to single-width by the sheer number of parked cars lining each side. The lead driver, not quite sure where he was headed, cast a curious gaze at his surroundings: *big houses, not seen a motor more than five years old, Range Rover central, there's money round here, he concluded, I could see myself here one day: wife, kids, Labrador, very nice.*

The happy-ever-after daydream didn't last long, interruption coming from his passenger barking directions to their final destination: a pub-turned-restaurant in the heart of the suburban village of Chislehurst. The pub occupied a pleasant location, facing on to a flat green open common. Directly opposite sat a picture-postcard perfect historic church, whose avenue of mature Yews dotted with ancient mossy gravestones on a photogenic lean made it popular for lavish weddings and snowy Christmases. With the pub's few parking bays already occupied, the lead driver, Pope, took a speculative punt and nosed along the lane beside it. Success. Just a very short distance behind he found the wide bell-mouth entrance to a school with its gates closed and secured for the night. *Perfect*, he thought. *No vehicles expected, nobody to complain we're blocking them in.* He swung his car off the road and into the bell-mouth. The following two cars did the same and drew to a halt beside him. Three abreast they switched off their engines, killed the headlights, and waited further instructions.

Sitting next to Pope was Kenton: former boxer, part-time door security and permanent behemoth. Kenton could have been forged from iron, his muscles as big and black as cannon balls, and just as deadly; a punch from Kenton would guarantee brain damage, Pope was certain of that. Thankfully for Pope, Kenton wasn't one for chit-chat, preferring to stare out the window. Pope welcomed the quiet; it gave him a chance to think. And Pope's thoughts led to the task in hand and the hope that Tony Flint would recognise his leadership skills. He'd coerced and cajoled the chaps together at such short notice: with four each in the two other cars plus Pope and Kenton they were ten in total, add in Jamie when he turned up. The first eleven, the top team. Pope felt sure Mr Flint would be impressed, and what with the success of the car depot gig the week before, Pope was confident he was on his way up to becoming a serious player in the organisation. Not like his dad, always on the fringes, petty thievery, a life of what-ifs and wannabes; Pope had more ambition than that. He was determined to make it.

Perhaps Pope's wishful thinking had distracted him, perhaps being the lead car he was too far ahead to notice, but he never spotted the grey mini-van with blacked-out windows following them. As for the car backing up the convoy, that had no one with Pope's ambition or professionalism inside, just four jokers treating it more like a stag tour than business. They didn't give the mini-van a second glance, and if they did they'd have written it off as just another private-hire service you see all over the place and then gone back to swapping the porn clips on their phones by Bluetooth.

The grey mini-van with the blacked-out windows drew to a gentle stop back beside the pub. To the rest of the world it appeared to be waiting for its fare to emerge from an evening's refreshment. From behind its black screen it watched the road ahead and waited.

*

Jamie loved the way the Mercedes drove: so smooth, so quiet, so powerful. Any other time he'd have been thrilled to glide the streets in his dad's motor. Not tonight.

Tony sat beside him; he hadn't said a word since they'd set off. With a face of stone, Tony occasionally gnawed on his thumbnail. His behaviour put Jamie on edge: *he's mad at me, I can tell, but there's more to it, he's thinking, planning, he's nervous and most of all, he blames me.* Jamie correctly read his father's emotions and his arms began to itch. No amount of rubbing relieved the irritation and he realised it was his conscience burning a guilty shameful pain inside him. His realisation triggered a memory from a few months earlier.

Bentley, moaning again. 'He's too young, no experience, it's not right.' Didn't he know he was right behind him and could hear him, or did he and that was the point? When Jamie came fully into his father's office, when Bentley faced him, there was no trace of embarrassment so that answered that question.

'It's fine,' replied Tony Flint in an attempt to mollify the very agitated Bentley.

'It's not, Tony, and if you're honest, you know it's not. You can't just go dropping a boy into the Executive.'

'I'm not a boy,' Jamie countered. He had little respect for Bentley: the fussy, pain-in-the-arse nuisance. 'I'm twenty-three.'

'See, he's twenty-three,' Tony fluttered an outstretched hand to bring his son closer to him, bringing him into the conversation formally. 'You, me and Lee were younger than that when we began running the firm, John.'

'That's totally different, Tony, and you know it. We'd grown up in it and around it since the moment we could walk, not to mention your dad dying so young, no age at all, we had no choice—if we didn't step up someone else would've. He, on the other hand, hasn't experienced the life, he knows nothing. You parachute him into Redlands' empty chair and you risk losing credibility with the men.'

'The men,' Tony's voice grew loud, a rage brewed within, 'will

do as they're bloody told, and as long as they keep earning and keep earning well, they've got nothing to complain about.'

Bentley didn't speak, but blew out his cheeks with a loud, dismayed sigh.

'Anyway,' said Tony, his voice calm again, an insincere chummy tone to it, 'He's going to get all the experience he needs. He's got himself a sweet gig lined up, could be a nice earner.'

The warm prickle of pride crept across Jamie's skin, he flashed Bentley a smug grin.

'God knows we need a big earner, ever since Redlands…' Tony's words petered out, as though he'd run out of things to say.

Bentley responded with a sympathetic nod as if to say he understood exactly what Tony couldn't articulate.

'And as we discussed John,' Tony seemed to have regained composure, 'Quinn has to be on the job with him.'

'I don't need no babysitter,' protested Jamie. This time it was Bentley wearing the smug grin.

'Let me explain about Quinn…' began Bentley.

*

'Let me explain about Bentley…' began Quinn. His black BMW X5 ate up the miles on the motorway with ease. Riding in the passenger seat, McLaren approved. It was like sitting in an armchair, or how McLaren imagined travelling business class might be.

They'd been driving about ten minutes. Quinn had offered McLaren the chance to stay behind but he figured *"in for a penny, in for a pound"*, and so far his association with Quinn had proven very lucrative. Quinn knew McLaren's decision to come with him was ultimately mercenary, but he was glad of the company nonetheless. That thought triggered another: he'd never worked alone, all his life he'd been side-by-side with Benny. Maybe that was why the gig with Jamie didn't feel comfortable right from the very outset: where was the trusted partner to cover his back?

The soft nappa leather seat was comfortable, the M-tech steering responsive and agile. As he changed lane Quinn caught his reflection in the rear-view mirror, he looked healthy and clean, back to his old self—better in fact! Thanks to the few days' enforced holiday on Cabbage Island he'd lost a few pounds and it showed on his face.

It was good to be home. It was good to be alive. So why risk it? Should anyone have asked him, *'Why can't you be grateful for what you've got, why can't you let it go and instead enjoy your second chance at living?'* how would he have answered? Quinn genuinely didn't know. A lifetime's conditioning gave the Pavlovian response *'It's a matter of respect'* but Quinn knew that wasn't true, not anymore. He didn't respect the Flint firm after the way they'd so easily cast him and Benny aside, after all they'd done for the Flints. Quinn had been genuinely happy and content with his life at the coffee shop; he certainly hadn't craved their respect in the years since. So, what was it forcing him to confront them? Redlands. It was Redlands. If he was honest, deep down, Quinn always suspected Redlands was at the heart of everything. Now he was convinced.

*

'But didn't you say this Redlands fella was dead?'

Quinn heard McLaren's question and was satisfied he was at least listening if not understanding, 'Let me explain about Bentley…' began Quinn. McLaren reclined in his big wide seat, ready for Quinn's story.

'Tony Flint, Lee Redlands and John Bentley all grew up together. Tony was the leader of the gang, him being the loudest and most belligerent. He was the one got them involved in most of their scrapes. Redlands was the brains: he was bright, he got into grammar school and could have gone to university but for his friendship with Tony—one too many adventures saw him expelled and that was that. But like I say he was bright. So you had Tony, the general if you like, mustering troops and mounting campaigns, and then you had Redlands the brains, the one who understood money: how to lend it, launder it and legitimise it.'

'And Bentley? Where's he come into it?' queried McLaren.

'Bentley's the negotiator,' replied Quinn. 'His skill: he can talk to people without getting emotional. He can see things from everyone's perspective all at once, like he can see round corners—'

'The big picture.'

'Exactly! He sees the big picture. So, he was sent in to calm down territorial disputes, or settle grievances. He's got this knack—two sides can go in, both deadly passionate in their views, and he'll mediate a solution between them so that they both walk out thinking they've won.'

'The Boss, the Banker and the Broker?'

'Exactly.' Quinn snapped his fingers as emphasis. 'That's it exactly.'

The car in front braked sharply. A fifty zone loomed. Red and white filtering reduced three lanes to two. Quinn, spotting the sunflower yellow camera hung from a gantry up ahead, dropped his speed to suit and let the filtering guide him across the narrowing carriageway. For most drivers travelling at forty-seven on an empty motorway is a painful experience, the landscape passes by at a walking pace. Quinn's foot itched with impatience. He needed to get to Bentley's, the sooner the better, but he daren't speed. The last thing he needed was one of those bright yellow vultures perched up there capturing him on film; the less people that knew about his visit to Bentley the better. To help pass the time, and also to consolidate his thoughts, he told McLaren about Benny beating Redlands to a pulp for his treatment of Zoe.

McLaren listened in rapt attention, then, 'Sounds like he got what he deserved. Listen I'm a dad of two daughters, I may not have been much of a dad I grant you, but I like to think if anything like that happened to them I'd react in exactly the same way.' And then, unexpectedly, he placed a hand on Quinn's forearm, just a quick fleeting gesture but enough to signal support and unity. Quinn nodded but didn't speak. He kept his eyes on the road ahead and fought back the moist tingling around his eyes but it was too late, he knew what came next.

'Benny seriously damaged Redlands,' Quinn said, hoping McLaren hadn't noticed his eyes wet and heavy. 'Broken teeth, broken bones, unconscious for days. He really went to town on him.'

'Good.'

'When he did eventually wake up,' said Quinn, 'he had a place in Florida, a villa on a golf course. He went there to heal and recover.'

'All right for some,' muttered McLaren.

'He wasn't there long. About a week into it, just about to tee off, he dropped down dead.'

'Couldn't have happened to a nicer fella,' replied McLaren. 'I'm sorry, I've no sympathy for nonces. None at all.'

'Nor've I,' said Quinn slowly, carefully choosing his next words, knowing that whilst Redlands' death may have been a blessing for the world at large it was also a curse for the Brothers Quinn. 'But this is where I think everything stems from.'

'Why? You didn't do it did you?' McLaren received a stern stare from Quinn in response. 'Okay, so you'll have to explain as I don't get it.'

The temporary filter lanes came to an end and the traffic shot out of the restrictions like corks from a bottle. Quinn floored the X5 and McLaren felt the sudden thrust of acceleration press him tight against his seat.

'It was nothing to do with what Benny did. Even the doctors said it was an aneurysm, a defect that may have been in him since birth. But Tony Flint wouldn't have none of it,' said Quinn. 'He was convinced the battering by Benny had somehow caused it or dislodged it or something, and it was therefore Benny's fault.' Quinn quickly corrected himself. 'Our fault.'

Deep down, Quinn had always suspected, he knew that now, but for the sake of... what? Appearances? Good relations? Who knows, but whatever the reason it seemed simpler to accept it as a tragic accident, a coincidence rather than anything else, but Jamie's words confirmed it wasn't, Jamie's words confirmed there had been plans in place. And that, Quinn finally admitted to himself, was why he was heading there tonight. Not for respect, but for revenge.

-29-

THE SMART-ARSE DRIVER OF THE THIRD CAR held up the video on his phone. 'Isn't that your mum, Dave?' he asked, pointing to the woman enthusiastically fellating a particularly well-blessed participant. Dave told him to fuck off, and the car rocked with howls of laughter.

In the second car, the occupants listened with dismay to the radio commentary of the Champions League match: Schalke had just taken the lead. In the first car, Pope and Kenton sat in contented silence.

Pope was lost in a fantasy where tonight's exploits fast-tracked him to the top of the Flint firm. Kenton, on the other hand, stared at the dark and vacant low-level buildings visible through the railings in front of him: squat two-storeys, wider than they were tall, glazed almost floor-to-ceiling, and remembered why he hated school so much. It was fair to say everyone in the convoy was occupied in one form or another.

None of them paid any notice to the grey mini-van with blacked out windows, or that it had edged closer to the school's bell-mouth entrance. It rested only one car's length away from them. And none of them noticed the other mini-van, this one dark blue, approaching from the opposite direction and also stopping about a car length away on the other side of the bell-mouth.

*

The fork scraped listlessly around the plate, any appetite lost with the pretence of politeness. Outside, not too far away, a boom suddenly rang out in the night, quickly followed by a second. Noticing them jump at the noise, the host offered calming words, 'Ignore it, fireworks probably, kids,' offered by way of explanation, then noticing their plate. 'Not hungry?'

He got a silent response in reply: just a tilt of the head, a turn of the lip, but it conveyed the statement clearly enough.

'What's wrong?'

Another silent response, but again body language got the message across.

'Don't worry. It'll be over before you know it. Any time soon.' The way he smiled was reassuring, but then... Bentley had always been a persuasive negotiator.

*

Jamie had followed Pope's directions to the meet. He'd arrived about ten minutes behind them but was unable to park next to them because of some stupid bloody mini-van hogging the road. He parked beside the kerb a little further along, got out the car and jogged back to Pope and the others. Tony stayed in the car; no standing out in the cold and damp talking to the foot-soldiers for him, he was strictly officer class.

'You know what you're doing?' Jamie asked Pope, leaning in through the open window of Pope's car.

Pope tried, and failed, to keep the contempt from his tone: of course he did and how dare Jamie talk to him like he was his fucking minion, and where's his thanks in mustering all these people with such little notice. 'Yes,' he snapped.

'Good,' replied Jamie, oblivious to Pope's annoyance. 'Bentley lives just around that corner, a few minutes away. You guys wait here until you here from me, understand?'

Pope signalled his understanding with a short sullen nod,

then flicked the switch to bring the window up: not necessarily the last word, but close enough to feel like a victory.

Jamie jogged back to Tony, not giving the silent, blacked-out mini-van a second glance. He got in, fired up the powerful Benz and moved off. What was Pope's beef, he wondered. *Who's he think he is? Known him since we were at school and he's acting like some sulky kid. He'd better have more respect for me than that once I'm on the Executive.*

Jamie was hauled away from his thoughts by his father angrily demanding, 'I said, how many?' Jamie's blinking gave away his puzzlement, realising he'd missed the start of the question, his father, also aware of his lack of attention, reframed it. 'In the cars, how many men?'

'Ten,' replied Jamie.

Pope would have been pleased to learn Tony Flint was indeed impressed with his organisational skills in herding up so many at such short notice. However, everything is subject to context, being in the right time and place. Praise for Pope was for later; now it was time to strategize. Tony Flint's lips drew back tightly across his dry teeth and in a voice little more than a whisper said, 'Ten? Practically everybody then.'

Jamie nodded, saying nothing but feeling somehow jealous of Pope without understanding why. Needing something to say, he asked, 'Do you think it's enough? For Quinn?'

Tony Flint preceded his response with a look that was pure undeniable disappointment in his son. 'Quinn is a handy bastard, I'll give him that, but even he can't take out ten men at once. He's not the fucking Terminator!'

Jamie nodded, desperate to win his father's approval. The nodding slowed until his chin rested on his chest, his head hung in shame.

"Bentley was right. You're not ready for it.' Tony didn't notice Jamie's face redden with shame in the darkness of the car. 'In fact, you're probably not right for this business at all.'

Jamie didn't respond; any fight had deserted him. He looked

away, turning to regard the street outside. He focused on a brightly lit poster at a bus stop in an attempt to hold back the prickling sensation around his eyes. His father had noticed but had no time for sentiment and snarled a new instruction at him. 'Drive. Get us to Bentley's. He's got that big Russian, bringing the troops up to eleven... twelve, maybe even thirteen because he's one big mean mother than Russian of his.' Tony paused, contemplated and then continued, 'The lad Pope, he's done good. He could go far, a lad like him, he's got promise.'

Jamie brought a hand to his face. It was a clumsy attempt to make wiping away a tear look like he was scratching his nose that fooled no one. He shifted the Merc into drive and pulled away.

BENTLEY LIVED AT THE TOP OF A GENTLE HILL, the toe-end of a gated cul-de-sac, one of eleven built in a red brick Arts & Crafts manor-house style back in the 1930s. All had neat lawns, mature trees and shiny new SUVs: the staple of the stockbroker belt stay-at-home mum. Outside Bentley's sat a fully-loaded Mercedes S-Class. Quinn knew who it belonged to. He'd expected to find it there after spotting the three cars waiting at the school nearby.

Deciding it would make them more invisible to the waiting trio of cars, Quinn and McLaren had left the BMW X5 parked up about quarter of a mile away and, keeping to the shadows, arrived on foot. Preferring not to announce their arrival through the controlled gate entry, they discreetly slipped in through the narrow pedestrian gate intended for the postman. They headed towards Bentley's house when Quinn saw, through the trees, Flint's big fat Merc parked on the driveway. They paused, then stepped away from the weak glow cast by the ornamental streetlamp. They took shelter in the dark and plotted their strategy, agreeing to split up. A smallish yellow moon hanging low in the sky behind them helped pick out their individual pathways and they approached separately.

Quinn walked around the side of the house neighbouring Bentley's place and, at the back, came to a wide terrace with cast iron furniture. Two footsteps later and a bright white light drenched the terrace: a motion activated lamp attached to the house had spotted him. Quinn spun away and pressed his back tight against the blind corner. He waited, trying to control his breathing, convinced it could be heard inside the house. Using his watch, he counted down the longest thirty seconds of his life, then peered around the corner. The terrace remained lit under sterile white halogen that burned bright enough to be the envy of any operating theatre. However, no response from inside. Quinn looked up at the rear of the property, squinting around the brilliant sharpness of the lamp, blinking away the bright spots burned into his vision. The windows were dark and empty. Nobody home. Quinn released his held breath and waited for the pulsing in his ears to fade.

He scuttled across the face of the property to the opposite corner, to the shared boundary with Bentley. A low retaining wall planted with glossy-leafed ground-cover shrubs provided him a step up to peer over the fence screening the two homes from each other. In contrast to its neighbour, Bentley's place threw warm welcoming shafts of light out across the garden: elongated rectangles extended outwards from the windows and held back the cold dark night. From Quinn's position in the shadows he could see across the garden and in through a ground floor window. Bentley was seated on a sofa in there, talking with two men sat in the sofa opposite. Bentley appeared relaxed—all smiles and friendly gestures—perhaps because Quinn knew him so well he could spot the insincerity; Bentley had always been persuasive. He couldn't see the men's faces, their backs to the window, but he already knew who they were, and from the way they were sitting Quinn could sense their tension.

Reaching over, using touch alone to guide him, he found the upper rail: a thick substantial length of timber fixed horizontally to stiffen the fence. Damp and slimy with moss, Quinn dug his fingernails into the rail and, once satisfied he'd secured a purchase on it, swung a foot upwards. The toe of his shoe caught the top edge of the fence panel and, with hand and foot as fixed points, he hauled himself over.

His landing was awkward. He dropped straight down on to woody, branchy foliage with a crackle and a crunch. Startled by his own noise he pressed himself flat against the fence, hoping the darkness would mask him. The sound had carried. Inside he saw one of the men react: they'd heard something, they were twitchy, their head flicked back and forth towards the window in a startled reaction. Quinn caught a clear view of the man's face: Jamie.

*

McLaren took the perimeter of the golf course with the practised stealth of the foxes prowling the deserted fairways. He'd identified some markers specific to Bentley's house and now looked for them above the treeline, intending to approach from behind. Above the hedgerow he came upon the first house, left dark for the night. Knowing he was on the right trail he continued to walk.

There was partial cloud cover above but some moonlight broke through, enough to see the difference between the neatly trimmed fairway and the rough: getting wet feet would be bad, tripping over a root and breaking an ankle would be a far sight worse.

It was getting late now, nothing much seemed to be happening anywhere. Far away in the distance the lights of the clubhouse penetrated the darkness, but no sound carried with it: low takings in the bar tonight.

Soon ahead of him, on the right, he could make out the back of Bentley's place. He stepped towards it, across the long unkempt grass. The cold damp sucked through his thin cheap trainers and waterlogged his socks. McLaren hissed a colourful obscenity but it proved fruitless: the damp didn't go away. Fighting his way through the bushes and the undergrowth, he reached a low-level chain-link fence and clambered over it with ease; its purpose was merely to mark the boundary and keep out the foxes, it wasn't designed for security. After all, who'd be stupid enough to get scratched and splintered hacking through the dense hedgerow to get in this way?

From the bottom of the garden, McLaren faced the rear of the house. He could make out his identifiers: the logo on the alarm box was the same as at the front, the number of chimney pots matched, the satellite dish was in the same place. This was Bentley's place, no doubt about it.

The garden was long and flat and mostly laid to lawn. McLaren kept to the border where the freshly pruned bushes made interesting silhouettes that he used for cover until he came to a small outbuilding: a shed or a summerhouse. It was a narrow timber weatherboard structure. McLaren dropped to a squat and leant back against it, deciding it would be the most comfortable spot to wait and watch the house from.

Confident he couldn't be seen from the house, he searched his pockets for a cigarette and sparked up. Confident he couldn't be seen, he still made a point of cupping the cigarette in his palm to hide the glowing tip.

*

The second time Jamie snatched a backwards glance towards the window, Bentley caught his eye and smirked at his jumpiness. 'It's only foxes. We get a lot in the garden this time of year.'

Jamie's eyes shot back an expression that made clear he was in no mood to be patronised. Tony ignored the pair of them, preferring to concentrate on the business in hand. From somewhere within the house a door slammed. Jamie jumped again. Bentley smirked.

*

A short distance away, the lads-on-tour continued their boorish banter in the warmth of the third car. In the second car, Schalke scored again: two-nil, who'd have thought it, maybe someone should have put a bet on? And in the first, Pope seethed about Jamie's attitude. Whether any of them noticed the side doors of the two mini-vans sliding open and the occupants clambering out was purely academic, because if they did it was too late by then.

-31-

IT WAS ONLY A ZIP-UP HOODIE made from the normal sweatshirt fabric; very expensive because of the brand, but a zip-up hoodie nonetheless. The gun felt heavy in its pocket and pulled the hoodie down on one side, stretching it out of shape. More for his own reassurance than anything else, he took the gun in his hand and held it at chest height, close to his body. He looked around. Nothing moving this side of the house, it was a largely blind gable end with no windows. The only possible source of light would have been a side access door, its upper panel glazed with a frosted floral pattern, but this too was in darkness. Quinn, knowing this to be a laundry room, had selected it as his point of entry. Clutching his gun, he raised his knees high and took long, careful steps, managing to get away from the fence with minimal noise. There was no light cast directly onto this side of the house, but that spilling from the back windows seeped across to pollute this dark corner, casting a steady low illumination by which Quinn could make out the narrow ribbon of grey concrete paving, two slabs wide, skirting the house and leading right up to the door but no further; any area beyond had been swallowed by the night.

He moved forward cautiously, left hand out in case of any unseen obstructions, and before long he came to the laundry room door. He reached for the handle, fully expecting the resistance of a locked door, when the glazed panel lit up and the door began to open.

Quinn didn't pause. The door jerked, starting its inward swing and he dove out of sight. Would his scrabbling to the darkest corner have been heard behind the door? Quinn maintained a crouch behind a small plastic shelter and felt his age bite through his knees. The shelter stood about waist height. It was bolted to the wall and secured by a thick padlock. Quinn assumed it was an external store of some kind; not that the contents were of interest, it was the cover it provided. Quinn didn't move. He kept himself out of sight. The anticipation gnawed away at him, making him twitchy: fight or flight?

*

Marko swung the door open then twisted his shoulders to look back behind himself: *Where've I left it?* His eyes scanned the countertops in the laundry room, quickly finding what he was looking for. He reached across for his joint, the boss's words still lingered in his ears: *'You're not smoking that disgusting stinky shit in my house.'* If Marko wanted a relaxing spliff to unwind at the end of the day, then he was relegated to the garden. Holding it delicately between his fingers he tested the temperature outside the open doorway. No need for a coat, he decided; he'd known proper cold growing up in Mother Russia and there was still some way to go before it came anywhere close to that, shirt sleeves would be fine. Holding the paper parcel up to his face he inhaled the dry aroma—*I'm going to enjoy this*—and he stepped outside into the night. He didn't see the jab until it hit him squarely between the eyes.

*

Rolling to his left, Quinn reached the door just as the big Russian stepped out; his eyes were shut and his hands held up close to his face. Quinn took his opportunity and, folding his big wide right hand around the barrel of his gun, slammed the pistol butt as hard and fast as he could into the middle of the man's face. The man's head snapped back with the impact, his nose burst wide open, blood exploded from it, but he remained standing. As if firmly rooted to the spot, Quinn's surprise piledriver of a jab hadn't moved the man a millimetre.

The man's chin dropped to his chest. Then he tilted his face towards Quinn; flame red eyebrows stood proud and aloft arching eyes wide and furious. The man seemed in a demented bloodlust; his red bushy beard dripped with blood and his bared teeth took on a claret tinge. With a guttural roar, he charged at Quinn.

His head drove into Quinn's diaphragm, winding him. In his airless reaction he dropped the gun, not seeing where it fell in the darkness around him. The momentum of the man drove Quinn backwards, pressing him up against the wall of the house. The abrasive brickwork scraped against his cheek and ear. With all the force he had, Quinn slammed the point of his elbow down against the Russian's neck. The man's forward pressure was halted by the blow. Quinn pushed him away then peeled himself off the brickwork, shuffling to a more strategic place to stand: the centre of the path, no corners or obstructions to be pinned against, plenty of room to swing arms and legs.

The Russian lowered his head again and charged. Quinn deftly sidestepped and the Russian toppled past, clattering over an unseen box of empty glass bottles and jars, and colliding with the low wall. Before he could regain his balance, Quinn's shoe connected with his ribs, a powerful kick; its connection fired a jarring pain back up Quinn's leg, yet the Russian seemed unaffected. Quinn doubted himself for a split-second, wondering if in the darkness he'd struck the brickwork instead of the man, but as they moved into the edge of the reflected light Quinn saw his damp dirty footprint stamped across the man's stomach. The man was Russian granite. And he was angry. He came towards Quinn, fists raised in front of his face.

Back in the early days, the Quinn boys had worked with an

old bare-knuckle boxer. He was a long way past his hey-day of the mid-1970s, but still handy enough for collecting late payments and evicting troublesome tenants, and besides they enjoyed his stories. From somewhere deep inside, his words came back to Quinn: *When facing a bigger, stronger opponent always start on the arms. Don't waste your time and energy getting in close to attack the body: that just puts you at risk. Always start with the arms.*

Quinn brought the outer edges of both hands down hard against the Russian's biceps, just below his mass of shoulder muscle. The Russian, expecting a head shot, was surprised and his temporary state of confusion gave Quinn the opening for a repeat hard, fast chop against the upper arms. The Russian reacted but Quinn pre-empted and dodged the flying fist. Another chop brought down in the same spot across the biceps. The Russian swung again, but this time it lacked the same vitality. *It's working*, thought Quinn. *He's got dead arms; he's finding them heavy to lift.* Quinn got in another swift chop, biting down on his lower lip to release the extra ferocity. The Russian made another lacklustre jab: easily ducked. Quinn's club-like fist shot out, catching the Russian on the side of the neck—not a bout-winning blow but it knocked him off balance. The Russian stumbled back a half-step then tripped over the threshold of the open doorway, collapsing on the laundry room floor. Quinn saw his opportunity and pounced.

Quinn's knees pinned the man down. With one forearm in a chokehold under the man's chin, the other gripping firm across the forehead, his lips rolled back and teeth bared. Quinn fought against the Russian's resistance. Through the tension in his arms he felt the man's neck snap and every muscle instantly turn limp. Quinn released him and let his head drop to the tiled floor with a heavy whack.

*

Jamie flinched at a noise he thought he heard deep in the house.

It was Quinn. He was in the laundry room. Killing the Russian.

'Did you hear that? Don't tell me that was foxes!'

Bentley looked at Jamie over the top of his glasses. 'It's probably Marko thumping about, relax.'

Tony Flint remained focussed and refused to waver. 'We've got a problem, John. What do you suggest?'

Bentley wrinkled his nose to manoeuvre his glasses back up to the bridge, and when the blinking stopped he spoke. 'So, from what I gather, Quinn's on the warpath and most of our men are parked mobhanded down the road ready to attack should he make an appearance: that's about the long and short of it, yes?'

Tony gave a long, slow nod and brushed a crumb from his trousers. He didn't respond, recognising the rhetorical question as one of Bentley's tics: thinking aloud whilst he processed problems and plotted mitigation. Jamie, however, was unfamiliar with his ways and couldn't help himself from blustering into the silence. 'I say we gather the troops, get tooled up and take the fight to Quinn and whoever he's working with.'

Tony turned to face his son. His shoulders moved in a slow ponderous rotation, unlike the back of his hand that shot out as fast as a cobra, striking Jamie across the mouth. 'Shut up, and get out!' The same hand that left its red mark across Jamie's face pointed to the door. 'Out!'

Jamie felt the imprint burn like a branding iron on his cheek, and he tried without success to avoid the smug curl to Bentley's lips and the satisfied gleam in his eyes. His father's arm was still outstretched, pointing in the direction of the door, but instinct told him it wouldn't stay like that much longer; if he didn't begin walking it'd lash out again. Beaten and dejected, Jamie left the room, closing the door meekly behind him with the gentlest of touches.

*

Tony Flint examined the back of his hand, absent-mindedly

rubbing his knuckles. If he'd been the sort of man for self-reflection he'd have wondered just what the Hell had got into him today. He'd never raised a hand to Jamie, not once in his entire life, and God knows there'd been times when the little shit could have done with it. Instead he'd waited on him hand and foot, attended to his every whim: whatever Jamie wanted, Jamie got. *But now he's in my world, in my business and this is the way things are.*

-32-

QUINN WAS INSIDE, stepping over the fallen body of Marko, out of the laundry room and into the main home. He went through a kitchen—untidy and neglected in the lady-of-the-house's absence—but his focus was squarely on the doorway beyond and the sounds beyond that. He paused, just for a fleeting second, long enough to draw a long stainless-steel carver from a block of matching knives.

He came into a wide panelled hall with a dining room visible through an adjacent open doorway. Light bled from beneath the closed door at the end of the hall and, on his left, under a blanket of darkness were the dark wooden stairs. A sobbing came from that direction.

He passed down the hall making barely a sound, his footsteps silenced by the plush carpet. He carried the knife dagger-style: its handle gripped in his left fist, the blade pointing outwards from the base of his hand. He brought it to his chest, the blade ahead of himself. He spun to face the foot of the stairs and the source of the sobbing: Jamie.

The tip of the blade hovered millimetres in front of Jamie's right eye, his lashes brushing across it as he blinked. Even in his terror he knew better than to cry out in fear. He sat still and waited for Quinn to decide what happened next.

When he was satisfied there was no one else nearby, Quinn sprang at Jamie and slammed the sole of his shoe squarely into the bridge of Jamie's nose. His head snapped back in urgent surprise, sending a spray of blood arcing across the wallpaper. He slumped against the stair treads like old laundry. Before he could cry out, Jamie felt Quinn's hands all over him, dragging him to his feet. Quinn's big, square, workman-like palms wrapped around his neck and began to squeeze, throttling him. Jamie's eyes bulged and began to roll upwards; consciousness escaping him. Confident he was suitably subdued, Quinn released his grip; not entirely, just enough to maintain control.

The collar tightened around Jamie's neck like a noose, the top button pressing hard into his throat. Quinn didn't move right away. Instead he gripped the shirt just long enough to force Jamie to remember their last encounter when Quinn had him in a similar stranglehold. He allowed the fear of their unfinished business to creep into his thinking. Then, twisting the collar to tighten the grip, he hauled Jamie up the stairs, backwards.

At the head of the stairs Quinn reached a small narrow landing. Several panelled doors led off, all firmly closed. Opening the nearest door, he hurled Jamie through. It was a bedroom, the décor chintzy and outdated. An out-of-fashion floral print dressed the small double bed, matching the curtains. A porcelain jug and bowl sat on an otherwise empty dressing table. Red droplets from Jamie's busted nose fell onto the beige carpet and bloomed outward like poppies in a field as the fibres swelled.

Jamie wiped the back of his hand across his face, smearing the blood, mucus and tears. 'What do you want?' he asked Quinn.

Quinn looked down on the cowering Jamie, his face a sticky confection of bodily fluids and emotions. Quinn took a quick glance over both shoulders, located the light switch and flicked it on. Illuminated by the low wattage bulb, Quinn took in his surroundings. The room was clearly a guest room used occasionally: very occasionally, thought Quinn, judging by the dated duvet and the small cuboid tv in the corner—a relic of a bygone age—but then Quinn wasn't there to spend the night. A room of such infrequent use was ideal as it was less likely anyone would enter unexpectedly. With a flick of the knife he gestured for Jamie to get to his feet. Jamie scrambled to oblige, untangling arms and legs, springing to his feet.

'How many are downstairs?'

Jamie opened his mouth, paused and then as if giving up any fight, replied, 'My dad, Bentley and Bentley's minder, Marko, the Russian.'

From Quinn's casual shrug at Marko's name Jamie knew the answer to the question was now two: Flint and Bentley.

'And how many are coming?'

'None.' Jamie dabbed his sleeve to his upper lip, it came away stained. Quinn's fixed sneer told him Quinn didn't believe him. 'It's true. There's no one.'

Jamie dropped to perch on the edge of the bed. It was a neat manoeuvre. He fell vertically, controlled, like a demolished tower block. Straight down, no cause for alarm. He held his composure for one second, two seconds, three seconds until Quinn lost patience and gripped his scalp, yanking his head back until he faced the ceiling. The thin chill from the blade's edge pressed against his exposed neck. Any pretence of composure was discarded immediately.

'Ten. There's ten men in three cars, tooled up and ready for the word. They're near a pub about a quarter of a mile away. And they've been instructed to kill you on sight.'

'And how can they do that?' chided Quinn. 'I've been dead for five days, remember?'

Jamie didn't respond. This time it was his turn to shrug his shoulders. He had nothing to say; he knew he couldn't deny it seeing as it was him that pulled the trigger on Quinn, point-blank.

'And then I hear you've been making a claim for all my stuff, what's all that about?'

Jamie shrugged again. Quinn's movements were quick and rapid. Jamie yelped. The knife tip withdrew from his upper thigh with a soft, wet slurp. Jamie's hands flew to the wound and pressed down. He rocked back and forth, mewling. Quinn raised the knife again, threatening to jab into his other leg. Jamie raised a bloodied palm to halt him and spoke: 'Reparations.'

'I was told by coming back to do the job, to babysit you, that was reparations.'

Jamie's laughter was contemptuous and sneering. 'You silly old fuck! You dead, that's reparations. Payback for Redlands. That's what it's all been about, all of it. You dead!'

Quinn rocked back. He tried getting his head around what Jamie had just revealed: it wasn't heat of the moment, it was a planned execution? He paused, trying to get his thoughts in order, but Jamie quickly filled the silence.

'It was my initiation,' said Jamie. 'A rite of passage, I suppose.'

Quinn, never one for a flowery turn of phrase, kept quiet. Instead he processed everything he'd just heard. He'd had all the pieces, but now they began to fit together and Redlands was at the centre.

*

A little under three years ago:

The restaurant wasn't far from their nightclub, on a main shopping street long since fully pedestrianised. Inside the lunchtime crowd filled it, tables pushed close together under the exposed brick and steel, more industrial urban chic to the point of cliché. Out front, on the pavement, a velvet rope suspended between chrome posts marked out the restaurant's external boundary. Several square tables and matching rattan chairs filled the space but only two of the tables were occupied, one of them by Quinn and his brother Benny. It was cool out here and Benny could smoke. Traffic noise was a distant but constant hum, and the passing shoppers moved by as steady and continuous as a river flow, slowing but never stopping. The constant churn of passers-by made it a more private place to talk than inside.

'You look good, mate,' said Benny.

Quinn, unsure how to take the compliment, ignored it and instead asked, 'You heard from anyone, about anything?'

Benny knew exactly what he was referring to: it had been a month, almost to the day, since their conversation with Bentley, since their excommunication. He signalled his response with a crinkle of the nose and a curl of the lip.

Quinn sought clarification. 'Nothing?'

'Nope.' Benny's head gave the slightest of shakes as if to say he hadn't but hadn't expected to. 'You know he's dead, don't you?'

'Redlands? Yeah.'

'Dropped down dead in the Florida sunshine a fortnight ago. Brain embolism, I heard. Gone before he hit the deck, out like a light, didn't feel a thing. It's not fair; he deserved something painful, long and lingering.'

'No remorse then?' A smile crinkled at the edges of Quinn's face.

'Nope.' Benny relaxed back in his chair. 'Nonces like him deserve everything they get.' A holidaymaker's carton of duty-free cigarettes lay on the table between them. He reached for it, tore open the packaging and took a brand-new packet. 'Thanks for these by the way, how much do I owe you?'

Quinn watched his brother grasp the small see-through tab between his teeth. He ripped away the packet's cellophane wrap and removed a cigarette. He flapped a dismissive wave as if to say, *'No charge'*. Benny, understanding the gesture, brought his face down towards the flame of his lighter and winked his gratitude over the top of his cupped hands.

*

The door swung open wide. The room was smallish, luxuriously minimal, with flat grey walls and a flat white ceiling. Low leather armchairs and a sofa made an informal area around a square glass coffee table. At the opposite end, a huge desk in glass and chrome dominated the space. The highly-polished brass plate beside the street door outside announced a corporate property holding company occupied the premises. The room looked every inch the executive office. It was in fact the centre of operations for the Flint organisation. The room was the top of the pyramid. All the tuppence ha'penny drug deals, all the protection, all the whoring, all the trafficking, all the scams, it all happened far away from there, but the money filtered through it all, layer upon layer, refining itself, getting cleaner with each cycle, washing up stage by stage like a mighty ziggurat until the pinnacle of respectable, legitimate finance: that very room. The office of Lee Redlands, deceased.

Tony Flint walked in without knocking—why should he? He owned the building. John Bentley looked up from the vast glass and metal desk. Flint was late. Bentley had been expecting him almost an hour ago. Bentley rose from the seat in greeting, ushering him towards the armchairs.

Tony Flint was a man in a perennial bad mood, but that annoyed him even more than usual: who did Bentley think he was, this was Lee's office, Lee's kingdom: the man had been dead less than a week and he was already acting like he'd moved in.

Bentley and his famed ability to read people sensed Flint was irked. With a quickness of mind he ran through every known issue, both business and personal, then every scrap of gossip he'd heard, hoping to identify the reason for Flint's displeasure. From the tense posture and one-word responses, Bentley realised he himself was the reason. Displaying his talent for mediation and strategic thinking, Bentley immediately changed approach.

'As you suggested, I've been looking through Lee's files,' he said, subtly identifying Flint as the one in charge. Immediately he saw Flint's shoulders relax slightly, his jaw loosen a touch.

Bentley looked over across at the desk, in particular towards the two large monitor screens sat side-by-side, both paper-thin on sleek silver pedestals. 'I've managed to get into the computer.'

Tony, as Bentley knew only too well, had no computer skills and absolutely no desire to learn but he nodded appreciatively and muttered, 'Good, good,' softly to himself. Bentley, happy to accept the praise, didn't mention how he had found the password.

*

Benny exhaled a fine jet of smoke through his nose, then spoke. 'Other than that one piece of good news, I've not heard a thing. Nobody's been in touch, nobody's returned any calls.'

Quinn rubbed a hand across his chin. It had taken on a grey shading, the same colour as the ash forming at the tip of Benny's gasper: *thirty hours since my last shave, twelve since flying out of Grantley Adams, two hours getting out of Heathrow and home, then straight here.* The scratching against his fingertips had the coarseness of sandpaper. It was a strangely pleasant sensation and helped him stay awake. He considered Benny's words then responded. 'Sounds like Bentley wasn't bluffing, sounds like Flinty's cut us off, full and final.'

'Yep, that's the way I see it.'

The sharp, fragrant burn of the freshly lit cigarette triggered Quinn's cravings, an affliction not unnoticed by his brother who wafted a hand in front of his face to fan the smoke away from the table.

'So how's it been?'

'What, you mean being left here to deal with it while you pissed off to the Caribbean on holiday?' A harder edge had crept into Benny's tone, a resentful and angry edge but then the illusion was spoilt by the start of a grin breaking through the mask. 'Bloody marvellous!'

Benny laughed. It was a throaty, hoarse chuckle triggering a smile from Quinn, a genuine smile, an automatic reaction. *I can't help it, he sounds like Dad when he laughs.* Benny raised his water glass and tilted it towards Quinn, who mirrored the gesture, they clinked glasses together in celebration: Brothers against the world, fuck 'em all!

'It's not been that bad actually,' continued Benny. 'In fact, I'm thinking of starting up the money-lending again, asking around

I think there's a market for it. It's a win-win.'

Quinn studied Benny's wide gormless grin, his cigarette clamped between his exposed teeth, and began to wonder if Benny actually knew what win-win meant.

*

The desk was exactly as Redlands had left it before heading away. A holiday beckoned, a month recuperating at his villa in Florida: a lovely hacienda-style property with ocean views. In the morning a man could stand on the terrace, look out to sea and watch the dolphins leap from the water in play. There were worse places that a man could drop down dead from a brain embolism than there. Redlands certainly lucked out when he checked out. But before he left the office for his permanent vacation, Redlands tidied everything with fastidious precision. This extended to a small black leather-bound notebook, the sort that held itself closed by a loop of tight elastic stitched into the binding, that got positioned square and parallel to the edges of the desk. Bentley spotted it as soon as he walked in and recognised it at once. He pinged off the elastic loop and flipped the notebook open. Slap, bang, there on page one, in a familiar neat handwriting, was a password. Mere minutes later Bentley had the computer unlocked and open, and he began perusing the assorted files within.

*

'Aha.' Benny was distracted by something, or someone, over Quinn's left shoulder. 'Here she is now.' Benny rose to his feet whilst Quinn was still struggling to understand what was happening. He rose too and looked behind, hoping whatever Benny was distracted by would be obvious to spot: it was.

Quinn was surprised to find a statuesque blonde standing immediately behind him. Her tight-fitting red shop uniform clung to her like haute couture. It defined and emphasised her impressive curves, leaving Quinn rather taken aback.

'Hi I'm Nicole,' she said offering a delicate hand, cold to the touch. 'I've heard so much about you.'

Quinn, unable to offer the same in response, merely smiled and looked towards Benny for an explanation. Benny understood the look and beckoned for Nicole to join them at their table. She did so without hesitation or comment, leading Quinn to conclude it was no chance meeting: it had been arranged beforehand.

Her hair was immaculate, and she smelt nice; even though Quinn didn't recognise her uniform it was no surprise to learn she sold cosmetics in the nearby department store. 'We met when I was browsing. She asked if I wanted a sample,' recounted Benny with such a coarse tone to underline the innuendo Quinn knew it was a line he'd been dying to use. They'd been out a couple of times since. 'I've invited her along this afternoon,' he said then quickly added, 'That's okay with you?'

She seemed pleasant enough and Benny seemed happy. Quinn knew Benny deserved a bit of happiness after recent events, especially after holding the fort for the three weeks he was in Barbados. 'Sure,' he said. Benny gave a smile of genuine delight.

*

Tony's eyes joined Bentley's by looking across towards the computer screens. 'Any joy?' he asked.

'Depends,' replied Bentley, returning his attention back to Flint. 'I only got here ten, fifteen minutes before you so I've not had chance to do a proper deep-dive. But I've managed to get his file directory open.' Tony wasn't following, and his impatience was obvious by his knee bouncing up and down like a road-drill. Bentley rephrased: 'I can see a list of everything that's on there.'

That was better, plain English, but the impatience still rebounded through Flint's knee, up-and-down, up-and-down.

'Such a shame,' murmured Bentley. 'And him still quite young. Tragic really.' Tony Flint gave a grumble that Bentley took as agreement. 'Mind you, he was never going to be the same after all those blows to the head he took, at his age. Hardly any wonder there was a blood clot in his brain.'

Tony Flint grumbled again.

*

They were going to a former associate's birthday party; him, an old man now, had chosen to mark the milestone with a small gathering at home to celebrate. It had been in the diary for several months and he'd been lucky with the date as it was shaping up to be a bright, sunny day. Perfect weather for a garden party.

Nicole made her excuses and headed for the restroom. Quinn took advantage of being alone with Benny. 'Do you think it's wise, us still going today?' he asked.

Benny threw back a quizzical look. 'Why wouldn't it? You and me have known Alan longer than anyone, long before we got involved with Flint, since when we was kids.'

Quinn bobbed his head in acknowledgement: that much was true, but he couldn't help feeling unsure given their current state of purdah.

'Anyway,' Benny added, 'I spoke with Alan yesterday, he says he's looking forward to seeing us there, so relax: it'll be fine.'

'I don't know…'

'Look,' Benny stubbed his cigarette out in an earthenware saucer on the table. 'Me and Nicole don't intend hanging around long, we've got plans. And you look absolutely knackered; you been to bed yet?'

Quinn shook his head. Benny continued, 'There you are then. We can all go, stay for an hour, show our faces, be polite. We can wish the old boy many happy returns, watch him blow out his candles and then we can leave. So even if there is anyone there, we won't linger long enough for it to be awkward.'

Quinn was too tired to argue and even if he wasn't, he couldn't find any flaws in Benny's proposal; it sounded perfectly reasonable to him. 'Okay, fine,' he replied. 'But I'll drive myself.'

Benny's head tilted in confusion. 'I told Alan we'd all be coming together in my car, you don't need to drive.'

'No, it's fine,' said Quinn. 'I'm shattered and I'm in no mood to drink. I'll take my car then that way I can come straight home and you and Nicki—'

'Nicole.'

'Nicole. You and Nicole can head off wherever it is you're going.'

'You sure?'

'I wouldn't suggest it otherwise.'

Benny nodded an acknowledgement. He withdrew a fresh cigarette and lit it. *There it is, that delicious scent, do the cravings ever go away?* thought Quinn.

'Hey hey hey, look at you, don't you look lovely?' Benny used an excited tone, louder than speaking but not quite a shout. He rose from the table with arms outstretched. Quinn glanced back over his shoulder and found it was Nicole. She'd changed whilst away from the table and was now returning in a pretty, patterned sundress and jewelled sandals. Quinn agreed with Benny: she did indeed look lovely.

*

Tony Flint smelt of expensive cologne and cheap cigars mixed with a hint of garlic. The scent was heavy and conjured memories of long lunches in fancy restaurants. It was the fragrance of money. Perched on his shoulder to squint at the screen, Bentley found the smell overpowering and began breathing through his mouth.

Tony leaned further over the top of Bentley, getting closer to the screen. 'I can't see anything. Where is it?'

'You can see everything the same as I can,' replied Bentley. 'We've been through every folder and—'

'It has to be here somewhere.'

'And I keep telling you, it's not.'

'Fifteen million doesn't just disappear. Redlands told me he was investing it offshore.'

'Panama. Yes, you told me.'

'Panama. I signed forms and everything.' Flint's voice was registering a tone of panic within it now. It hadn't gone unnoticed by Bentley. 'Where's the forms? Find them and that'll take us to the account.'

Bentley sucked down a deep breath. He wanted to speak clearly and without emotion, he could sense Flint's temper was getting dangerously short. 'They aren't there. If he was taking the money offshore, he obviously wanted to keep it untraceable. Maybe he was intending on making a back-up, but I guess he hadn't anticipated getting beaten to a pulp.'

Beside him, close to his ear he could hear Tony Flint's low growl. Bentley pressed on. 'Without the back-up I don't know what to suggest. There's no way of tracing any account. It's gone.'

Tony Flint's sweeping arm sent the monitor screens tumbling off the desk, clattering to the floor. 'Fuck!'

Bentley let Flint vent his rage and remained silent. In a graceful movement, amidst the carnage Flint rained down across the room, Bentley crossed his legs placing one knee over the other, hoping it would smooth away the straight square edges in his trouser pocket.

*

The car stood on its side in the hedgerow, its wheels still turning. It had come off the road at enough speed to flip it on edge, its own momentum sledging it into the unmade bank. Blue paint smeared along the tarmac for a dozen or so metres. Tiny cubes of broken glass followed in its wake like a faraway meteor shower. The crows, over their initial surprise, regrouped on the telephone wires up above the wreckage, their feathers jagged, black and stiff.

He jumped out of his BMW, phone in one hand already dialling for an ambulance. He ran to the front of the upturned Audi and dropped to his hands and knees, trying to peer past the white shatter-pattern of jagged crazing that seconds before had been the crystal-clear windscreen, and seeing nothing.

They were only a few miles from the town centre and this single width lane was a back route mostly used by locals. It took the driver between flat featureless fields: empty hectares waiting for the wheat and rapeseed to grow back. There were no buildings or passing traffic anywhere to be seen. He'd never felt so isolated, alone and useless. There were no sirens yet, just the caw of the crows calling their friends back to the wires to watch the drama unfurling below.

With the base of his fist, using his phone as a hammer, he smashed out the windscreen. It peeled away in one long clinging piece and at last he could see clearly.

The female passenger, a make-up demonstrator in a department store and new to him today was unmistakeably dead. He'd only been introduced to her an hour earlier and struggled to remember her name: Nikki, Nicole, something like that. Still strapped in her seat, suspended high above the ground her head hung at an unsustainable angle for any living person. The car had ploughed into the edge of the field's bank when it flipped, embedding the pillar of the driver's door into the hard clay earth. The driver's head had bounced and scraped and shredded against the unforgiving ground.

He looked at his lifeless, unmoving brother: face in ruins, body smashed. He howled at the sky. The crows took flight again and a siren in the distance grew louder.

-33-

THE SMALL CHAPEL SEEMED A CATHEDRAL: empty, cold and cavernous. Just two people sitting side-by side in the front pew: Quinn and Zoe. A simple coffin was presented in front of them. It was of pale timber with brass fittings and surprisingly small for a man so large in life. Nearby lingered a vicar whose name Quinn never caught. That was all. Nobody else came.

The anonymous vicar, a wiry man with the spidery limbs of a long distance runner, kept an embarrassed distance from them until eventually time forced him to approach. 'I'm sorry, but I really think we should make a start,' he said, having already granted them a fifteen-minute extension. 'I have another service at eleven, so you know…' He tailed off, hoping they'd get the hint.

Quinn glanced again at the door. It had a historic styling: arched, dark aged wood with black iron studs and straps. His eyes lingered but it didn't open. He returned his attention to the vicar and gestured consent to begin his brother's funeral.

Neither Benny nor Quinn had been religious, and Zoe hadn't been brought up to follow any specific belief. Nonetheless here they were. Somehow it seemed fitting, in the crematorium with the incumbent from the local parish church. Quinn thought Zoe may get some comfort from the vicar's words, and she thought the same for him: the shared thought that in that moment the other was getting solace was in its own way comfort enough for each of them.

The vicar asked with a timid tremor to his voice if they cared to sing a hymn. Quinn's silent glare made clear hymns wouldn't be necessary; the vicar took this as a blessing, knowing it would save time and wouldn't cause any delay to his eleven o'clock commitment.

The vicar spoke some more words that Quinn tuned out like white noise, preferring the company of his own thoughts. As if resurfacing from a hypnotist's trance he found himself murmuring 'Amen' in unison with Zoe and the vicar. The curtains closed. Benny was gone. All over. Less than twenty minutes start to finish.

Zoe reached across, her tiny hand seeking Quinn's. He clasped it and together, hand-in hand, they walked out to the garden of remembrance. He was aware how delicately he'd folded his fingers over hers. He was terrified of squeezing too tight and crushing her fine, thin bones, as fragile as porcelain. He realised, there and then, that he'd already committed himself to protecting her, to keeping her safe from harm.

*

The vicar saw them to the door, shook both their hands, muttered pleasantries then left to prepare for his eleven o'clock guests. Quinn and Zoe found themselves alone, unsure of what to do next. Quinn draped his arm across Zoe's shoulder. She welcomed the warmth and snuggled closer. They began a slow aimless wander along the main avenue, neither speaking, either side of them floral arrangements from earlier services flanked the pathway—a *"Granddad"* here, a *"Mum"* there. *Maybe I should have ordered some flowers,* thought Quinn. *But what was the point? Benny never liked flowers, and there's no one here to see them.*

Without speaking, Quinn gently guided them in the direction of the carpark: time to get away from there. They followed the path as it veered to the right, rounding a neatly manicured hedge, only to find it obstructed.

'John?' said Quinn to the man blocking their path. 'What are you doing here?'

John Bentley held his hands behind his back, and shuffled from foot to foot, 'I just wanted to say—you know—I'm sorry for your loss. For Benny...' He'd dressed for the occasion in a dark raincoat and a black tie. He sounded sincere.

Quinn muttered, 'Thanks'.

Neither of the men mentioned the lack of people in attendance, or that the excommunication was full and final, somehow agreeing without words that it was unnecessary.

'I liked Benny. Always did,' added Bentley. 'There was nothing personal between us, just business, you know that, don't you?'

Quinn made a noise: just a response to fill the gap, no more than that. He had no opinion to offer either way.

'I'm sorry how things turned out. He made his choices, but all the same... You know. He was a good man, I liked him. I wanted to let you know that.'

'Thanks, John. Cheers.'

'If there's anything I can do, anything you need,' offered Bentley. 'You've got my number.' Quinn nodded a grateful acknowledgement, but Bentley hadn't quite finished. 'You know you're welcome to come back in from the cold, don't you, if you want. Think about it, I can make it happen.'

'Thanks, John. I'll let you know,' replied Quinn, but he never did. Instead Quinn had no contact with Bentley until the day he appeared in his coffee shop almost three years later. So why Redlands? Why now?

*

'Are you going to kill me?' Jamie's question snapped Quinn from the thoughts tumbling around his head.

'I haven't decided yet,' answered Quinn truthfully. He pressed his fingertips against his temples, almost as if the gentle pressure could squeeze out the answer for him.

Quinn spoke slowly, his tone measured. 'You said reparations, you said initiation. What did you mean?'

Jamie, even now, played it tough. He cast a sullen scowl upwards at Quinn. A subtle half-roll of the massive shoulders looming over him immediately broke his resistance. He dropped back on his knees, deflated. Frowning at the floor, he spoke.

'Initiation. My Dad wanted me on the firm, Bentley didn't. So I needed to impress Bentley. I came up with the gig at the car depot: that was all mine. A high-value, high-profile gig to prove I deserved my place on the firm.'

'That was a nice job,' admitted Quinn. 'But what was I doing there? You didn't need a babysitter. Tell me the truth.'

Jamie still refused to look at him, 'That was their idea. To begin with I figured it was because you're a fat old fuck who's been out the game too long. If it all went wrong, we all could have out-run you, left you behind.'

Quinn knew exactly what he meant. 'The sacrificial goat. The Law won't investigate too hard as they'd have me.'

'That's it. They look like they've done something, we get away with the gear, everyone's a winner.'

'Except me,' murmured Quinn. 'But why me?'

'Reparations. I told you. For Redlands.'

'What about Redlands? And why now?'

Jamie drew the long breath of the condemned man: an honest answer would have serious repercussions with one party, a denial would have just as serious repercussions with the other, but if you're committed to certain death anyway then take a long breath and let your conscience decide which way to go. 'He's dead. You killed him.'

'I never did,' protested Quinn. 'I'm not sorry he's dead, but I never killed him.'

'If not you, your brother did,' spat Jamie. He tilted his face up to meet Quinn's, the muscles across his cheeks tight with defiance. 'Between the pair of you, you battered him to death.'

'Rubbish.' Annoyance had crept into Quinn's voice. He'd wanted explanations not childish arguments. 'He died in Florida.'

'A couple of weeks later; it was your battering that caused it!'

'Nonsense. Absolute nonsense. That's what the doctor said, was it?'

'No. It's what my dad said. That's all that matters.'

Quinn nodded a reluctant agreement: it'd make no difference whether an army of doctors, specialists and experts said Redlands died of natural causes. If Tony Flint had made up his mind there was no way of changing it. Except... there was. The one person, the only person capable of ever persuading him to do anything—John Bentley, realised Quinn.

But then Jamie spoke again and any thought of mediation was quickly forgotten. 'I was wrong, though. I wasn't to leave you behind. I was told to kill you.'

'Because of Redlands?'

'Yeah, but more because of the money. Off-shore, the Panama account.'

Quinn's head reeled. 'I've absolutely no idea what you're talking about.'

'You wouldn't do,' snapped Jamie. 'Why would you? You're a nobody!'

The back of Quinn's hand struck Jamie's face with such speed and force it sent him crashing to the floor. 'I'm losing patience, Jamie. I want answers, and I want them now.'

Jamie's right eye was half-closed but he could see Quinn was deadly serious. With one hand held outwards to placate Quinn, he used the other to lever himself back upright. 'All right,' he said, sitting himself more comfortably. 'From what I understand, Redlands had invested everything the firm—my dad—had in a secret off-shore fund in Panama right before you and your brother gave him a beating.'

Quinn didn't understand. 'But what's that got to do with me?'

'Because,' even this late in the game Jamie couldn't help

himself, his voice dripped sarcasm and contempt, 'all the account information, all the passwords and numbers, all died with him. So, the way the logic goes, you battered him, you killed him, you lost the account information, you cost us fifteen million.'

A rushing giddiness rocked Quinn. He struggled to comprehend the sheer lunacy he was hearing, but Jamie hadn't finished. 'My dad's had loads of lawyers and investigators trying to get the bank to open their books, give him the account. Spent fortunes, called in favours from all sorts, got nowhere, and rather than give up and walk away you came back up on the radar.'

'Me?'

'You were still in reserve. Retaliation against your brother had been almost immediate, but for whatever reason you were left behind. So, to earn my place on the firm, to win their approval, first come up with and pull off the perfect gig and second, execute you. Sorry, man: it was business.'

Quinn didn't hear Jamie's flippant apology and didn't care; he hadn't heard anything beyond the first few words. 'Benny... I knew... I always knew.'

This time Jamie saw the blow that struck him. Quinn's fist as big and heavy as a hammerhead connected with his temple. Everything went black and he slumped to the floor.

-34-

THE FIRE WAS LOW. The smouldering firewood, as white and as fragile as a chrysalis, cast a warm glow. Bentley dropped on a new log and a flurry of sparks rose like shooting stars, snuffing out as they fell back to their ash bed. The heat chased out any residual moisture deep inside the timber with a crack and a snap, and small darting flames curled around it.

Bentley settled back in his armchair. 'Should feel the benefit in a minute or two,' he said to his guest.

In the neighbouring matching armchair, Tony Flint nodded silently. He watched the fire reawaken, spellbound by the dancing flames.

'There's a lot of noise out there, maybe I should go check?' Bentley said aloud, but mostly for his own benefit.

'Leave it,' snarled Flint. 'It's only a few bumps, probably just Jamie sulking. What we need to do is work out what we're going to do here.'

Flint extended an arm, the bulbous belly of a heavy crystal brandy glass cradled in his palm. Bentley took the hint and reached for the bottle.

Flint was hauled from the chair with such searing ferocity he hadn't even time to feel the hands around his neck. The stranglehold, tight and deadly, lifted him with little resistance. His body arched backwards across the head of the armchair, until his left foot stopped him: the back of his shoe snagged against the chair. A sudden yank as though tugging on a stuck and stubborn rope had him moving again. His shoe, ripped off in the tussle, dropped to the seat cushion. His head, almost yanked from his shoulders, dropped to the ground.

Flint looked up at the moulded plaster ceiling and sunk into the soft carpet. He tried to recapture his breath. A heavy object pressed against his throat and he began to choke.

Bentley looked on in a mix of shock and awe: Quinn had crossed the room unnoticed with gentle stealth, but the demented fury now across his face was all too apparent. Bentley, momentarily frozen in the few seconds of explosive activity, stood between the armchairs with a cut-glass decanter of cognac ready to pour. His brain re-booted, taking in everything he saw before him—Quinn: eyes wide, nostrils flared, jaw clenched. The flat of Quinn's shoe pressed down on Flint's throat. From the set of his body, from his stance, from Flint's reaction, Bentley knew he wasn't using his foot to merely restrain Flint; no, he was channelling all his weight and power and anger down through his foot to literally crush the life out of Flint.

'Stop!' shouted Bentley. 'Stop it now, you hear me! Stop it now!'

Quinn gave no reaction at all.

'Stop! I said stop!' shouted Bentley again.

This time, Bentley's plea penetrated Quinn's rage. He regarded Bentley through quizzical eyes, as though roused from a deep sleep, then looked down seeming almost surprised to find Flint beneath his shoe. Slowly, gingerly, Quinn raised his foot and brought it to rest neatly on the ground beside Flint's face, trapping him by his hair.

Quinn paused, his lips twitched searching for the words to say. Then they came. 'He killed Benny, John. My Benny. He killed him.'

Bentley gave a sympathetic nod. 'I know' he said. 'I found out after it happened, after you'd left us.'

A silence fell between the two men, hanging long enough to become awkward. 'Is he dead?' asked Bentley, attempting to break the unsettling quiet. A cough and a snort from the prone Flint answered his question. The signs of life broke Quinn from his trance. His two strong arms scooped Flint up and dumped him back on the armchair. Flint sagged forwards, unconscious. Both men left him as he was.

'What's this all about, John?' demanded Quinn.

'I've no—' began Bentley but knew as soon as the words passed his lips there was no point in pretending anymore. Instead, he sat down and took off his glasses. He rubbed his hand across his eyes, squeezed the bridge of his nose, then felt ready to begin. 'He told me he'd instructed the hit on Benny, about six months after the event. You were gone by then. I figured it'd be better for all concerned if I let sleeping dogs lie, so I kept it quiet.'

Quinn gave a low growl, undecided whether he agreed with Bentley's decision or not. He'd taken up a standing position. He stood with his back to the fireplace and kept a vigilant eye on both armchairs and their occupants. The heat of the fire hit him squarely from behind like a stiff warm breeze.

'A bomb, to all intents and purposes,' continued Bentley. 'A small explosive charge was planted in Benny's car, designed to disable the engine block and cause the car to flip at high-speed. They didn't get you, though.'

'Me?'

'Tony had been told you'd be travelling together, coming in the same car. But by the sound of it there was a last minute change of plan and you drove yourself. Lucky escape.'

'Not for Nicole.'

'Who? Oh… Benny's new fancy piece, I forgot about her. Yes, shame, dreadful shame but… there you go. That's the world we live in, I guess.'

'I don't,' responded Quinn. 'I was out, remember? You came to me, brought me back.'

Bentley wrinkled his nose and drilled a curious finger into his ear as if mining for the right reply. 'Yes I did. You're right. And I've told you why. To babysit Jamie, to bring him back safe from harm.'

'Lies!' roared Quinn. 'Lies, lies, lies.'

If Bentley was taken aback by the response, he didn't let it show. Instead he pursed his lips, ran his tongue across his teeth and waited for Quinn's outburst to pass. Beside him Flint groaned, he was awake again. He delicately massaged his throat. Bentley gave him a cursory look, then turned his attention back to Quinn. 'What do you expect me to say?'

'The truth,' replied Quinn. 'I know I was set up. I know Jamie was under orders to kill me.'

Bentley shrugged. 'Sounds like you know everything already. So what do you want?'

'He killed Benny,' Quinn's voice wavered. Bentley gave a solemn nod to confirm. Quinn's voice cracked further when he spoke the words, 'And he wanted to kill me too?' Bentley nodded again.

Quinn lunged at Flint. Flint reached out from his armchair, his hands towards Quinn's wrists trying to fend off any purchase, slapping away any hands from landing on him. Dull blows echoed around Quinn's thighs. He glanced down to find Flint kicking him. Stuck in his armchair, both arms and both legs lashing out, Flint resembled an upturned beetle: all limbs jerking randomly, achieving nothing. From his standing position, Quinn easily reached through the flailing. He grabbed a handful of hair on the top of Flint's head and yanked him forwards. He tumbled out of the chair like a deadweight, collapsing on the rug at Quinn's feet. Quinn unclenched his fist and stretched his fingers apart; several stray strands of silver hair fell from his hand and floated gracefully to the floor. He reached across to the chimney breast where the brassware glinted in the firelight.

*

The prison mouse hid just to the left of the window. Using skills self-taught during a lifetime inside he'd approached it with cunning and care, successfully not spotted by anyone.

Having heard raised voices, McLaren failed to overcome his inbuilt urge to snoop. He scurried from his safe hidey-hole to a new vantage point and hoped it would give him a clearer view of the commotion.

He crouched to peer over the window ledge. Inside he saw a room panelled in a warm, reddish coloured wood, with one wall dominated by a red-brick chimney breast dressed in polished horse brasses. A pair of matching leather wingback armchairs sat in front of the brightly burning fire. It reminded McLaren of a cosy country pub. The room looked inviting—apart from the man being killed on the hearth rug.

The startled-looking man was stocky, fiftyish, golfing casuals and of doughy complexion. From what Quinn had told him, McLaren correctly identified him as Bentley. Therefore, he assumed the man underneath Quinn, the one being beaten to a pulp with a brass poker, must be Flint.

Bentley started to turn in his direction and McLaren ducked down. *This is dangerous, too much light, they'll see me.* McLaren resumed his position beside the window, but for good measure took half a step for extra distance. McLaren considered. *Should I get inside? But I'm no fighter, I'm here as look-out only but… but…*

Unable to find any justifiable reason compelling him to stay, he moved around the side of the house. Two paces on, approaching the door in the expectation of the solid, dependable paving beneath his feet, his ankle buckled. His foot had landed on something raised, too small to land his whole shoe on, and he staggered, his balance lost. As he stumbled his foot slid back whatever it was he'd trodden on. It slid across the path with a metallic rasp. With his senses already overloaded, curiosity gnawed away at him. He squinted in the hope it'd relieve the darkness, and swept the path, crouching with outstretched fingertips before him until he found it. Cold, damp and heavy. Just from touch alone he knew it was a gun. He'd never touched a gun before and wasn't quite sure whether he should now. He picked it up with straight, cautious fingers and held it up in front of his face. The starlight above mixed with the low-level light pollution bleeding from the house gave enough illumination to see its shape. It looks like the one Quinn had, he thought but then he wasn't an expert and as far as he was concerned they all look the same. Thinking it may come in handy—if only for resale value later—he stuffed it into his waistband, and for extra safety double-knotted the drawstring cord of his joggers.

McLaren moved forward and cautiously tried the door. As he'd expected, it was locked. Only it wasn't. The resistance gave way and the door swung open to reveal the large dead man lying on the tiled floor. McLaren's light pressure on the door had pushed aside the man's foot wedging it shut. *Jesus fucking Christ, what's going on in here?* Gingerly, McLaren tiptoed over and across the dead man. The soulless bulging glassy eyes stared endlessly at the kitchen ceiling. Out of respect for the departed, and because of some bullshit superstition he'd made up on the spot, McLaren stepped sideways and around the dead man rather than cross his line of sight. McLaren opened the hallway door. He stood on the threshold, taking in the hallway and the room beyond. The door at the back of that room was closed but through it, if he controlled his breathing and kept himself still, it was possible to make out the muffled thumping of Flint's death.

*

Quinn raised the poker above his head and swung it down hard for the last time. It struck the fragmented remains of Flint's skull with a dull, damp thwack. He dropped the poker and sat himself down in the chair previously occupied by the deceased, perching himself upright against the elegant straight back of the seat. He tilted his head in puzzlement as though it was the first time he'd ever laid eyes on his big, square hands, resting on his lap: thick veins, swollen from the exertion criss-crossed the backs splashed in blood not his own.

Bentley turned his face towards the window. *What was that? Someone there?* Bentley convinced himself he'd seen nothing: *a trick of the light, I'm just being too jumpy.* He poured himself another cognac, hovered over a second glass, just for a moment, then decided to pour it no matter. 'Here,' he said offering it to Quinn. 'For your nerves, help calm you down.'

Quinn gave no response. Bentley offered the glass a second time to Quinn, again no response, Quinn's attention hadn't lifted from the rope-like tangle of veins across his blood-soaked hands. Bentley placed the glass on a small low table between the chairs and muttered, 'I'll leave it there for you.'

The fire cast an uplit glow across Quinn. It dragged long dark shadows in directions where shadows don't usually fall. His nostrils flared wide, his teeth bared, his breathing heavy and loud: the massive adrenalin release swirled inside of him with no sensation of dissipating. Combined, it gave him a ghoulish, Halloween appearance.

Bentley sat quietly in the chair beside him. He did his best to appreciate the subtle burn of the cognac vapours in his mouth and waited to see what happened next.

-35-

'WELL, YOU'VE DONE WHAT YOU CAME FOR,' said Bentley matter-of-factly. Quinn didn't respond. He continued staring into the fire. He gave no sign whether he'd heard Bentley at all. Bentley crossed one knee across the other and habit-bounced his raised foot back and forth. He looked down at his bobbing toes and reminisced. There once was a time when they were all friends. There once was a time they were all close. Times had changed. Past his foot on the edge of his vision, the hands and forearms of Flint had taken a dark purple complexion. Nature had taken over the process, lividity was setting in, blood lay still in his veins.

'I said, you've done what you came for.'

Again, no response.

'You're going to have to get rid of him, you know that,' persisted Bentley to the unresponsive Quinn. 'And you're paying to replace my carpet; that'll need doing before the wife gets back next week.'

Quinn's head turned in a slow rotation to look Bentley in the face, the firelight reflecting and sparkling against the tears in his eyes. *Tears for what?* wondered Bentley, but he didn't ask, and the moment passed unremarked.

'I can tell Marko to get rid,' said Bentley, pointing his toe at Flint's corpse, unaware Marko was just as dead. Quinn didn't feel the need to correct him and used the moment to think, then responded, 'I'll take care of it, my rubbish to clear away.'

The simple truth was he didn't trust Bentley. He knew it would be a typical Bentley trick to use it against him for threats or coercion at a later date. Quinn planned to find McLaren and they'd both take Flint back to Sheppey for one of McLaren's burials at sea off the coast of Cabbage Island.

'All right then,' Bentley replied. 'And I'm serious about the carpet. You're paying for that.'

*

McLaren crept through the house without making a sound; as light of foot as a ghost. The noises behind the closed door had stopped almost the moment he reached it. He waited, pressed against it, but silence: *either something's happening or nothing's happening, but whatever it is I shouldn't be here.* He peeled away with a new motivation: *I'm alone in a rich man's house, no one knows I'm here, may as well make the most of it.*

With one ear tilting towards the silent closed door he floated around the room. Then adjoining rooms. Drawers and doors were opened, contents rummaged through in the search for anything small and precious, then carefully put back to hide his intrusion. He found a blue canvas shopping bag in the kitchen and decanted his findings into it. No big prizes so far: just some cash, designer sunglasses, a few ornaments of silver and glass, and a couple of phones. Upstairs though, that's where the good stuff was, he was sure of that, that's where he'd find the jewellery.

His steps were light and cautious, he stayed tight to the wall and made it to the upper level without a single creak. Quinn's gun was heavy and he found the way it dug into his waistband uncomfortable. He placed it in the bottom of the bag for safekeeping and convenience. In what he imagined was the style of a posh lady, a duchess perhaps, he hoiked the long red rope handles over one shoulder and squeezed the bag close to his body, pinned underarm between bicep and breastbone. At once feeling more comfortable, he began the upstairs sweep.

*

It took every ounce of strength to lift the dead Russian off the floor. The heavy, unyielding flesh offered no help but every resistance. Quinn manhandled him into a fireman carry, draped over one shoulder like a roll of old carpet. All the weight bore down through his knees making every step shaky and awkward.

Quinn slammed the Mercedes' trunk lid down, the Russian dumped inside. Returning back to the house, his strides seemed as bouncy and rubbery as though he was walking on the Moon, his muscles and his balance recalibrating after bearing such a heavy load. He came back out with Flint across his shoulder: a much quicker pace for a much lighter man. He placed Flint in the passenger seat; that'd have to do for now, the sprawling mass of the Russian having filled the boot space.

Bentley had promised to retrieve the proceeds of the car depot gig whilst Quinn cleared the house of Flint. Quinn returned to the living room and saw the two leather armchairs, the open fire, the bottles of drink on a silver tray and the spilt bodily fluids of Tony Flint seeping into the carpet. What he didn't see was John Bentley or his money.

'John?' he called out.

'In my office, just coming.' Quinn spun on the spot seeking out Bentley's voice behind him. He traced it to the corner of the adjacent dining room, a narrow door hung ajar. 'Sit down, I'll be out in a minute.'

Bentley liked his office. It was the only room in the house off-limits to everyone. The cleaner was forbidden from entering, as far as he was aware the children never set foot inside it, even Helen knew better than to go in there: quite often she would call out to say she'd made him a cup of tea and leave it on the sideboard outside the door to get cold waiting for him, rather than bring it in. But that evening something seemed amiss and he couldn't quite put his finger on what. Everything was exactly as he'd left it, only it wasn't, but it was. *Am I being paranoid?* he mused, surveying the room for any signs and finding none. Scolding himself for letting the heightened emotions of the night get to him, he opened his desk drawer and removed a set of keys.

Quinn got himself comfortable in the same leather chair as before. The open fire had a hypnotic effect on him, the way the flames danced low and slow speculatively around the edges of the logs. He felt the heavy pull of drowsiness on his eyelids. A dull thud on the floor beside him snapped him wide awake with a start. Quinn looked down to the carpet to find a black nylon holdall. Packed solid, its contents formed sharp angular corners in the thin fabric: nice, very nice.

'There you go. Take it and leave. We're done, we'll never see each other again,' Bentley's voice came from behind Quinn's shoulder. Quinn, still admiring the bag on the floor turned to face Bentley.

'Or you leave it… and walk out with this.'

Bentley stood a few paces from Quinn gripping Zoe around her elbow. Somewhere deep within the scrambled mess of his brain, where thousands of questions were being processed at once, Quinn wondered why Zoe was letting Bentley pilot her like some bizarre marionette. Then he saw her eyes: glassy, foggy, spaced-out.

Bentley spotted this. 'She's all right, I just gave her a few of the wife's Temazepam to calm her down. She'll be right as rain tomorrow.'

Drugged? He's brought her here and drugged her. But why? How?

*

Two days earlier a message had flashed up on Bentley's phone: just three words. Three words he'd been expecting and they provoked an immediate reaction. *"I have her."*

Bentley left his coffee untouched and his pastry only nibbled. *That'll keep Helen happy; good for my diet!* He left them where they sat on the kitchen table and headed straight to his car.

Buckled up, engine running, Bentley opened an app on his phone and used it to locate Marko, his big red-bearded Russian. *He's still near Rochester High Street; they've not gone far.*

The traffic was patchy—the A2 in parts rammed solid with slow-moving vehicles but inexplicably opening into wide open stretches with hardly another driver in sight, and thankfully the God of Green Lights was on his side most of the way. It didn't take too long to reach the general region where Marko was meant to be but the app, unlike the ones in the movies, couldn't pinpoint a precise location to the exact blade of grass.

Each time Marko didn't answer his phone Bentley's frustration intensified. With no alternative, Bentley resorted to driving around; sweeping the network of residential streets in the vague hope he'd soon spot a massive hulk of a man with a flaming red beard. After five minutes of this Bentley's patience was at breaking point. He pulled over and began dialling Marko again. Waiting for the voicemail prompt to finish so that he could leave Marko a message tearing him a new arsehole, he spotted her— Zoe.

She flashed past very quickly, but it was definitely her driving the little white Fiat. He couldn't see Marko anywhere nearby. *Useless prick, she's got away from you.* Bentley pulled the tightest U-turn he could manage, gripping hard to keep the wheel pulled as far right as it would go. The off-side wheel scraped against the high kerb opposite and he winced, both at the crunching noise and also the prospect of how much it'll cost to polish out the damage. Once straight, he headed off after her, muttering, 'Want something doing…' to himself.

In under a minute he was right behind her. Her driving was fast and erratic. She was panicked and she lacked concentration. She was spooked and spooked bad. Looking in his rear-view mirror he saw no sign of Marko. She'd done a good job shaking him off but she wasn't giving up the chase just yet.

With a sudden, urgent squeal of brakes she brought him to

an abrupt halt. She'd misjudged the timing of the traffic lights, not expecting the van in front of her to stop on amber. Forcing the little car to throw on its brakes to the maximum she'd come to a very close stop behind the van, and Bentley an even closer distance to her.

Bentley took his chance. He stepped from his car and sprinted to the small Fiat in front, hoping to get there before the lights changed again. 'Zoe, Zoe,' he panted breathlessly, tapping against her window.

Zoe threw a curious glance sideways to the middle-aged man at her door, all time watching the road ahead. Her foot hovered above the accelerator, ready to gun the engine at the first glimpse of green.

'It's me, John Bentley. I'm a mate of your uncle.'

The name was familiar, if out of context. Remaining primed for a quick getaway, she turned to face him. Immediately recognising him she lowered the window by no more than an inch. 'You came to the coffee shop a few weeks ago?'

'That's right,' he nodded. 'That's me. Now listen, your uncle, he's in trouble.' Bentley had made his voice loud and his speech clear, hoping it'd carry and give it authority. 'He asked me to find you, make sure you're safe.'

The traffic lights changed, the lamp glowed green and the van pulled away but Zoe's foot remained hovering over the pedal; a buffer of uncertainty stopped her shoe landing squarely on it and getting her away.

'He wants you to come with me, stay at mine, he says he'll meet us there as soon as he can. You'll be safe there.'

Bentley knew she was wavering. He could see she'd lost focus and was struggling to work out what was happening. Bentley pressed his advantage. 'Tell you what, I'm going to get back in my car and head home. If you want my protection, like your uncle wants you to have, then follow me. If you don't, if you want to do your own thing, that's fine too.'

From the biting of her lip, from her eyes tilting skyward, he could tell she was trying to weigh her options and knew it was time to add a convincer. 'You can go your own way, but you'll be on your own. I won't be able to protect you once you've left here though, not once you're out of sight.'

He fought back the urge to smile. *This is too easy, it's almost unfair.* With her uncertainty mounting he returned to his car, leaving her with his killer line, 'It's entirely up to you'. He signalled and passed her with a friendly wave then took up the position in the lead. He began to drive away.

Ten seconds later he flicked his attention to the mirror: she was right behind him, the lost puppy keeping close. This time he didn't fight the urge to smile, and allowed it to spread across his face, triumphant and smug. He'd always been a persuasive negotiator.

*

'I know she's all you've got left. I know what she is to you. So…' The smugness on Bentley's face enraged Quinn more than his goading tone. 'What's it to be? Cash or Zoe? Your money or your life?'

'I'm going to tear you apart. I will kill you, you realise that?' replied Quinn.

Bentley laughed: a nasal, snide laugh that thinned his mouth to a prissy, pissy slit and made his glasses slip. He bumped them back to the bridge of his nose with a blinking gesture that wrinkled his face. 'No you won't, so don't threaten me,' he spoke with a genuine calmness. He wasn't scared of the big man. 'Marko!' he called, again a moment later, 'Marko!' and then a third time 'Marko!' only louder.

Relief flushed through Quinn. The balance of power was tipping towards him. 'Don't waste your breath. Marko's not coming, John. He's dead.'

Bentley's face blanched, his paunchy cheeks pallid and dough-like: could this be true? 'Marko! Get in here now!' he cried at the top of his voice.

From the hallway, there came the creak of floorboards, and a figure filled the doorway.

-36-

When Quinn had loaded the car outside with dead passengers, upstairs the prison mouse deftly moved from room to room without making a single sound; not a squeaking hinge, not a creaky floorboard, not a stiff drawer runner, pure silence. Rooms were searched. Contents lifted, examined and returned back from whence they came. It was an exercise in experienced and expert burglary, and the shopping bag began to swell with the goodies found. So far he'd been right about upstairs being Treasure Island: in the first room he'd entered, laying on the dressing room table, he'd found a jewellery box generously filled with lots of sparkly treats as well as a pair of his-and-hers gold Omega watches. This was proving a very lucrative trip. He emptied the bathroom of all Mrs Bentley's prescription drugs—Diazepam, Temazepam, Valium, might get a few quid for these—and promptly moved on.

The second bedroom looked promising but failed to live up to expectations. First impressions, the room of an older child, but it failed to yield anything of value; no electronic games or computers, leading to the conclusion that the child must have flown the nest and taken it all with them. The third bedroom yielded the same disappointment. The fourth, well it was fair to say he wasn't expecting to find *that* in there!

'Jeez,' he muttered, shocked by the scene before him: a young man lay face down on the floor, the pale carpet around him spotted with blood-red blooms. McLaren examined the young man; he didn't appear to be moving. He watched the young man for about thirty seconds, and all the time pondered: *Quinn, ever since I met him there's been bodies everywhere he goes.* The young man hadn't moved. McLaren concluded the room must be safe: *the lad might be unconscious, he might be dead, but as long as he stays down, I'm safe.* McLaren placed the shopping bag on the carpet and started opening drawers.

*

Jamie had come to. He blinked away the strange state between unconscious and awake, and tried to understand his surroundings. The side of his face pressed against something coarse but also sticky, his sight was blurred by a white-out filling the edge of his vision, his senses were dominated by the iron taste of his own blood and the smell was dusty and dry. The realisation struck him: *Carpet. I'm on a carpet. I'm face down against the carpet.* The gaps in his understanding were plugged by memories, each triggering the next in rapid succession: *Quinn did this to me. Quinn.* Messages flew back and forth telling his brain that fingers and toes were still connected and functional, but any thought of trying them out, of hauling his aching carcass to its feet were immediately cancelled by the sight of the door slowly opening inward.

Jamie closed his eyes and played dead. If Quinn was making an inspection, he didn't want to give him any reason to look too closely, otherwise he might finish the job he'd started. Jamie drew in a long, deep breath and held it.

The footsteps were gentle and very quiet, probably too quiet to be heard in normal circumstances but Jamie's awareness was so elevated by the experience he could hear them distinctly pad softly towards him. Then they stopped, they were close, he could smell the sweet, acrid odour of hand-rolled cigarettes clinging to his visitor and hear a mucal bronchial rattle in their breathing: this wasn't Quinn, he was certain of that.

Something with weight, not a lot, but enough for its placement to cast a rolling wave of air across his face was dropped very close by. It landed with the gentlest of thuds. There followed a couple of metallic clinks. Jamie correctly guessed it was a bag, half filled with loose contents settling against each other on landing. The footsteps padded away from him, and slowly in his head he counted down from twenty before attempting to open an eye. Just a crack, a sliver, his vision filled with the black fuzz of lashes and confusion, but enough to assess the situation.

It was safe. He could breathe again, and he quietly exhaled the air he'd been holding for so long. He opened his eyes fully. Directly in front of him was a blue canvas shopping bag decorated with ladybirds in vibrant reds and bold black dots. It was so close to him it virtually obscured everything. Without moving, other than flicking his eyes right, he could just about see around it and make out the small rodent-looking man ferreting through a chest of drawers on the other side of the room. Jamie propped himself up on his elbow, he moved with glacial speed—partly due to a curiosity to make sure everything still worked after his encounter with Quinn, but mostly because he didn't want to disturb the little man.

*

McLaren was annoyed. After hitting the motherlode in the first room it had been diminishing returns in every room thereafter, this one being the worst of the lot. The top two drawers he'd opened were only filled with rolls of wrapping paper, ribbon and greeting cards, and this third one held a variety of hats and caps. People hide things in the strangest of places, as every experienced burglar knows, and McLaren didn't give up the search. He lifted the hats and shifted the caps and bingo! A small square blue velvet box lay tucked away in the far corner. It looked old: the fabric rubbed and smooth on the corners, the curly silver embossed writing missing in parts. McLaren's palms twitched in anticipation; maybe Granny's Victorian pearls are in there, or Granddad's gold fob-watch, items too old fashioned for nowadays-tastes but sentimentality stops them being got rid of. He reached in, excited at the prospect of discovering the contents when a voice took him by surprise.

'Stop. Slowly turn around. Hands in the air.'

McLaren froze, then threw a glance across his shoulder. The young man was sitting up, cross-legged on the floor. McLaren knew at once he'd looked through his bag because he was pointing Quinn's gun straight at him.

McLaren slowly rotated on the spot, turning to face the young man. Instinct and obedience raised his hands upwards, a reflex passive gesture that he wasn't aware he was doing until he noticed he still clutched a floppy straw sunhat in one hand. He released it then instantly regretted it: his imagination flashed full of thoughts of duelling with pistols—when it flutters gracefully to the ground, when it touches down, it's the fastest finger first, the quickest on the draw. But the wide-brimmed sunhat simply settled at his feet and the young man eyed him with growing levels of suspicion and contempt.

'Where's Quinn?' the young man said, and McLaren said, 'Never heard of him,' and neither were convinced by this as an answer.

*

Bentley couldn't believe what he was seeing. Quinn could: McLaren was the first to enter, immediately followed by Jamie. Jamie's left forearm locked around McLaren's neck, trapping him close. His right hand pressed a gun against McLaren's head.

'Evening all,' said Jamie.

Quinn seethed at himself. *I should have taken care of Jamie properly, tied him up or something, not left him to sleep it off.*

'Move!' Jamie nudged McLaren forward with a knee to the lower back and, always obedient, McLaren began to walk. Jamie maintained a firm hold around his neck and, when satisfied they'd entered the room far enough, he gave it an extra squeeze to stop McLaren.

Quinn immediately recognised the gun. It was his. It was the one he dropped on the path outside. Right now it didn't matter who found it or how, there'd be time for that later. Right now it was time to assess the situation. Jamie's behaviour was erratic and evasive: one second he had the gun pressed against McLaren's head and the next he was threatening those in the room with it, arcing across in a fan before returning it to McLaren's nugget.

Half of Jamie's face, vertically, sported a stippled pattern coating of dried blood from the carpet; coupled with his eyes that had taken on a wild animal-like quality, Jamie resembled a savage warrior from some mystical tribe. He didn't look of rational mind. Instead of speaking, Quinn stared him down. He fixed unblinking eye contact onto Jamie. He could tell Jamie was beyond reasoning, he'd escalated to his nuclear option, this was his do-or-die moment. Quinn didn't flinch or break eye contact, but side-stepped using slow deliberate scissor movements—left leg across, right leg across, open, closed—until he came to a stop exactly where he wanted. He'd shuffled around to block Jamie's direct line of fire at Zoe, making himself her human shield. The eye contact and the silence continued and all the while he questioned whether he could rush and disarm Jamie without him harming Zoe.

Jamie spotted the black nylon holdall on the floor, and puppet-steered McLaren to it. He reached for it and threw the strap over his head, then crab-walked with McLaren backwards to the door.

'Who the bloody hell is that?' said Bentley, pointing at McLaren, curiosity finally having got too much for him.

'No idea, John,' replied Jamie. 'One of his mates, best ask him,' he added, waggling the gun barrel back and forth between McLaren and Quinn. 'I found him upstairs; he was robbing you, John.'

'I knew it, I bloody knew it,' Bentley's voice sounded victorious, odd given the circumstances but that penny had been falling for a very long time and it had eventually dropped. 'I knew someone had been in my office.'

'It doesn't matter who he is,' confirmed Quinn. 'All that matters is that you're going to let him, and us, go. Now.'

'Oh I am, am I?'

'Give it up son,' was Bentley's contribution. 'Come on. This won't end well. You're outnumbered here.'

A smirk twitched under Jamie's eye. 'You're forgetting something,' he replied. 'I've got ten men waiting for me outside.'

Jamie wrestled McLaren to his knees and rested the tip of the gun against his head. His free arm brought up a mobile phone. Using the skill and dexterity of the tech-savvy young, his left thumb scrolled contacts until he reached the one he wanted: Pope. He touched the screen to make the call and raised it to his ear. He heard the dialling tone, and then Pope's voice greeted him. 'Yes.' *He wasn't still sulking was he? Moody sod*, thought Jamie.

'Pick me up from Bentley's house. You know where that is?' commanded Jamie.

Another one word answer in response. 'Yes.'

What is it with him, the sullen git? 'I'll be outside. Hurry up,' demanded Jamie, any attempt at civility forgotten. Pope made promises to be there soon.

Jamie cut the call, not wanting to speak with him anymore but resolving that words would be had later about attitude and respect. He began to shuffle backwards out of the room, with the money in the holdall strapped diagonally across his chest, he dragged McLaren backwards by the neck. A few more footsteps to the threshold then he'd jettison McLaren and be off into the night to regroup with his crew.

One footstep, two footstep, almost there, three footstep, four—

Everything went black again for Jamie: his systems shut

down, his knees buckled and he collapsed to the floor—again.

Behind him stood a man; a man with a narrow face, straight black hair and a long chin. '*Guten Abend*,' he said.

-37-

IT HADN'T BEEN DIFFICULT FOR THE HUNTER TO FIND THEM; that was why he was the best. He'd followed them to the railway station, and then observed them make other plans to get off the island. He'd watched them board the rather shabby-looking pleasure boat and waited patiently for its return a few hours later. The skipper, a fat man in a leather jacket, told him where he'd dropped them off—eventually. He'd been a tough nut to crack, but he did in the end, they always did. Waterboarding, somehow appropriate given the location, and when put to the bouncy soundtrack of Bobby Darin's *"Beyond The Sea"*, his buyer would pay handsomely for that video, he was sure. Arriving in Rochester, it was simple for the Hunter to pick up their trail once again.

He'd stood in the darkness just a few metres downwind of the small man, breathing in the foul stench of his tobacco. And when the big man wrestled the brute with the magnificent red beard, he'd almost intervened at the point the red beard looked to be winning. It would have been very unsatisfactory for the trail to end on a kitchen floor, so he stepped forward. The big man, however, dominated, and he returned to the shadows and waited. When he saw the holdall brought out, he knew he'd reached his objective. Luckily the big man's approach had been as subtle as tornado; every door he'd come across flapped wide open. The Hunter simply followed in his wake, into the house, and waited for his opportunity.

*

The Hunter wore glossy black loafers; they looked European, elegant. With a side-sweep of one he pushed the gun, dropped by Jamie. It spun and skittered across the carpet, coming to a halt beneath a sofa against the wall. In his hand he held a gun of his own, a different model to Quinn's. Where Quinn's was hefty and vulgar, a blunt instrument to strike fear by sight alone, the Hunter's was sleek and compact with a long slender barrel: it was discreet and designed for purpose not for show. He held it steady and close to his body with an assured self-confidence, not the chaotic indiscriminate jabbing of Jamie. Everyone in the room could read the body language; he was an expert.

'Get the bag,' he said, giving McLaren a gentle nudge at the same time. With a grunt and a tug, McLaren quickly removed it from under Jamie and handed it to the Hunter.

'Who are you?' demanded Bentley, affronted at being held at gunpoint in his own house by a stranger.

'All you need to know is my employer is the man you stole from,' replied the Hunter, 'and I have been tasked with recovering it.' He ducked under the strap, letting it cross his chest diagonally. 'Is this all of it? My employer knows exactly how much you stole from him. Believe me, you do not want to see me again.' Bentley nodded his confirmation that it was all there.

'In that case,' replied the Hunter, 'my business is done, and I will leave now.'

McLaren, his voice trembling, asked, 'Are you going to kill us now?'

The Hunter gave him a quizzical look, the way a cat would to a trapped mouse, as though he was mulling over the choice: life or death?

'Ordinarily I should, but no,' he replied, and McLaren gave a gasp of relief. 'No,' repeated the Hunter and looked directly at Quinn. 'I have given the matter considerable thought as I will need to explain to my employer why I've left you alive, and convince him you pose no further threat.'

Quinn didn't know what to feel: should he thank him or shake his hand or attack him just in case? With absolutely no term of reference to go by, he responded, 'I don't understand.'

'It is my debt repaid to you,' the Hunter began. 'You will recall our earlier encounter, in a parking lot,' said the Hunter. 'You did not see me watching you, you thought I had fled the scene.'

Quinn nodded; it was beginning to come back to him. He waited for the Hunter to explain further.

'There was a body. A very large man. It was unprofessional of me to have left it in such a public place. Sloppy work. But I watched you load it into a car and take it away. You did me a great favour by doing that, clearing my mistake. Not killing you tonight is my repayment of that favour. Agreed?'

'Agreed,' confirmed Quinn.

The Hunter kept his gun pointed at Quinn, but his free hand gently patted the bag resting against his hip. 'As for my employer's instructions, he wanted retribution enacted against whoever perpetrated the crime against him. It looks as though you have taken care of that task for me also.' The free hand gestured towards the carpet stained with Tony Flint's blood.

At their feet, a weak groan reminded them of the young man. The Hunter, using a flick of his long chin to point, directed their eyes to Jamie on the floor. 'He is the only loose end. As I say, my employer wants retribution against those that robbed him. I must deal with him.' He lowered the barrel of his gun, point blank, barely inches from Jamie's head. McLaren and Bentley braced themselves for the noise and mess.

A metallic click. The hammer had drawn back, but it didn't fire. Quinn's large, square workmanlike hand wrapped around the Hunter's delicate artisan's hand.

'No,' said Quinn. 'I have plans of my own for him.'

224

The Hunter stared at him, as if staring into him. 'If I give him to you, do you guarantee he will be no further threat to my employer in any way whatsoever?'

'I do,' promised Quinn. The Hunter gave a slow nod. Quinn could tell it signified his warranty had been accepted but was also that it was binding; and he knew at exactly what cost.

The Hunter walked backwards using slow, deliberate paces. At the threshold he turned and fled. The sound of the entrance door opening and immediately slamming shut could be heard through the house seconds later.

'Seemed like a nice bloke, after all,' remarked McLaren.

-38-

'WELL,' SAID BENTLEY after the mysterious German had departed leaving them as confused as when he arrived. 'I guess that's our business concluded. That's that then.'

Quinn raised himself to his full height, and rolled his shoulders back to their full expansion. 'Your money or your life, was that what you said? Snatching and doping up my niece? Concluded? We haven't even started yet.'

Bentley leapt to his feet, his index finger poking his glasses back to the top of his nose, then it rotated out to point at Quinn. It pointed with intent, as though Bentley believed he had right on his side, that Bentley wasn't afraid of Quinn and was ready to confront him.

'Firstly,' the finger jabbed forward for emphasis. 'That was a joke, banter, it's what people say... money or your life... It was a joke, forget about it.'

Quinn's brow lowered, his jaw tensed, thoughts brewed. 'That was no joke. You wanted to set your Russian loose on me.'

'Only because you didn't get the joke and started getting aggressive,' Bentley snapped back. 'Anyway, you killed him, so that makes us even I reckon.'

Somehow, in some way, that perverse logic made sense to Quinn. His shoulders loosened and his stance followed, but then there was something else. 'Zoe: you kidnapped her. You drugged her!'

'Kidnapped? What the bloody hell are you talking about,

kidnapped?'

Quinn looked across at Zoe. She had slumped on a sofa against the wall. She sat upright, but her posture was loose and languid, her eyes were looking at the floor, her demeanour unconcerned by the chaos going on around her.

'She came here under her own free will. Her car's in the garage, the keys are in the ignition; go and check if you don't believe me,' protested Bentley. Quinn gestured to McLaren with a nod of the head. McLaren understood the unspoken message and went to investigate. 'And she's not drugged. She's had a few tranqs to calm her nerves, she's had a fretful few days. In case you've forgotten we've just had a visit from a hired assassin. No wonder she's a bit highly strung, poor love.' Bentley held a long sympathetic gaze in the direction of Zoe.

McLaren returned. From the doorway he gave Quinn a clear nod confirming Bentley was telling the truth about Zoe's car.

Quinn was conflicted. Bentley sounded very plausible, but then he always did. Bentley had given a good account for everything, it all stacked up, but something didn't quite sit right with Quinn, something he couldn't pin down.

Bentley had been watching Quinn. He could read the internal questioning and uncertainties taking place within him. From the twitching of the small muscles around his eyes and the rubbing of his finger and thumb, he knew Quinn's resistance would crumble and he'd fall in line, and it'd be sooner rather than later. Bentley knew that for certain; he'd always been a persuasive negotiator.

*

Quinn, aided by McLaren, manhandled the unresponsive and out-cold Jamie up and out of the house, dropping him on the back seat of the Mercedes: its third fare of the night.

Bentley had been right: Quinn crumbled. Quinn fell into line. And it was very quick: no more than a couple of minutes and

Quinn was taking instructions, master and servant relationship restored. Bentley had spoken to both Quinn and McLaren. 'Returning to what I said earlier, business is concluded. There's no money anymore, it's been returned to the Fatherland, so there's no point you being here. Get rid of him,' he gave the unconscious Jamie a kick to identify the subject, 'and then you can come back here, and take Zoe home. And don't forget—you owe me a new fucking carpet.'

Quinn had an idea, he got behind the wheel of the Mercedes and told McLaren to follow him. 'Oh, and bring a bottle.'

Quinn didn't lead them very far. Close to Bentley's place the main road dipped steeply and then immediately climbed again, just as steeply: a peculiar little valley with the local railway station at the bottom. Quinn parked up in a side road at the top of the slope, McLaren slotted in behind him in Zoe's little Fiat. Quinn lifted Jamie into the driver's seat, then wiped the car down for fingerprints.

'You going to kill him?' asked McLaren, his tone scared but thrilled.

Quinn looked at Jamie; he appeared to be sleeping. In sleep he looked younger than the man he pretended to be, but Quinn offset any romantic redemption with the memory of him raising his pistol and firing from point-blank range. 'No, I'm not,' replied Quinn, reaching across to strap the seatbelt across Jamie's torso. 'I thought I'd give him the same chance he gave me: fifty-fifty. That seems fair.'

Quinn held out his hand and gestured with flexing fingers. McLaren understood and handed him the bottle he'd brought from Bentley's: an unopened litre bottle of expensive premium vodka. The label was printed entirely in Cyrillic lettering: for the briefest of seconds Quinn wondered if it was a present from home, from Marko to Bentley. He twisted off the cap and leaned into the car. With his left hand he pinched closed Jamie's nose, with his right he pushed the neck of the bottle into his mouth and upended it. When the overspill began, he clamped his hand across Jamie's mouth and reflex action took over: swallow or drown. He swallowed. Jamie awoke with an urgent hungry gasp, his throat burning with the intensity of the alcohol. Quinn repeated the process: nose pinched shut, bottle upended, forced swallow, gasp. Quinn examined the bottle: *two thirds gone, that'll do.*

'You're probably better off asleep for this, Jamie.' He delivered a sharp fast rabbit punch to the side of the head in the genuine belief he was doing him a favour. Quinn wiped clean the bottle and cap and dropped it in the footwell of the car, then told McLaren he was ready.

'Wait, I've an idea,' chirped McLaren. He scurried around to the passenger side. He removed Tony Flint's shoes and placed them in the footwell neatly side-by side then raised his legs, planting both feet squarely on the dashboard. The luxurious leather seat whirred smoothly on its motors in response to McLaren's press of the button. It brought the seat closer to the dash. The result was minimal. The seat had come forward two or three inches; not much, but enough to keep Flint's feet firmly planted and his knees bent. He slammed the door shut and wiped all surfaces of prints. 'All done,' he confirmed.

'What's that all about?'

'Wait and see,' replied McLaren, 'Wait and see.'

*

The main road on the hill was a historic throwback, being the principal route through since the Middle Ages. Over the years it had been widened, surfaced, resurfaced and lit as the traffic and population demands but it essentially followed exactly the same route as that of the carriages that ferried the gentlemen in powdered wigs lamenting the loss of the American colonies. Horses, unlike engines, don't like long steep slopes to climb and gentlemen in carriages don't like long steep slopes to descend. It was for that reason that the main road on the hill, at around the halfway point, took a deceptively sharp bend of almost right-angled proportions. In the olden times it gave the horses chance to rest, in the modern times it gave the drivers a nasty surprise.

Quinn and McLaren set the Mercedes into drive and let it go. Gravity soon took a role and the car accelerated: quicker and quicker, faster and faster. At the infamous bend it clipped the high concrete kerb installed many years ago as a warning to drivers of the dangers ahead and the car bounced a wheel off the road. It came back down on the footpath and the powerful traction of the big Mercedes motor pulled the car in that direction. It shot at speed across the footpath and up a shallow grass verge. It collided at some force with a sturdy mature tree. The tree remained stoically upright and unmoved. The car folded and crumpled around it until motionless.

Quinn and McLaren, squeezed into the small tiny Fiat, crawled past the wreckage under the boughs of the mighty chestnut tree. Airbags had been deployed on impact, filling the voids like big white clouds. Jamie's face rested on one, as though fast asleep on a deep soft pillow.

'Look, see,' said McLaren pointing across to the passenger side, the excitement in his voice due to his scheme paying off. Quinn saw what he was pointing at, and gave a nod of appreciation to McLaren. As planned, Tony Flint's feet had been planted on the dashboard when the car crashed. The airbag had shot out at a speed of over two hundred miles an hour, ramming his knees like pistons through his face. His skull had been shattered as easily as an eggshell into a thousand tiny pieces. To anyone investigating, any trace of the damage inflicted by Quinn was long gone; it'd take a lot of time and money to prove it was anything other than a drunk-driving accident.

'Let's get out of here,' Quinn said to McLaren, then added, 'And thanks.'

-39-

HER HEAD WAS FILLED WITH COTTON WOOL. She was trapped on the inside of her body looking out, unable to interact, unable to make that connection of being active in the present. She was on autopilot; she somehow knew what was going on, but at the same time didn't. The sofa was comfortable. It was large and plump with faded red cushions and gold brocade. Cosy. She could just curl up here and sleep. Sleep like that man in that fairy story she vaguely remembered, sleep for a hundred years.

Where's my uncle? He was here a minute ago, oh well, I daresay he'll be back again soon enough. At least John Bentley's here, funny little John with his V-neck sweaters and his jeans too baggy round the bum, at least John's here. He's been good to me; he's always been good to me. When I was running away, getting chased there he was, he found me, he saved me. And Dad's funeral, he was there, he came. And when I was at school, needing money he was there to help out, offering part-time jobs, waitressing… that night, Redlands… Bentley got me that job. He's always been there.

*

Bentley stood at the window and watched Quinn and McLaren drive away to dispose of the bodies. *So long as they get them far away from here, I don't care what they do with them.* When the red dots of their taillights disappeared from view, he pulled the curtains closed with a tight tug and turned back to face the room. *That stain across the carpet will never come out, he noted. I'll need to get on to someone first thing in the morning to get it replaced double quick.*

And then his eyes fell on Zoe. He'd virtually forgotten about her, she'd almost become part of the furniture sitting quietly in the corner like that. 'Zoe, you okay, love?' he called out to her.

She flicked her eyes up at him, but she didn't respond. Bentley's mind returned to suppertime and the tablets he crushed under the curve of a teaspoon. *Did I put too much in her food? Oh, she'll be all right, just needs to sleep it off.*

*

Through the fog filling her head, she heard her name being called… Zoe. It took an effort, her eyes as heavy as stone, but she traced the source of her name. Bentley. Him again. Him who has always been there. Him who turned up out of the blue in the coffee shop and set them down this path. Him who turned up at Dad's funeral. Why? To make sure he was really dead? Him who turned up at home offering her money, a lot for three hours work, just to waitress at Redlands' birthday party. Him. He's always been there. Always.

Her eyes were too heavy and she let them drop. Her field of vision fell to the floor, and then she saw it beside her foot, poking from underneath the sofa: black, metallic, deadly.

*

Bentley looked at his watch. Surely they must be back soon; this was taking too long. He wanted Quinn back and his assurance it had all been dealt with; he didn't like the uncertainty. He turned and pulled apart the curtains but saw no returning vehicles. The frustration was driving him mad. Then he heard the click…

On the opposite side of the room, the girl Zoe held a gun

tightly between both hands and pointed it straight at Bentley. Although her eyes, her face, her expression were spaced out and vague the gun was held steady and firm. He shuffled to his right but the gun followed him, he shuffled to the left, it followed him still. *Maybe*, he wondered, *she's not as out of it as she's been letting on.*

Zoe was most definitely still two beats behind the pace of the world, still trying to wade through the swamps in her consciousness to catch up with everyone else, but one thought was coming through loud and clear: Bentley was always there.

'Come on Zoe, put that down. You'll hurt someone with it,' said Bentley in a soft, friendly voice. 'Come on, put it down. You aren't thinking straight.'

'You,' she replied, her voice strong and clear. 'You're always there. You've created this, all of it. It's all your fault.'

'Zoe, love, I don't know what you're talking about,' Bentley raised his hands above his waist and took a tentative step forward. She jabbed the gun in his direction and he stopped, mid-step.

'You set my dad up. You set my uncle up. You set me up.' Zoe's voice had taken on a wail, the emotions washed through her.

Bentley assessed the situation: he was alone in the house with a young, small, doped-up woman. He could easily overpower her, get the gun off her. From this realisation, the status of power changed. Bentley knew it was just a matter of a few actions and he'd be the dominant one. He took another step forward, this time not flinching when she jabbed the gun at him again.

'You set me up, promised me money for waitressing. Only it wasn't for that, was it?'

Bentley's awareness of the shifting powers gave him a confidence he hadn't had earlier; she might hold the gun but she didn't have what it took to follow this through. 'So you've finally worked it out then, have you? It was Redlands' birthday, we all knew his sordid little secret, what his tastes were. So, what better for his birthday than a nice treat for him to enjoy? Don't play dumb, you knew what you were getting into…'

'You gave me to him? He tried to rape me.'

'You knew exactly what was going on. Why else would you have been given so much money?'

'I trusted you. All my family did. You lied to us.'

'I thought you'd be up for it,' goaded Bentley. He could tell she was getting distracted; he took another step forward, then another, just a few more well-placed words to confuse her focus, slow down her reactions, and then he could snatch the gun from her. 'A lot of money to show an old man a good time, just like your mother.'

He saw the flash of the gun muzzle before he heard the fearsome burst, before he felt the hot metal bore a hole through his thigh. 'You fucking bitch,' he screamed. 'I'm going to fucking kill you.'

She fired again and again but the shots went wild, shattering the crystal decanters of brandy and cognac on the table nearby. The thick glass exploded into a fine powder; splinters hung in the air momentarily then fell to earth like raindrops. The expensive liquor sprayed up across the curtains, drenching them and sweet-scented amber pools ponded on the carpet and soft furnishings.

Bentley gripped his injured thigh, pressing his hand tight against it to stem the bleeding. He looked down in a state of confusion at the steady flow of blood sluicing between his fingers. He let out a roar then leapt towards Zoe. She cowered on the sofa, gun in front of her and pulled the trigger, once, twice, but just hollow clicks. It was empty.

-40-

QUINN GRABBED BENTLEY'S SHOULDERS and pulled him off of Zoe. He threw him across the room. Bentley collapsed in a heap beside the fire.

'What the bloody hell is going on here?' demanded Quinn.

'It's him,' replied Zoe, her voice coming in pants as she desperately tried to catch her breath. 'He pimped me out to Redlands. He knew what he'd do to me.'

Quinn strode across to where Bentley lay. 'Is this true?' Bentley didn't respond. Quinn pulled a log from the top of the firewood pile. He gripped it at one end, like a club, and raised it above Bentley's head. 'Is it?'

Bentley shuffled away from Quinn but butted up against the chimney breast, no more space to manoeuvre. He looked to the ceiling and took a deep breath. With Quinn rampant and looking for blood he realised he'd no alternative. He made the choice to confess. 'Yes, Redlands had to go, he was a liability. We all knew what he was like but Tony Flint wouldn't hear a word said about him. So I needed your brother's help; he was a hothead, everyone knew that. I figured let Redlands get caught in the act and get his punishment, then Tony couldn't defend him.'

'But he still did, though.'

'Yes, he still did. So then I figured you and your brother could help me again. Flint, Redlands and me: we held this firm together when Old Man Flint died, we made it what it is today.

But it was always me that had to sort out all the shit, smooth out all the problems, and did I ever get any thanks for it? Not once.'

McLaren gently took the gun off of Zoe and passed it to Quinn. Quinn stood directly over Bentley, feet widely planted, big and imposing, toying with Bentley, deliberately messing with his mind. Quinn tossed the log into the fire where it puffed up a cloud of fine powdery ash. Previously slumbering flames suddenly awoke and danced around it. By freeing up his hands, Quinn popped out the spent, empty magazine and with a reassuring click re-inserted a fully loaded magazine from the spares he'd carried in his pocket. In one long outstretched arm he lowered the gun to Bentley's eye level and, with a tilt of the head, indicated Bentley should resume his story. Bentley obliged.

'I was sick of it, always playing second fiddle to Flint and Redlands…'

'Let me guess, you wanted them out the way, so you could be in charge?'

'I'm a bit old for that now, it's a young man's game,' replied Bentley. 'It's time for me and the wife to retire. Go and live on a tropical beach.'

Quinn twisted to investigate the noise behind him. Zoe was on her feet and McLaren was holding her hands, guiding her. 'I'll take her out to the car, catch us up when you're ready,' he told Quinn.

Quinn returned his attention to Bentley. The pieces were beginning to fit, he could start to see the bigger picture. 'You knew I'd kill Flint for arranging Benny's murder. You could have told me years ago if you'd wanted him out of the way. Why'd you wait until now?'

Bentley grinned. 'Now you're starting to get it. Flint was one hundred percent certain you and your brother killed Redlands. He took out Benny straight away. You dodged that one and believe me he wasn't happy about it, but I managed to hold him off going for you. Bided my time. I needed him to be primed and ready.'

Quinn took a cushion from a nearby chair and stripped it down. He threw the empty covering to Bentley, who caught it and pressed it against the wound in his thigh then wrapped it around and tied it off in a tourniquet. 'What do you mean: primed?' asked Quinn.

Bentley gave a patronising laugh that Quinn didn't appreciate. Quinn kicked him on his good thigh and Bentley knew not to laugh again.

'Flint hated you because of Redlands, but it wasn't enough. So I'd drip feed a little poison here and there, every now and then. I wanted to get him to peak levels of hatred, just at the right time.'

'And this is the right time?' asked Quinn.

'Certainly is,' replied Bentley. 'I'd watched him over the past few years spend fortunes, calling in favours, doing anything to try to get Redlands' Panama accounts reopened, but he got absolutely nowhere. Well, that was always on the cards.'

'The right time?'

'His treasure hunt in Panama proved fruitless, and he held you responsible—sorry about that, it was kind of my fault. But it meant at last I could set you two off against each other, and his trying to get Jamie in the Firm and you still floating round the edges like a bad reminder: it was the perfect opportunity. So, Flint gets Jamie to kill you, he's got it out his system, he'll give up his Panama treasure hunt and let it go. Or you kill Flint, he's gone, out the way. Either way it's happy days for me. I'll book flights for me and the wife and we're out of here to spend the best years of our lives overseas in the sunshine.'

'And that's it? All of this just so you can put your feet up on a sun lounger?' Quinn's voice couldn't hide his bewilderment. 'But we've just lost the money, it's been reclaimed, you won't get far without that funding you. I thought the whole purpose of the car depot gig was because the Firm was skint.'

Bentley couldn't hold back his snide laugh this time. 'You stupid ignorant bastard. You just don't get it, do you?'

Quinn had seen and heard enough. 'I'm leaving now, John. I'm taking Zoe and I'm gone. You won't follow me; you won't contact me. Understand?'

Bentley nodded, then raised an arm towards Quinn. 'Help me up will you, before you go?'

Quinn bent at the waist and leaned in towards Bentley. He planted one hand for support against the chimney breast and extended the other to pull him up. Bentley clamped on to the offered hand, and felt the strength as Quinn began to pull him to his feet. However, Quinn was unprepared for what Bentley did next: twisting as he rose, he grabbed in his free hand the end of the log from the fire. The end he grasped like a bat, as yet uncharred, still wrapped in bark. The opposite end glowed red. His swing caught Quinn a glancing blow just above his ear. Orange sparks flared around Quinn's head and his nostrils filled with the bitter smell of burning hair.

Quinn swiped at Bentley's hand, simultaneously releasing his grip on him. Bentley toppled backwards, his head striking the slate hearthstone. The log flew from Bentley's hand, turning end-over-end in its long trajectory until it struck the curtains which billowed, absorbing the momentum of the flight. The log fell to the floor.

Quinn looked down at Bentley; he appeared unmoving, unresponsive. Thinking it probably for the best, he left him where he lay. Quinn exited the room and headed to the small Fiat outside. He didn't notice the burning log combining with the alcohol-soaked curtains. Ignition promptly followed. The flames quickly took hold and began to climb.

-41-

THE FIRE QUICKLY SPREAD, devouring the curtains and the soft furnishings. It didn't take very long before it hungrily licked and lapped the timber panelling lining the room. It leapt from surface to surface, wall to wall. Within minutes the room was ablaze and the fire had begun to spread out across the house.

In the street outside, Quinn made plans with McLaren. McLaren would drive them all in Zoe's little Fiat to where they'd parked Quinn's X5 a few streets away. Then Quinn would take Zoe in the X5 and McLaren would follow on in the Fiat. Upon arrival and regrouping back at Quinn's place in Rochester they'd think about what to do next. It was a plan. It'd work.

When McLaren had been sent out to check the story of Zoe's car, he'd stashed his shopping bag of stolen trinkets in the back of the Fiat. He hoped Quinn would let him keep them, otherwise the night had been a whole lot of trouble for no reward. The smell of smoke reached him on the still breeze and he looked around for its source. The windows of the lower storey to Bentley's home flickered orange and red, the fire was now getting out of control. He knew it was time to go.

'This place'll be swarming with police and fire fighters any minute now, we need to get moving,' warned McLaren, twisting the key and revving up the engine. 'And this is no flying machine; we need to be out of here now, before anyone comes. We can't outrun anything in this.'

Zoe murmured some kind of protest from the back seat, a

defence of her beloved little car. McLaren reached out a paternal hand to gently pat her knee, as if to assure no offence intended. She took it in the spirit it was offered and slipped into sleep.

'Come on,' called McLaren.

Quinn remained standing. He had one foot planted in the car's footwell, the other firmly anchored on the pavement. He watched the flames dancing in the windows, and listened to the old house creak. Something was on his mind. Something had been troubling him, gnawing away at him.

'Come on, let's go,' shouted McLaren.

'What did he mean?' asked Quinn. 'Bentley. He said he knew the attempts for the Panama accounts were fruitless.'

'I don't know, probably because he's been there. Come on, get in the car, we have got to get out of here.'

'He laughed at me when I said there was no money.' Quinn kept looking at the house.

McLaren eyes darted up and down the street, so far he'd not spotted any activity from the neighbours but he knew it wouldn't be far away, not once the fire reached the upper floors; then they'll all be out for a gawp and a stare. He knew they needed to be gone, and he urged Quinn to get in the car.

Quinn stood motionless, half in, half out, and turned towards McLaren. 'What do you mean: he's probably been there?'

In his panic it took a second or two for McLaren to understand the question, then, 'Bentley? I saw something in his desk when I was going through his office. A folder. Official looking. It had Banco Panama printed on it.'

Quinn began running back to the house. McLaren looked on confused. 'We need to go,' he pleaded.

Quinn stopped on the path, in front of the cute arts-and-crafts red-brick arched entrance. 'You go: take Zoe home, get out of here. I'll catch up.'

McLaren didn't need telling twice, and released the handbrake. The little Fiat gave a small sharp squeal as it leapt from a standing start and then sped towards the road's gated entrance and the way home.

Quinn watched them drive off, rooted to the spot until he was sure they'd got away safely. Then he pulled the neck of his t-shirt over his nose and mouth, flipped his hood up and tightened the cords until a small hole was left for his eyes. He took a deep breath and headed inside the house.

*

Bentley awoke with a shock and a start, as though an electric current had been channelled through him. He gasped in a deep breath, only to cough it straight back out. Instead of the lungful of clean fresh air he'd been expecting it was heavy and sooty and suffocating. His eyes stung and began to stream. He looked around; the room was dense with smoke. Flames attacked most surfaces. He needed to get out. He struggled to his feet and then immediately stumbled back on to his knees, he hadn't anticipated the structural strength missing from his injured leg. *Nothing else for it*, he thought, and began to crawl on all fours in the direction of the door.

Fucking Quinn, he cursed. *Fucking Quinn ruining everything.* It had all been so neatly planned. Bentley's memory flickered back to the beginning. He'd only wanted Redlands publicly exposed for the depraved pervert he was; surely Flint would disown him then. But him dying, well that was so much better. A brand new path was plotted for Bentley the day Redlands dropped down dead.

The heat around him was intense. His eyes blinked away hot stinging tears, his throat constricted, every breath created a new searing pain. Blisters burst open on the palms of his hands, and his clothing felt as heavy and as dry as straw, ready to combust at any second.

It had all been so easy. Redlands was a neat freak and a fastidious recordkeeper. Find the record, find the fortune. If Tony Flint had arrived on time it'd be a whole different story now. Ifs and maybes: *if ifs and ands were pots and pans there'd be no need for tinkers*, that's what his old grandmother used to say. He'd not thought about her for nigh on thirty years, but he knew she was right. Tony Flint was late that morning getting to Redlands' office and nothing now could change that.

It had rained that morning. Bentley remembered it clearly, he'd bought a coffee and a Danish in the Pret opposite while he waited for Flint. When he still hadn't arrived, fifteen minutes after the agreed time, Bentley gave up and went in alone. Redlands' office was like something off the telly: very swish and modern. Bentley had always resented it, he'd never had an office. *But I'm the face, John, I'm the respectable face of the business. That was rich, a fucking nonce claiming he was the respectable one.*

Redlands had had a big status symbol desk of chrome and glass: of course he fucking did, he wouldn't have had anything less. The office was pristine, like a photo shoot, everything neatly laid out and ordered, right down to the magazines fanned out on the coffee table like some swanky hotel lobby. But there, its edges perfectly parallel to the desk top, sat Redlands' notebook. Bentley snapped off the elastic loop and there on the first page, in Redlands' neat upright handwriting, were the passwords to the computers. He had tapped them in, and the screens blinked into life. Still no sign of Flint. Bentley had idly flicked through the pages of the notebook looking for anything that might be of currency; some salacious gossip, possibly? His eyes had locked onto a word about two-thirds into the book. That word was *"Panama"*—could it be? Suddenly a new plan had plotted its route in front of him. He had slipped the stiff small book into his trouser pocket and waited for Flint to arrive.

Around him burning remnants of paper—the glossy gossip magazines Helen loved so much—rained down on him, gently fluttering down with the grace of autumn leaves. They brushed past his ears, scalding them, snapping him out of his daydreams. Ahead of him, crossing the hallway, the shape of a man, a big man, a man entering the house. Why, is it a firefighter? Bentley attempted to cry out for help but his throat was too parched to make a sound. It couldn't have been a firefighter, it had to be a trick of the light, my fevered imagination, they weren't wearing a helmet, or an air-tank: what kind of maniac runs into a burning building?

-42-

BENTLEY COLLAPSED IN HIS FRONT GARDEN. He'd made it; he was out. The cool damp grass seeped through his clothes, soothing his stinging back and shoulders, it felt good. He looked up at the stars and gulped down lungfuls of clean, fresh air. It tasted refreshing and moist, and made him cough. He spat out a thick black clod of mucus, then looked back to see his home ablaze. In the distance he could hear sirens: *they must be coming here*, he thought. In the houses all around, the homes of his neighbours, windows were lit, and shocked, concerned faces populated them. *Marvellous. Now I've got a bloody audience. I should get out of here.*

A recent conversation replayed itself in Bentley's head. *'Pick me up from Bentley's house, you know where that is?'* That's what Jamie said, wasn't it? And what else had he said? *Ten men, tooled up and mobhanded? I need to make contact with them, get my Firm onside, make that bastard Quinn pay for what he's done.*

Bentley had a plan and he had a thirst for revenge; it was enough to get him to his feet. He tried to run but his leg wasn't up to it. Despite this, he moved as quickly as he could, wincing through the pain, knowing he'd get to inflict it tenfold on Quinn. He hadn't done any proper exercise for years. Helen had been going on at him for ages to do something about it and now he was starting to regret not listening to her. Just the short distance to the gated entrance of his private road was hard work but Bentley persisted, driven on by a fear of what lay behind him and the desire to command his loyal crew of ten to start cracking skulls.

His anger and fury at Quinn spurred him onwards. *Quinn's going to pay for what he's done to me.* At last he came upon, and sidled through, the unlocked pedestrian gate and found the bright white LED headlights of Pope's car waiting as promised. Lactic acid had begun to spread through his body, his breathing was heavy and laboured and the last few strides out towards the car made his legs ache but he didn't care: tired muscles were a small price to pay. He'd won. Gripping thoughts of the suffering he intended to inflict on Quinn as tightly as his shit-eating grin, he threw open the back door of the car and clambered aboard.

'Come on. Let's go,' he commanded, and the car lurched away at great speed. His hand flew to the ceiling searching a handle to steady himself with.

A needle-sharp point dug into him, just below his ribs. 'Mr Flint,' said a heavily accented voice beside him in the shadows. 'We're going for a little ride now.'

*

The driver of the grey mini-van was a whippet-thin man with sharp features and narrow eyes. In this country he went by the name Dan, the girls seemed to like that. Tonight, in the van, with five fellow countrymen, speaking in their mother tongue, he was Bogdan again.

Dan was smarting. Dan wanted revenge. Earlier he'd discovered his brother had been murdered. Andrei—Dan and Andy to the girls loving their dark brooding Balkan looks. Andy had been slaughtered like a dog, in a garden shed in the corner of a tatty carwash. Their business lay in ruins. Retribution must be swift and decisive, there was no question of that. The carwash survivors told of the big man, of Flint. All it took was a few phone calls to discover where the Flint organisation called home—and when the Flints began mustering a convoy, it seemed the ideal target for an ambush.

From his observations, Dan fancied the front car for himself, the one with just two inside: the leader would always be at the head of the convoy, the soldiers following behind. *I will avenge you, Andrei.*

*

The men moved quickly, nimbly, organised. Five from the grey van, five from the blue. Ten men. Ten loaded shotguns.

Keeping close to the wall with the shadows for cover, they skirted the three cars unnoticed. On Dan's nod, they tightened their circle and raised their weapons. Someone in the back of the second car sensed the light change outside, a flicker of a shadows passing the window, but put it down to branches moving in the wind and turned his attention back to the football commentary. The flicker lingered, casting a darkness over the window. By the time he looked out he was eye-to-eye with the gunmetal. There was no time to shout a warning: in unison, the shotguns blasted one barrel then the next. Before the boom had stopped echoing off the school walls, the men were back in their vans. A polite flash of the indicators and they carefully pulled away from the kerbs and trundled away.

In the days that followed, when the police went door to door seeking help with their enquiries, no one remembered anything out of the ordinary: *a loud bang, yes, I heard one or was it two, but put it down to kids letting off fireworks, I remember when fireworks was one night only, but it goes on for weeks now doesn't it, no I didn't give it a second thought, sorry.* See anything? *No. Wait, there may have been one of those people carrier things, you know, with the black windows, but going very slowly, I expect it was picking someone up from the pub, perhaps you could ask them. Registration number? Why would I? it was just a taxi, you see them all the time round here.*

Pope opened his eyes and uncurled from his tight flinch. His eardrums numbed from the shotguns' blasts but that was the only damage he'd incurred—physical damage at least. It hadn't even occurred to him what the repercussions from facing a death squad might be on his mental health; right at that moment he was relieved to be whole and breathing. The car's back doors opened and closed quickly. A sudden see-saw lurch from the back seat rocked him and he knew he'd been boarded. A hard, metallic edge poked into the side of his head, just below his ear. He instinctively knew it was the barrel of a gun pressed against him.

'Don't look around. Drive. Now,' an accented voice demanded of him, adding, 'I'll tell you where. Drive... now!'

Pope rolled the car out of the wide bell-mouth, back onto the road and followed the instructions to a hidden-away seclusion of lock-up garages.

'Stop here,' commanded the voice.

An attempt to turn and look at the owner of the voice got halted by an abrupt poke in the temple with the gun. Pope flicked his eyes to the rear-view mirror, but it was too dark to distinguish any discernible features.

On the edge of his peripheral vision Pope could see a matt black pipe pressed hard into the side of Kenton's face; another gun held by the other back seat passenger. These weapon-wielding maniacs had matched his crew one-to-one and massacred them all, but why? Pope waited, expecting instructions from the unseen hijacker behind, but none came. Instead, his phone rang. Linked to the car's Bluetooth, the chimes echoed through the car's speakers and the name *"Jamie Flint"* displayed on the centre console screen.

'Answer it,' commanded the voice. The gun barrel grinding hard against Pope's ear added emphasis to the demand. 'Remember, happy: all is normal.'

*

Dan was pleased with his team's work. He told them to get in the mini-vans and get away. Go quietly, go discreetly and in different directions. Be invisible: they were good at that.

Dan was satisfied that the threat to their business had been resolved; now it was time to get personal, now it was time to get retribution for Andrei. Dan climbed into the back of the lead car; his cousin Gheorghe got in the other side. Gheorghe had brought his knives tonight: good. He was considering which of them to slice and dismember first, they would suffer, they would feel his anguish.

But then the driver's phone rang, distracting him from his musings. He spotted the caller-id flash up on the car's central screen—Jamie Flint. *Could I claim the greatest scalp of all, a genuine real-life Flint?* He leaned forward, knocking the rim of the barrel against the driver's head as a reminder, and in almost a whisper spoke into his ear. 'Answer it.' Could he get up close to a Flint family member? Better not scare him off. 'All is normal.'

*

Jamie's disembodied voice filled the car: 'Pope, it's me. You all right?'

A cold, jagged nudge from behind prompted Pope's response. 'Yes.'

'Good,' replied Jamie. 'Pick me up from Bentley's house, you know where that is?'

'Yes.'

'I'll be outside. Hurry up.'

Another nudge in the back from the shotgun. 'Coming. I'll be a few minutes. I'll be waiting for you.'

Jamie cut the call. Silence filled the car and Dan smiled. *A few minutes, Andrei, a few minutes and I'll have Flint, they will pay.*

'You know where you're going?' asked Dan, the gun gave another tap to Pope's ear. 'Show me. SatNav.'

Pope sat completely motionless, every muscle frozen except for his thumbs. He gripped the steering wheel and kept his hands as still as possible. He didn't want the gun to think he was pulling a fast one. His thumbs flicked the scroll-device on the steering wheel, and in front of him the centre console screen skittled through various screens before he reached the SatNav home screen. Another screen opened by his remote thumb found Bentley's name in a long list of others and as the cursor hovered over it. It flashed to confirm it had been selected. A bright blue line snaked over the screen, laying out the route. Quarter of a mile away, it said. Three minutes away, it said.

'Happy?' asked Pope.

'Very,' replied Dan. He gave a double-tap of his foot, the pre-arranged sign, and the knives plunged into the throats of Pope and Kenton

*

Behind them, Bentley's home burned. It tore through the night sky like a rising sun. 'Mr Flint, we're going for a little ride now,' said a heavily accented voice.

Bentley turned in the direction of the voice, seeking its owner to correct their mistake. He could just about make out their silhouette in the darkness, backlit by the glow of the rising flames. The car sped away aggressively, a knife blade reflected the flash of a passing streetlamp and Bentley reconsidered. He closed his mouth and paused for a moment's thought: he'd always been a persuasive negotiator...

-43-

Three months later:

ON THE ISLE OF SHEPPEY, the traffic still thunders up and over the new bridge, still blind to what awaits them on the other side. The big ships still bring in new cars from the Continent. The chalets and the caravans still sit facing the sea waiting patiently for the summer season to kick off. Life, on Cabbage Island, by and large carries on unchanging.

But there has been a change. A small café is under new management. It's nothing grand, it's not even close to the seawall to catch the passing tourist trade, instead located in a light industrial area. Builders frequent it; they like it, they come from the site opposite. It used to be a hand carwash, but now they've just poured the footings for a block of three new units.

The first change implemented by the café's new management was to terminate the employment of the former serving staff: the sullen ex-waitress removed her attention from her phone to receive the news, then went back to her screen and skulked off, never to be seen again.

In the small café, which is under new management, Dori Musatova sits at a table in the far corner. No longer are the tabletops sticky to the touch, now they are dressed in traditional red and white checked waxed cloths. Viktor sits opposite his mother, his school books spread across the table in front of him. She never used to get the chance to help him with his homework when she worked every hour God sent, and she's already seen the positive difference it's had. If Viktor works hard, he'll do well in England, she's certain of it. Back home in Chișinău she was an accountant for the local government. It feels good to use her skills again, to engage her brain: far better than working from six 'til six, six days a week unloading boxes. With the day's bookkeeping done she closes the ledger: not a bad day's business, not great, but certainly not bad, and besides there's the added unquantifiable value of being a family business to consider. Dori steps behind the counter and returns the ledger to its shelf under the cash register. The proprietor has a little fun with her, stepping first left then right to obstruct her path, he wrinkles his nose and it wiggles his gingery moustache. She giggles and playfully slaps his shoulder, he grabs her and they kiss. Viktor rolls his eyes.

McLaren looks out from his position behind the counter: master of all he surveys. He bought the café and the flat above with the generous sum that landed in his account, wired all the way from Panama. A new start at a new life: a good woman to be with, and a legitimate business to take pride in. Well, mostly legitimate, there's still a healthy under-the-counter trade to be had in tobacco and cigarettes—very popular with the builders over the road, no need to trouble his new wife with it.

*

In Rochester, a pretty green coffee shop with gold writing recently re-opened, just in time for the first of the year's weekend-long festivals. Neighbours, if asked, let it be known the owner and his niece had been on holiday, somewhere in South America. Quinn was glad to be home, grateful for the return to normality. And grateful for the return of Zoe: she'd spent the past few days in Sheppey, showing Dori and Viktor how to use the machinery to make good coffee. Apparently Viktor was a good learner and picked it up quickly, he could become a coffee magnate one day with a chain of stores, a lad with a bright future. Quinn put it down to her being a good teacher.

Quinn wiped some stray droplets off the countertop, and flipped the cloth across his shoulder. It had been a quiet morning so far, not too many customers, but he wasn't unduly worried, not with the Sweeps Festival happening soon. Music: that's what's needed to brighten the place up, he decided. He flicked through the app Zoe had downloaded to the laptop, finding a playlist that suited his mood just right, pressed start and waited. A second later it began. Clear smooth trumpets began to play in the empty shop. He closed his eyes, savouring the perfect, melodic introduction of the song.

Interrupting his appreciation, the chime of the bell and the swoosh of the street door opening. He raised his eyes to see who'd entered.

'Brendan Quinn. It's been a long time.'

Did You Enjoy This Book?

If so, you can make a HUGE difference.

For any author, the single most important way we have of getting our books noticed is a really simple one—and one which you can help with.

Yes, you.

Us indie authors and publishers don't have the financial muscle of the big guys to take out full-page ads in the newspaper or put posters on the subway.

But we do have something much more powerful and effective than that, and it's something that those big publishers would kill to get their hands on.

A committed and loyal bunch of readers.

Honest reviews of our books help bring them to the attention of other readers.

If you've enjoyed this book I would be really grateful if you could spend just a couple of minutes leaving a review (it can be as short as you like) on this book's page on your favourite store and website.

Author's Note and Acknowledgements

I should make it very clear from the outset that none of my characters are based on real people. Similarly, my Isle of Sheppey in this story – as well as the other locations – are concoctions of my own fantasy and fiction so I apologise for dropping dead bodies and a cast of assorted reprobates on them. I'd like to reassure anyone thinking of visiting that in real-life they're very lovely places.

It's been a long journey to get to this point and I am grateful for the help, guidance, collaboration and inspiration of so many people along the way. Firstly, I'd like to thank Peter Oxley and Simon Finnie at Burning Chair for having faith in me, giving me this wonderful opportunity and working tirelessly in getting this book to you. Pete and Si's encouragement, guidance and support has been there in abundance from the very beginning and I've always felt that I'm in very safe hands with them.

I would like to express how enormously grateful I am to Leslie Gardner for being so generous with their time, support and advice: thank you, it was so kind of you.

I am ever grateful to my wife Rebecca, and our two boys, for being there and giving me the support and encouragement to keep following this dream.

And finally, thanks go to you for taking the time and trouble to read this book. It's more appreciated than you may ever realise. If you enjoyed it, your feedback would be gratefully received so please do leave a review and tell your friends. And, please do feel to get in touch with me: you can find me on Twitter at @ mattwross, on Instagram at mattw_ross, or contact me through the publisher here at Burning Chair. I'd love to hear from you.

About The Author

Matthew Ross was born and raised in the Medway Towns, England. He still lives in Kent with his Kiwi wife, his children, a very old cat and an extremely bouncy puppy.

Several years ago he ticked off a lifelong ambition and tried his hand at stand-up comedy. He enjoyed the writing more than the performing and got approached by a leading stand-up comedian to provide material for their nationwide theatre tours, Edinburgh Fringe shows and their appearances on shows such as 'Mock The Week', 'Have I Got News For You' and 'The News Quiz'. Unfortunately, his writing ambitions got put on hold "temporarily", something he regrets because of the momentum gathering behind him. However a grown-up proper job, losing his father, and having his babies got in the way - what was a temporary postponement in time became a total derailment. But the itch wouldn't go away and he wanted to write again. So, he joined the Faber Academy 6-month Novel Writing course in 2016 under Richard Skinner's tutelage and it changed his life.

Matthew has been immersed in the building industry from a very early age helping out on his father's sites during school holidays before launching into his own career at 17. He's worked on projects ranging from the smallest domestic repair to £billion+ infrastructure, and probably everything in between. He drew influence from his experiences and the people he's met over the years when writing his darkly comic crime novels, "Death Of A Painter" and "The Red Admiral's Secret" featuring the misadventures of beleaguered builder Mark Poynter and his crew of idlers, slackers and gossips (published by Red Dog Press). "Death Of A Painter" was selected by *The Sun* newspaper as one of its picks of the week, describing it as "a chaotic comic caper that's as funny as it is brutal."

Matthew enjoys reading all manner of books - especially crime and mystery; 80s music; and travelling, and can't wait for the next trip to New Zealand to spend time with family and friends.

About Burning Chair

Burning Chair is an independent publishing company based in the UK, but covering readers and authors around the globe. We are passionate about both writing and reading books and, at our core, we just want to get great books out to the world.

Our aim is to offer something exciting; something innovative; something that puts the author and their book first. From first class editing to cutting edge marketing and promotion, we provide the care and attention that makes sure every book fulfils its potential.

We are:

- Different
- Passionate
- Nimble and cutting edge
- Invested in our authors' success

If you're an author and would like to know more about our submissions requirements and receive our free guide to book publishing, visit:

www.burningchairpublishing.com

If you're a reader and are interested in hearing more about our books, being the first to hear about our new releases or great offers, or becoming a beta reader for us, again please visit:

www.burningchairpublishing.com

Other Books by Burning Chair Publishing

Killer in the Crowd, by P N Johnson

Push Back, by James Marx

The Fall of the House of Thomas Weir, by Andrew Neil Macleod

By Richard Ayre:
Shadow of the Knife
Point of Contact
A Life Eternal

The Brodick Cold War Series, by John Fullerton
Spy Game
Spy Dragon

The Curse of Becton Manor, by Patricia Ayling

Near Death, by Richard Wall

Blue Bird, by Trish Finnegan

The Tom Novak series, by Neil Lancaster
Going Dark
Going Rogue
Going Back

10:59, by N R Baker

Love Is Dead(ly), by Gene Kendall

Haven Wakes, by Fi Phillips

Beyond, by Georgia Springate

Burning, An Anthology of Short Thrillers, edited by Simon Finnie and Peter Oxley

The Infernal Aether series, by Peter Oxley
The Infernal Aether
A Christmas Aether
The Demon Inside
Beyond the Aether
The Old Lady of the Skies: 1: Plague

The Wedding Speech Manual: The Complete Guide to Preparing, Writing and Performing Your Wedding Speech, by Peter Oxley

www.burningchairpublishing.com

Burning Bridges

Made in the USA
Las Vegas, NV
08 June 2022

49950880R00156